The Last Little Blue Envelope

The Last Little Blue Envelope

maureen johnson

HARPER TEEN
An Imprint of HarperCollinsPublishers

To all the jars. You know who you are.

HarperTeen is an imprint of HarperCollins Publishers.

The Last Little Blue Envelope
Copyright © 2011 by Maureen Johnson
All rights reserved. Printed in the United States of America. No part of this book
may be used or reproduced in any manner whatsoever without written permission
except in the case of brief quotations embodied in critical articles and reviews. For
information address HarperCollins Children's Books, a division of HarperCollins
Publishers, 10 East 53rd Street, New York, NY 10022.
www.epicreads.com

alloy**entertainment**

Produced by Alloy Entertainment
151 West 26th Street, New York, NY 10001

Library of Congress Cataloging-in-Publication Data
Johnson, Maureen, 1973-
  The last little blue envelope / Maureen Johnson. — 1st ed.
    p. cm.
  Sequel to: 13 little blue envelopes.
  Summary: Seventeen-year-old Ginny Blackstone precipitously travels from her home in New Jersey
to London when she receives a message from an unknown man telling her he has the letters that were
stolen just before she completed a series of mysterious tasks assigned by her now dead aunt, an artist.
  ISBN 978-0-06-197679-7
  [1. Voyages and travels—Fiction. 2. Swindlers and swindling—Fiction. 3. Letters—Fiction.
4. Artists—Fiction. 5. Aunts—Fiction. 6. Interpersonal relations—Fiction. 7. Europe—Fiction.] I. Title.
PZ7.J634145Las 2011   2010033580
[Fic]—dc22   CIP
                                                                                                                      AC

11   12   13   14   15   LP/RRDB   10   9   8   7   6   5   4   3   2
❖
First Edition

London is a riddle. Paris is an explanation.
—G. K. *Chesterton*

Prologue

It was that time of day again. Time to stare at the question, the two lines of black on an otherwise blank page.

Question: *Describe a life experience that changed you. What was it, and what did you learn? (1,000 words)*

This was the most general college application essay, the one that required the least research. Ginny had completed all the other steps—asking for transcripts, groveling for recommendation letters, two sittings of the SAT, one AP exam, four essays on various subjects. This essay was the very last thing she had to do. Every single day for the past three weeks, she opened the document and stared at the question. Every day, she started to type the answer, then erased what she had written.

She took a deep breath and began to type.

My aunt Peg died last May. At least, that's when
we found out about it. She left the country two years
before, and we didn't really know where she was. But
then we got a call from a man in England who told us
she had died of brain cancer. A few weeks later, I got
a package that had thirteen blue envelopes in it. . . .

How exactly was she supposed to explain what happened over
the summer? One day, thirteen little blue envelopes containing
strange and very specific instructions from her aunt showed up, and
then Ginny—who had never been anywhere or done anything—
was suddenly on a plane to London. From there, she went to
Paris, to Rome, to Amsterdam and Edinburgh and Copenhagen
and across Germany in a train and all the way to Greece on a slow
ferry. Along the way, she had met a collection of stone virgins,
broken into a graveyard, chased someone down Brick Lane, been
temporarily adopted by a strange family, been fully adopted by
a group of Australians, made her stage debut singing Abba in
Copenhagen, been drawn on by a famous artist . . .

. . . it was a bit hard to summarize in one thousand admissions-
committee-ready words.

She looked at the calendar she had made for herself out of
sticky notes on the wall next to her desk. Today's note read:
Sunday, December 12: FINISH ESSAY!!!!! NO, SERIOUSLY,
THIS TIME FINISH THE ESSAY!!!!!! And a few lines down,
the due date: January 5. She pulled it off the wall and tossed it
into the trash. Shut up, note. She didn't take orders from anything
that had a glue strip.

Ginny put her feet up on the edge of her desk and tipped her chair back. She had always thought applying to college would be exciting. Living away from home, meeting so many new people, learning new things, making a few poor life decisions . . . the thought of it had kept her going all through high school. But after last summer, college didn't seem like such an adventure anymore. She started idly scrolling through the websites of the colleges she was applying to. All of them were trying to sell her a future in the same way they might try to sell her some mascara ("Longer, fuller lashes! New formula! Look!" *Close-up of unnaturally long lashes, thick with something*) or a weight-loss product ("I lost 25 pounds!" *Image of woman twirling around in dress next to picture of her former self*).

The photos were all the same, for a start. Here was the one with the smiling and carefully composed group wandering down the tree-lined path in the sunlight. The close-up of the person at the microscope, the wise professor leaning over his shoulder. There was the one of cheering people in matching shirts at a basketball or football game. It was like there was a checklist that all the schools had to follow. "Have we included 'professor pointing at blackboard full of equations'? Do we have 'classroom of smiling, engaged students staring at nothing'?" Worse than that were the catchphrases. They were always something like: "We give you the keys to unlock the door of success."

She dropped the legs of the chair back down to the floor and flipped back to the blank page and the question.

The letters arrived last May . . .

. . . and were promptly stolen by some dudes on a beach a few months later.

Ah yes. That was the other problem with this essay—the horrible ending. In August, she was on the Greek island of Corfu, standing on the white sand of a gorgeous beach. The only envelope she had left to open was the very last one, and she decided to do this just as soon as she had a little swim. She had been on a ferry for twenty-four hours, baking in the sun on the deck . . . and the water here was so very, very beautiful. Her friend Carrie decided to swim naked. Ginny went into the warm, clear waters of the Aegean wearing her clothes. They left their backpacks in the care of their three male friends, who fell asleep on guard duty.

High above, on the white rocks overlooking the water, two boys on a scooter stopped and surveyed the scene. Ginny was bobbing up and down in the waves and watching the ocean meet the sky. She remembered the sound of Carrie screaming and yelling. She remembered climbing over some rocks to find Carrie dancing around in a towel, naked and crying and saying something about the bags being gone. Ginny looked up to see the scooter ripping away from the scene, back up the rough path, back to the road above. And that was it. Letter number thirteen had been ripped right out of her life by some petty thieves who wanted her crappy backpack.

Lesson learned? Do not go swimming in the Aegean and leave the single most important document in your life in a bag on the beach. Take that, College!

Her eyes drifted away from the essay to the little red light in the corner of her screen. The light that symbolized Keith.

Keith was the actor/playwright she met when she was following the directions in her third letter, the one in which she had to give five hundred pounds to a starving artist. She found Keith's play in the basement of Goldsmiths College and she bought all the tickets for the entire run, making him the first person to ever sell out the tiny student theater he was working in (also accidentally ensuring that no one would ever see his show). He was intense, hilarious, bizarrely confident, handsome . . . in a scruffy-poor-London-art-student way. But most mysterious of all, he was fascinated by *her*. He called her his "mad one."

To be clear—and she reminded herself of this fact daily—Keith was not her boyfriend. They were "kind of something." That was how they had left it, in those exact words. Their relationship was deliciously and frustratingly ambiguous, always flirty, never defined. When Ginny first returned to America, they were in touch every day. The time difference made it tricky—he was five hours ahead—but they always managed it.

Around Thanksgiving, he got into some show he called a "panto," so between rehearsals and his school schedule, his time online had decreased dramatically. For the past few weeks, Ginny had perched herself at her desk every night, waiting for that little light to turn from red to green, signifying that he was online. It was seven thirty now, which meant it was twelve thirty in London. Tonight was probably going to be one of those nights he never came online at all. She hated those nights.

She checked her email instead. There were several messages, but the one that caught her eye was from someone named oliver273@ easymail.co.uk. Someone else from England was trying to reach her—someone she didn't know. She opened it.

What she found was a picture. A big blue square that filled the screen. It took her brain a moment to realize that it was a scan of a piece of blue paper with very familiar handwriting. It took almost a full minute more for her to fully accept what she was seeing.

Dear Ginny,

Let me tell you about the division bell. The division bell will tell you a lot about England. You like to learn about England, right? Of course you do.

See, in Parliament, when they have a vote, they shout aye or no. The Speaker says, "I think the ayes have it" or "I think the noes have it," depending whichever side is at its shouty best. Sometimes, though, when it can't be determined which side has won, they have to have what is called a rising vote. A rising vote means just that--you have to rise up and stand on the yes side or the no side so you can be counted. There is an adorable, kindergarten-like quality to this, right?

Following on the kindergarten theme . . . sometimes members of Parliament are out at recess when these votes happen. Instead of being in the sandbox, though, they are usually at the pub. So, local Parliament pubs are sometimes outfitted with a division bell, which rings when one of these votes is about to take place. When it rings, the members hurry back and stand on the yes or no side.

The division bell is ringing for you today, Gin.

You've done a lot in the last twelve envelopes, if you have in fact completed all that was contained in them. For all I know, you've read these letters from your sofa in New Jersey. But I trust you. I think you're exactly where I suggested you should be: on a ferry in the Greek Islands.

If you really wanted to, you could go home right now. Maybe you've had enough. Or . . .

. . . or you could go back. Back the way you came. Back to London.

Do you want to go on? Ding, ding. Yes or no?

I'll be honest with you, from here on out, things get a little weird. If you are ready to stop, do it. Take it from someone who knows--if you feel the need to go home, listen to that need and respect it.

Think it over on the beach for a while, Gin. Should you decide to go on, you can go to the next page and . . .

At this point, the letter stopped. At the bottom, below the image, was a short message:

Sorry to interrupt. You don't know me, and likewise, I don't know you. As you can see, I possess a letter (actually, a series of letters) that seem to belong to you. But since this last letter contains very important information, I have to be sure that I am speaking to the right Virginia Blackstone. If you think this letter belongs to you, please let me know. My name is Oliver, and I live in London. You can reach me at this address.

For a moment, she did nothing. No movement. No speaking. She waited for the information to sink in. This was a page of the last letter. This was a task undone. This was the universe more or less demanding that she return to England at once and finish what she had started. This was fate. This was her brain going into hyperdrive.

The old Ginny had never traveled and knew no one in England. Old Ginny would think, plan, be cautious. But new Ginny needed a distraction, and a reason to see her kind-of-something non-boyfriend . . . and she knew someone who knew how to make unlikely things happen.

She got up and started to pack.

Delusions of London

Ginny tried to process what she was seeing. She had been drifting in and out of sleep, so the line between dream and reality was a little unclear. She blinked a few times and looked out the window again.

Nope. This was not a dream. They were really there. Two massive, inflatable snowmen—fifty feet tall or more—hovering two stories up, their leering smiles pointed toward the street below. Big, white monsters of cheer, floating like clouds. It was unclear whether they had come for good or ill, whether they were ascending or descending. They were as wide as the road and blocked out the sky.

She pointed at them dumbly.

"Those are the giant snowmen of Carnaby Street," her uncle Richard explained. "Festive and disturbing, just the way we like it here. Don't look them in the eye."

Ginny and Richard were in a black cab making its slow way

through the streets of London. They turned onto Regent Street—a seemingly endless line of stores large and small. The sidewalks were packed to capacity, easily five to ten people across. Strings of lights poured down over storefronts, waterfalls of them in red and silver and blue. Overhead, intricate patterns of lights and wire had been webbed between every streetlight, forming pictures of musical notes and sleighs. The bleary film of exhaustion over Ginny's eyes added to the sparkle.

"It was probably a mistake coming this way," Richard said, looking out the window at the traffic. "But I thought you should see Oxford and Regent streets during the holiday rush. I don't recommend actually shopping here. Today's bad enough, but tomorrow, Christmas Eve . . . it's going to be a mad day for us."

By "us" he meant Harrods, where he worked. Harrods was the biggest, baddest, most famous store in London. Richard ran a department that mostly dealt with rich and famous people. He was the guy who had to make the arrangements when the Queen wanted to go shopping, or when TV stars or rock musicians or people with titles needed to send out a bunch of complicated baskets full of improbable things. Since Christmas was the hardest time of year for him, it was probably not the best time to have his American niece drop in, but he didn't seem like he minded. When she had called him and asked if she could come over for Christmas, he'd accepted instantly.

It had been a tricky negotiation on the New Jersey side of things, but she approached it with a confidence that she had never known before. She pitched the idea to her parents: Going to England was an extremely educational and culturally expanding experience, and she could spend it with her *relative*. Wouldn't that be better than sitting around in Jersey for the two weeks that school was off? One phone call from Richard, with his smooth do-not-worry-I-will-take-care-of-everything delivery, sealed the deal. Everything was easier when you had a responsible adult with a fancy accent involved.

Ginny had uncovered the fact that she even had an uncle late in her stay in England over the summer, when Richard revealed that he and Aunt Peg had gotten married right before her death. Richard definitely didn't look like he was someone she would be related to—this tall, suited English guy who knew exactly how wide ties, collars, and lapels were currently being worn, probably down to the millimeter. Yet he was so warm and easygoing, so weirdly apologetic about everything. And handsome, with his softly curling dark hair, his wide eyes, and arched brows. Even his gently receding hairline added to the soft openness of his face.

"I've arranged for a proper roast dinner on Christmas," he went on. "I'm not making it. That would be a disaster for all concerned."

"Roast dinner?" she repeated. The jet lag was just creeping in at the sides of her thoughts, making everything a little hard to process.

"Oh, roast dinner . . . that's the best part of Christmas. You have your turkey, your roast potatoes, your carrots, that one Brussels sprout, the bucket of gravy . . ."

The cab driver was nodding along to this with an expression of almost religious contemplation.

". . . anyway I ordered the whole thing from work. I'll bring it home with me tomorrow. They do a good job in the food halls.

11

And I have some time off in a few days. We should go and do some more holiday things. Are there places you want to see? Tower of London, or . . . I don't know. Do you want to ride on the London Eye? I've never done that. I never go anywhere that visitors might like, except for Harrods. Do you want to go to Harrods? Please say no. You've been there, anyway. Anywhere else . . ."

Ginny nodded contentedly. As they drove farther north and east into Islington, she started recognizing more and more. There was Angel Tube station, here was the street full of shops, the little pub on the corner. . . .

"It's right here, second one in with the black door."

Richard was talking to the driver. She had fallen asleep again, her face mashed against the window. They had arrived at the house with the six steps leading up to it, the lightning bolt–like crack running down them. The plant pots were still there, full of twigs and dusty soil. She immediately reached for her purse, but Richard was ahead of her, holding out a few twenty-pound notes to the driver.

Stepping out of the car snapped her back to reality. It wasn't that it was any colder than it was at home, but there was wetness in the air as well. Richard's house still had that strange, blank quality, that feeling like it had been furnished from an office-supply warehouse. The plain pine furniture, the low, industrial carpet. There was a large new television but not much else of note in the living room. It had the air of a house that was waiting for its occupant to show up. There were no decorations.

The kitchen was in a mild state of disarray—take-out containers, bottles stacked on the counter waiting to be recycled, piles of bags sitting on top of the trash. All the signs of a man on his own who had been running nonstop for weeks.

"I've got to get back to work," he said. "I'm sorry you're going to be alone for the rest of the day. Here's your key—you probably remember, the square one is for the top lock. Genuine Harrods key chain, enjoy that. And there's plenty of food. . . ."

He indicated the kitchen with a general sweep of his hand. Ginny caught the little silver glint of a wedding ring on his left hand. She had managed to miss that ring when she first met him. God, she'd been clueless the first time she was here.

"I'll be fine," she said. "Promise. Sorry I'm busting in when you're so busy."

"Don't be. I'll be back around eight. Maybe nine . . . but I'll try for eight."

As soon as he was gone, Ginny dragged her suitcase up the steps. It was not an elegant trip, banging and clunking, smacking into the wall. The door to her room—Aunt Peg's room—was open and waiting for her. It would always be strange coming into this room. The pink walls had an odd glow in the pale morning light. The glint of the wrappers and various pieces of trash that Aunt Peg had collaged on the walls stood in stark contrast to the large poster print of *A Bar at the Folies-Bergère*, Aunt Peg's favorite painting. Richard had stacked towels and extra blankets on top of the patchwork quilt Aunt Peg had sewn.

Ginny dropped the suitcase under the window and sat on the floor with her back against the bed, looking up at the walls, the ceiling, taking it all in. There were two things she had to accomplish while she was here. Thing One: Get the letter. That was all arranged. She would meet Oliver at a coffee shop tomorrow at two and he would hand it over.

Which meant that she had today to accomplish The Other Thing.

In the two weeks that she had planned this trip, Keith had spent less and less time online. Their conversations, when they had them, had been short. Normally, this would have devastated her, but since she was on her way back to England, she had decided to use this to her advantage. The thing about her Keith seemed to like the most was the fact that she sometimes just turned up out of the blue, with some very unlikely story. So she hadn't mentioned that she was coming. Today, she was going to appear on his doorstep.

This was a maneuver that required preparation. She had managed, through some creative questioning, to find out that he would be at home this afternoon. The timing was right. She also brought the proper tools. She reached over and unzipped the suitcase. Her favorite outfit was on top—a new black dress with white dots. With her new black boots and a pair of silvery tights, it was by far the greatest outfit she had ever owned.

Time for a shower, which required a wrestle with the shower-spigot attachment in the bathroom. She had soaked the ceiling many times with this contraption over the summer. Richard had also kept all the toiletries Ginny had purchased on her last visit and had stacked them on an empty shelf in the bathroom. One quick and not-too-serious spray-down of herself and the bathroom later (already an improvement on her previous technique), and it was time to get dressed. She made sure the seam of her tights lined up perfectly along her toes (an often-neglected detail). Then the boots. She examined the final product in the mirror. It was . . . good. She looked good. Not like a tourist. Not like someone who was trying too hard. She looked like herself . . . maybe just a little dressier than normal.

Quick hair check. When she got home from England in August, she felt the need to change herself a little. She had worn her hair very long for her whole life, and 80 percent of the time, she wore it in braids. The braids had become her signature, and the signature felt very tired. She impulsively chopped four inches off the bottom and dyed it a deep shade of auburn. Everyone loved the hair, but she still wasn't used to it. She kept looking for it, expecting it to hang down lower, to get in her way when it was windy out, to be there to twist and curl when nervous. Still, it had a nice, deep shine. It was more . . . mature.

There was one more thing to get out of the suitcase—a small present wrapped in red paper. She carefully examined it to make sure the wrapping had not been ripped. The present had been tricky. She had to get something meaningful, but not *too* meaningful. Something personal, but not *too* personal. She had searched long and hard for it, and finally found it.

During the summer, Keith found her in Paris. They had kissed once. That had happened in a graveyard, on a stone monument shaped like an open copy of *Romeo and Juliet*. Copies of *Romeo and Juliet* were common, but the one she'd found was antique, from 1905. It had a blue leather cover and was illustrated in bright, jewel-like colors, with gold endpapers. It was the kind of thing you could give to a theater student, just because it was a nice thing for a theater student to have. And it was the kind of thing you could give to someone as a way of remembering your first kiss.

The paper had made the trip with no damage at all. She

15

wrapped it in a plastic bag to protect it from any rain, put it in her messenger bag, and grabbed her coat and her keys. It was time to make her second entrance into Keith's life. This time, she was ready.

Surprises and Explanations

The route to Keith's house was perfectly preserved in Ginny's memory—past Indian restaurants and dozens of newsagents, down street after street of rows of houses, all in various stages of repairs. Unlike New York, which was a city of big buildings and apartments, London was a city of houses, rows and rows of houses with little gardens in the front, houses that had known many families, known wars, known different eras and levels of wealth.

And there it was, the house she remembered so well, the house she thought about so often. There were the cheap black blinds, askew as always. There was the gold plastic window in the front door, the trash bin out front that was always overflowing, the little stone wall, and the shabby, tiny front garden, which always seemed to grow a thin crop of crumpled candy wrappers. As a little nod to the season, a string of Christmas lights was draped somewhat haphazardly around the upper windows, strung from one window to another across the front of the house. It blinked in an irregular pattern, one that suggested to Ginny that it probably wasn't supposed to be blinking at all.

Out front was Keith's small, battered white car. She peered inside the front window to see if it was as trash filled as ever. It wasn't. He'd obviously given it a cleaning recently. Aside from two plastic bags and a few script pages on the front passenger seat, it was clutter-free. The first time Ginny saw this car, it had been stuffed with an entire theatrical set, including an inflatable palm tree (deflated, thankfully).

There were lights on in the two upstairs windows, and the muffled beat of music escaped the glass. *Someone* was home. It might be Keith, or it might be David, Keith's lovesick roommate with the horrible on-off girlfriend, Fiona, the human cotton swab. She got closer and listened carefully. The noise was coming from the window on the left—that was Keith's.

For the first time since she'd cooked up this idea, she felt a surge of nervousness. This had all felt so hypothetical up until this point. In the time between turning out her light at night and going to sleep, she had imagined this moment, the exact way she would knock, his face when he opened the door. . . . Now she was *really* here, and in a minute, she would *really* see Keith. Imagination was about to collide with reality.

"Relax," she told herself. "You have the advantage of surprise. Just *be normal*."

Of course, the first step toward normalcy probably didn't include sneaking around in front of the house, looking through the car windows, and talking to herself.

She reached up and knocked hard on the plastic panel. One of the windows above slid open a little bit.

18

"THE DOOR IS OPEN!" Keith yelled out.

Ginny looked up to see if he was peering down at her, but there was no head sticking out of the window. He was just letting whoever it was come in. While that didn't seem especially safe, it did work to her advantage. She pushed the door open slowly.

Instantly, she was overwhelmed by the familiar smell. Detergent, a spicy incense, some kind of dish soap, wet clothes, theater dust . . . it was Keith smell. The door opened onto a hall and a set of stairs. The little foyer area was crammed with things—plastic bags full of newspapers, Keith's sneakers, umbrellas, books. There was, for some reason, a hammer in the middle of the floor and rolls of toilet paper piled in the corner. T-shirts and boxers were spread over the heater on the wall to dry.

"Top of the steps!" he called. "Just come up!"

Ginny steadied herself and quickly checked her warped reflection in a cheaply framed poster for Keith's last show, *Starbucks: The Musical*. Someone's black scarf had fallen just at the foot of the steps, marking the line she had to cross to continue. She stepped over it and made her way up the steps.

Keith sat on the sofa, his legs stretched out and his feet balanced on a plastic crate. The first thing she noticed was his hair. It was a little shorter, and not quite as shaggy as it had been over the summer. The haircut made it look darker and brown, not quite so reddish blond.

He was half-scowling at a computer screen, squinting a bit as he typed away feverishly. He was so intent that he didn't notice her standing in the doorway. He turned and opened his mouth, ready to call out again, and caught sight of her in his doorway.

He actually jumped back an inch or two.

"Hi," she said, grinning. "Remember me?"

For almost ten seconds, Keith did nothing but stare. Ginny clung to the door frame.

"There is something terribly, terribly wrong with you," he finally said. "And I intend to have you put in a home. Are you going to come in, or are you going to hang in the doorway like that?"

He pushed some papers off the sofa to make room for her. She came in and sat down carefully, barely able to look at him directly at first. The sensory overload took some time to get used to. He wore a black sweater, ragged jeans, and a pair of bright socks with visible holes. She smiled at his toes poking out.

"Why didn't you say you were coming?" he asked.

"I wanted to surprise you," she said. "Do you let every weirdo who knocks come into your house? You didn't even look."

"I thought you were here to audition," he said. "People have been coming here to read for the last few days."

"Audition?"

"New play about the financial crisis. It's called *Break the Bank*. It's the evolution of something I started a while ago called *Bank: An Opera of Greed*."

"Aren't you in that . . . panto thing?"

"Ah," he said. "I had an . . . artistic disagreement with the director of the panto. As it happens, I take issue with the objectification of women in *Cinderella*, and the reliance on shoes as a means of identification. Surely you understand."

"You got fired?"

"Fired is such an *accurate* word. Also, I didn't like being the back half of a horse."

20

Ginny smiled and sat back into the couch. Rain was coming in through the half-opened window, but Keith didn't notice or care. She reached into her bag and pulled out the present.

"What's this?" he asked. "Is it a lump of money? Did you bring me money? You want to back my show again, don't you?"

"Yes," she said. "It's a lump of money."

Keith held the gift for a moment and squeezed it lightly.

"You're embarrassing me." He looked down at the package. "I didn't know you were coming. I don't have anything for you."

This was definitely a first—Keith, *embarrassed*. His cheeks even flushed a bit.

"Open it!" she said.

He tore through the paper, revealing the blue cover. He looked puzzled for a moment, then ripped off a few more strips until it was fully revealed. For a moment, he said nothing at all, just opened it and looked at the pages, the illustrations. When he finally looked at her, his eyes were wide and his expression raw and open.

"I don't know what to say, Gin. It's . . . it's lovely."

His embarrassment was catching. Ginny felt her face get hot, and she found that she was gripping bunches of her skirt in her fists.

"I know it's one of your favorites," she said.

"Well, who doesn't like a romantic suicide pact?"

"Only bad people," Ginny said.

"Exactly." Keith looked up partway, avoiding her face, instead tracing the outline of her new haircut. "Your hair. You changed it. You look like a news presenter."

"Is that a good thing?"

"Clearly you don't know about my childhood obsession with the woman who did the weather. My heart still flutters when I hear the word 'precipitation.' I don't think I've ever seen you without braids. I thought your hair just grew that way."

He turned back to the book and flipped the pages for a few moments. From the way his eyes were flicking across the pages, Ginny could see he wasn't reading. He was thinking. The moments ticked on. Ginny managed to inch her way closer to him, until she was right at his shoulder. He didn't turn to her directly, but he was moving toward her in barely perceptible increments. This was it. Her whole body was tingling. She could feel a kiss coming, the way you could feel a heavy rain approaching.

The door opened downstairs, causing them both to start a bit. A female voice called up a muffled hello. Keith glanced toward the noise, set the book on the coffee table, and stood up. Ginny assumed this horrible interrupting person was here for an audition until a voice called from the downstairs hall.

"It is foul out there! David had better thank me! I stayed late for him and got stuck in the rain!"

"Fiona?" Ginny mouthed.

"No." Keith shook his head and crossed the room. "She's gone. Been gone for ages. They split up right after you left. That's why the grass out front started growing again."

"He's got a new girlfriend?" she said quietly. "Thank god. You must be happy."

"Yeah. He does. It's a relief. She's a lot nicer. But then, your average angry snake is nicer than Fiona. I'm sure she's happier wherever she is now, burning orphans or whatever she does with her time."

There was a quick footfall on the steps and then a girl appeared in the doorway. The new girl was extremely pretty. Like David, she had very dark black skin. She was a few inches shorter than Ginny, with skinny jeans, scuffed-up brown boots, and an enormous, slightly ragged gray sweater. She wore no makeup, but her cheeks glowed brightly from the cold and damp. Her hair was a free-flowing halo of spirals that rose up high, at least six inches or more, all around her head. Moisture from the rain was trapped in the tips of her hair, which she was rubbing in disgust.

"Remind me to never . . . oh! Sorry! I'll go wait downstairs until you're done."

"It's all right," Keith said. "It's not an audition. This is Ginny. The famous Ginny Virginia."

"No!" the girl exclaimed. "Was that you, with the letters? Your aunt is an artist?"

"That's me," Ginny said, oddly flattered that David's girlfriend had heard of her.

"Oh! Keith's always talking about you!" The girl came in and sat next to Ginny. "I'm Ellis. So nice to meet you! Did you just . . ."

"Kind of a surprise visit," Keith said with a proud smile. "As is her way."

"This is so exciting! What are you doing here? Just visiting for Christmas? Sorry I'm such a mess. Just had my last day of work. I took a Christmas job at H&M and now I am *finished*!"

She threw her arms into the air in triumph before collapsing on the sofa in the place Keith had just vacated, pulling off her boots. Ginny forced a polite smile. David's new girlfriend was nice, but she was also settling in. She had no

23

I-have-just-interrupted-a-personal-moment radar at all.

"People are so horrible when they shop for Christmas," Ellis continued. "They do things you would not believe. David wanted me to pick up a shirt for his sister. I got the last one and a woman tried to rip it out of my hands, and when I didn't let go, she pulled her hand back, like this. . . ."

She demonstrated.

"That looks more like a punch," Keith said. "Are you sure this was H&M you've been working at, and not some ultimate fighting league?"

"It's hard to tell some days. But I got the shirt. He had better appreciate that."

Keith began pairing his socks, putting them into little tucked bundles. Ginny had never seen Keith do his laundry before, but he certainly never struck her as a sock bundler. He placed each pair onto the mantel, making a little pyramid out of them.

"What's this?"

Ellis picked up the copy of *Romeo and Juliet* and started paging through it. This was too much—the book was private. Keith glanced over, but he didn't ask Ellis to stop. His pyramid of socks was getting out of control. It was going to fall apart at any second. Yet he just kept folding and piling.

"A Christmas present from Gin," he said finally. "It's brilliant, isn't it?"

"It's so lovely," Ellis said, replacing it. "You have to tell us all about your plans for while you're here. We'll have to go out and show you around. There's loads to do in London at Christmas."

"Holly-eating contests and Christmas tree fights . . ." Keith's voice was a low mumble. Ellis picked up a spare sock and threw it across the room at Keith. He half-smiled and pulled it off his shoulder. Suddenly, all in a second, Ginny understood everything. She knew why Keith was off-line so often, why the door was really open, and what "kind of something" actually meant.

Ellis wasn't David's girlfriend. She was Keith's.

The room was unbearably hot. The rain at the windows far too loud. She needed to get out of here, to get some air, to sleep . . . to do anything. She just had to get out.

"You know what?" she said. "I'm . . . I didn't sleep on the plane. I think I . . ."

"Would you like a cup of tea?" Ellis said quickly. "Or a coffee?"

"No." Ginny stood. She was unsteady on her feet.

"Oh, look at you!" Ellis said. "God, you're exhausted. You should just take a nap right here."

Keith finally reentered the conversation, a bright expression pasted on his face. "The lengths you'll go to for a ride in my magnificent automobile! I can hardly blame you. Come on, then. I'll take you back."

"It's really nice meeting you," Ellis said, hugging Ginny. "Feel better. Some sleep will help. And we'll see you again, right? We'll make plans!"

One of the small mercies in all of this was that the ride from Keith's to Richard's only took about five or ten minutes. Keith was very chatty when they first got into the car, rattling on about his plans for *Break the Bank*. Ginny nodded and tried to act interested in "the collaborative writing process, you know, based on our collective disillusionment with the traditional financial structure, you know, hearkening back to the communal voice in theater that we haven't had since, you know, the seventies."

The rain had let up a little. Now it was fine and misting. Ginny fixed her gaze on the view—the rain, the glimpse of Christmas trees through open windows, the guy with the shopping bags of wine hanging off the handlebars of his bike, begging for disaster. When they pulled up to Richard's, Keith let the engine run for a second, then reached for the key to turn off the car.

"So, I'm off home for the next day and a half," he said.

"Where is that again?" Ginny said. She was trying to sound casual and unbothered, but her voice was dry.

"Reading. Just doing the Christmas thing. I'll be back on Boxing Day and we should . . . we'll do something."

"Cool," she said. "I'll be here. Thanks for the . . ."

She waved her hand to indicate the general miracle of automotive transportation.

"No sweat," he said.

She was halfway up the cracked steps when she heard the car door open. He was leaning sideways across the front seats and waving to her to come back. She returned and leaned down into the opening.

"Thank you for the book," he said. "Merry Christmas, yeah?"

"Merry Christmas," she replied. And then she turned and skipped up the steps so he couldn't see the tears that fell freely down her face.

Pairs of Shocks

The next morning, Ginny woke up in a cold room. She stared straight up the wall, at the strange landscape Aunt Peg left behind—the wall of trash she had collected up and collaged, a jarring vista of different materials, some wrinkled, some smooth, some reflective, all different colors and words and shapes and materials. It was probably supposed to look like something, but from this angle, it was all confusion.

She was not going to mope. She was going to get up. Today she had to do what she really came here to do. She was in London. It was Christmas. She had a letter to get.

In the kitchen, Richard had left a cheerful note against a mug about how happy he was to have her here, and how she should think of this house as her own. She opened up her computer, half-expecting a long message from Keith, with an excruciating explanation of the day before, but there was nothing from him. There was one from Oliver, confirming that he would be at the café above Foyles bookshop on Charing Cross Road at two P.M. That was what she needed to focus on. Getting the last little blue envelope, and getting on with her life.

She arrived at Charing Cross a full two hours early and wandered down the street of book and music shops. Foyles was a massive place, with a large, urban-folksy coffee bar—heavy wood tables and real cups and wine and cookies and indie newspapers. It was very crowded, so she waited in the corner until a table was free, then claimed it and sat.

At exactly two o'clock, a tall guy stepped into the café. That's probably what Ginny noticed first—his extreme height. He was well over six foot. Ginny wasn't sure what she had been expecting, but he turned out to be a very pleasant surprise. He had an angular face and almost jet-black short hair. He wore a long black wool coat, which looked very well-made and expensive, and under that, a gray dress shirt and slightly loose black pinstripe pants. He had a well-worn leather bag with him, strapped over his chest. His face was pale, and he was thin, with dark, intense eyes. Though he had to be somewhere around her age, the effect made him look older and placed him in some unknown territory between stockbroker and rock star. He was, without question, the most *English*-looking guy Ginny had ever seen. She wasn't even sure what that meant, really. She only knew that from now on, when calling up an image of an English guy in her mind, this would be the picture.

Oliver surveyed the room from his natural vantage point and quickly focused on her. He strode over to the table in about four steps and pulled out the chair opposite Ginny. As he sat, he adjusted his coat, revealing a flash of rose-colored silk lining and a fancy embroidered label just on the inside. And yet, for all the weird formality of his clothes, there were three tiny pins on the lapel of his coat—one said BOWIE, one was a small lightning bolt, and the other had a picture of a skull and writing that was too small to read. He pulled his bag onto his lap.

"Virginia?"

His accent was much crisper than Keith's, and he was more polite, hesitant. He was *fancier*.

"Ginny," she said. "Hi, I'm . . ."

She always did that, introduced herself twice.

They sat staring at each other for a moment. He put his hands on the table and knotted his fingers together. When he reached forward, Ginny could see that though the coat was custom-made for *someone*, it clearly wasn't Oliver. The arms were too short by several inches, exposing his arm with every move.

"Did you want a coffee?" he asked.

"No, I'm fine."

He nodded, looking oddly relieved.

"So," she said. "How did you get the letters?"

"I was backpacking in Greece. My bag broke on the way to Corfu. I met some guys in town who were selling things out of the boot of their car. The things were used—it was perfectly clear that they had to be stolen, but they were cheap. And I was kind of desperate. Anyway, I bought your backpack. If you want it back . . ."

"It's okay," Ginny said. It was fine with her if she never saw that thing again. It was green and pink and hideous and over-sized—the physical embodiment of embarrassment.

"The bag has a lot of very strange hidden pockets," he went on.

"I didn't even find them all until I got home and was emptying everything out. The letters were in one of them, along with some receipts, and a few coins. . . ."

He opened his bag. First, he presented her with a small stack of crumpled receipts and a small handful of euro coins. Ginny took one of the receipts and stared at it. It was an artifact, a long-forgotten fragment of the summer. She'd spent eight euros fifty somewhere in Germany. She hadn't stayed in Germany at all, just moved from one train to the next in order to go south to Greece. But somewhere along the way, she bought a Coke and a small pizza in a train station.

"I brought it all," he explained. "But these are probably the only things you're interested in."

Oliver reached into his bag again and produced a clear plastic bag full of very familiar-looking blue paper and airmail envelopes. Ginny's heart beat faster as she reached for it and removed the contents, all the hand-painted envelopes Aunt Peg had created with such care. These were her paintings. The girl walking toward the castle on a hill from letter #4. The tiny pictures of cakes from letter #6. Here was her picture on letter #9, a girl with two long braids, her shadow cast all the way across the envelope. The strange picture from envelope #12 that had puzzled her at first, because it looked like a purple dragon coming out of the water. It wasn't until she reached Greece that she realized it was a picture of an island. And now . . .

She shuffled right back to letter #1. There was no #13.

"The last one," she said, holding up the letters apologetically. "Um . . . the last one isn't here."

Oliver gave himself a thoughtful chin-pinch before answering.

"When I found the letters," he said, "I did a bit of research, just out of curiosity. I read about the auction of your aunt's paintings. I take it you found them even without the last letter. You got a lot of money from the last sale. But what mattered to you more, doing the things in the letters, or getting money?"

It was an odd question, but not one that Ginny minded answering.

"Doing the things in the letters," she replied. "The money was nice, but it didn't matter."

"So the experience was the valuable part? If you had a choice between the experience and the money, you'd choose the experience?"

Ginny nodded. Oliver's gaze had drifted to a spot just over her shoulder. The questions felt a bit odd. The letters were so personal. Only a few people knew about them in detail. Here she was, talking about them with a total stranger—albeit a total stranger who had brought them back to her. It was fair enough. If she had found these letters, she would be curious too.

"I guess? Yes. I . . . yeah. I would."

Oliver nodded and leaned in, putting his forearms on the table and getting closer to Ginny.

"There's something in the last letter—well, there are several things in the last letter—but the most important thing is that there's another work of art. It's in three pieces. They're all in different locations out in the world, so that they can get exposed to different elements. It's based on a piece done by Mari Adams. You know Mari Adams, right?"

Ginny definitely knew Mari Adams. She was a famous artist, much loved by Aunt Peg. Aunt Peg had met and befriended her, and sent Ginny up to Edinburgh to meet her. Once you saw Mari, you never forgot her mane of orange-red hair or the tattoos on her feet that bore the names of her pet foxes, or her tattooed face.

He reached into his pocket and set a card down on the table—a familiar dove gray card. It read: CECIL GAGE-RATHBONE, JERRLYN AND WISE, ART AUCTIONS. This was also a name Ginny knew well.

"This is the man who handled the sale," he said. It wasn't a question. She couldn't figure out why, but for some reason, this comment put her on edge.

"Right," she said slowly. "He did."

Oliver looked at her intently.

"A finder's fee doesn't seem out of line," he said. "I suggest that we split the proceeds from the final piece of art. I made us an appointment. We're due in forty-five minutes."

Ginny simply didn't know how to process this. She grabbed for her braids, but, of course, they were gone. So she laughed—a weird, gurgling laugh. "You're kidding."

"We should go." Oliver plucked up the card and put it back in his pocket.

"You seriously can't be . . . serious."

"I'm completely serious. If it wasn't for me, you wouldn't know about this at all. In return, I will help you collect the art. Besides, you told me you don't care about the money. So what's the problem?"

"What if I said no?" she asked.

"Then I go home," he said.

"And the letter?"

"Remains lost. Your choice."

"I need to think about this," she said, hooking her ankles around the legs of the chair to support herself. "Can we talk about—"

"Look," he cut in, "by working together, we can both get what we want. But I assure you, I will leave in a minute, and you won't see me again. You'll never see the letter, and you'll never know what was out there. This is your time to decide. Right now."

He pushed back his chair and stood, waiting. From her seated position, he looked ridiculously tall, and aside from a little twitch above his left eye, utterly composed and serious. Ginny looked around at the many people in the coffee shop, all busy with their shopping bags and their strollers and their phones and computers. She wanted to scream out, to tell them all what was going on, tell them the whole story. They would be outraged. They would cluster around him and shake him down for the letter. He would be thrown out into the street, probably without his coat, and forced to run, coffee mugs flying after him and shattering at his heels. But that is not the way the world works. She had no doubt that he meant what he said. If she walked away from this now, he would go away, and that would be it. Forever.

She stood up.

The Devil's Bargain

"It's an absolute pleasure to see you, of course," Cecil Gage-Rathbone said. "*So* happy that you got in touch. Do come through. Coffee? Tea? Something else?"

The offices of Jerrlyn and Wise were richly but tastefully decorated for the holiday. A large tree decked in silver and gold horns and sugared fruit sat in the corner, and various holiday-oriented antiques dotted the room. Cecil looked exactly the same as before, and like everything else around this building, he had been expensively decorated. There was the artfully arranged and unmoving hair, another flawlessly tailored suit, silver cufflinks gleaming at his wrists.

"I'll have a cup of tea," Oliver said.

Ginny shook her head tersely. She felt like she was being kidnapped and was afraid to speak, to say the wrong word.

"Could you bring us some tea, James?" Cecil said, to a man sitting at a desk in the hall.

The Jerrlyn and Wise building looked like it was an old house built sometime around the 1800s. Cecil's office was a small room, probably an old pantry, with an entire wall of built-in shelving for cups and plates. This had been reappropriated to display antique silver spoons and a collection of auction catalogs. The walls had been hung with massive gilt-framed pictures of things like ship-wrecks and drooling dogs and pale children, bringing disaster, rabies, and anemia to every inch of the space. There was just enough room in between these tragedies for his massive mahogany desk and two wingback chairs.

"Please," he said, ushering them into the room. "Please, have a seat. And I don't think we've properly met, though we spoke on the telephone."

He extended his hand to Oliver, who shook it confidently. Ginny began to understand why he was so dressed up. He had been prepared for this meeting.

"Virginia, I hope you've been keeping well."

"I'm great," Ginny said. The words caught in her throat a bit. She sank into the chair closest to the door.

Cecil settled into his chair and assumed his version of a casual position. "You've come about another piece of Margaret's? I'm delighted to hear about this, of course. The success of the previous sale combined with the obviously limited availability of the artwork . . ."

This was a polite way of saying, "Your aunt is dead, so she can't paint anymore, and that makes the price go up."

"And Mr. Davies . . . were you involved with Margaret's work in some way, or are you . . ."

"I'm a friend of Ginny's," Oliver said. "I'm helping."

Ginny dug her nails into the arms of the chair.

"I see," Cecil said. "So, have you come here today with the new work?"

"The piece can be delivered just after the New Year," Oliver said. "Say, on the first? And we'd like to sell it immediately. The next day if possible."

For just an instant, Cecil looked surprised. There was a flicker of movement in the eyebrow region, which Ginny suspected was highly Botoxed.

"That doesn't leave us much time to photograph it and show it to the interested parties. It would be better if we could wait a few weeks."

"We'd prefer to do it quickly," Oliver said.

"Well," he said slowly, "of course, we can do things that way, if you wish. The element of surprise might work in our favor. And this is what you want, Virginia?"

This was her chance to tell him exactly what was going on. But Oliver would simply get up and walk away, along with her letter.

"Yes," she lied. "That's what I want."

"Well." Cecil adjusted the position of some papers on his desk. "In that case, please tell me all about the piece. I have to know what I'm selling."

"I think it's best if you see it," Oliver said. "It's a bit hard to describe."

There was a subtle knock, and James entered from the hallway with a silver tray bearing a small china tea seat and two cups. Cecil poured a cup and offered it to Ginny. She shook her head tersely. Oliver took a cup, topped it heavily with cream, and relaxed in his chair like he owned the place. Cecil put a lump of brown sugar in his tea and stirred it slowly.

"This is a bit unusual," he said, "but the last collection also had a bit of an unusual story. The buyers may appreciate that. I certainly look forward to seeing it. Is there anything you can tell me?"

"We'll be splitting the proceeds of the last sale, fifty-fifty," Oliver said.

"This is an agreement you've reached?" Cecil asked. "I have nothing to reflect this in my notes."

"That's right," she mumbled.

Cecil paused for a moment, then opened his desk drawer and pulled out a notepad.

"Of course," he said. "We can arrange that. I'll have legal draw something up and it will be ready for signature when you bring the piece in. Will that be acceptable?"

"If it's all the same . . ." Oliver reached into his leather bag once again, this time producing a few pieces of paper. "I've already had something drawn up. Very simple. We could just sign it now."

Cecil drew one of the papers closer to himself with just the tips of his fingers, then spun it around to read it.

"It is, as you say, very simple," he confirmed. "Just a moment."

Cecil took the contract and slipped around his desk and past Ginny's chair. He was gone for over ten minutes, during which Oliver and Ginny ignored each other's existence entirely. Oliver did something with his phone. Ginny shifted around, trying to turn away from him as much as she could in her chair. She read the spines of every catalog on the wall. She counted the spoons. Maybe Cecil would come back with the police. Or a gun. They had to have some old guns around here. Instead, he returned with some photocopies and a resigned expression.

"This appears to be in order," he said. "Basic, but acceptable. I have four copies here. If you'll just sign them all where indicated . . ."

Ginny scrawled her name as quickly as possible and pushed the papers away. Oliver wrote slowly, in small, steady script.

"Well," Cecil said, taking the copies, "as I work for the seller, I'll abide by your wishes. I'll arrange for the sale on that day and do what I can to get the previous buyers back in the room. You will have the piece on the first, yes?"

"That's right," Oliver said.

"Then I'll arrange for one of our teams to come for it. First of the year . . . normally we wouldn't do that, but we work with the circumstances. Unless there's something else I can help you with?"

"No," Oliver said, standing. "We should be on our way."

"Then James will show you out. Thank you so much for coming in."

Outside, the sky was the same color as the sidewalk and the stone walls in front of the houses. Oliver strode away from Jerrlyn and Wise with a long, easy step, stopping in front of one of the many small mansions that lined the street and sitting down on the low wall that surrounded its front garden. He pulled a pack of cigarettes and a silver lighter from his pocket with a sweeping gesture that Ginny suspected had been rehearsed in front of a mirror. She stood directly in front of him and folded her arms.

"I want my letter," she said.

"I can't give that to you just yet. The letter is the key to getting the art. If I give you the letter, you can just go and get the art. Don't worry, though. The letter is of no other value to me, so the minute we're done, you'll get it back."

"The minute we're done with what, exactly? How is this sup-posed to work?"

"We go to Paris. That's where the first piece is."

"Paris?"

"Nothing's properly open on Christmas or Boxing Day, so we'll start nice and early on the twenty-eighth. I got us two train tickets. Don't worry—they were cheap. Only fifty pounds. I fig-ured I could contribute that to the cause."

"You think I'm going to travel with you?" she said. "To Paris. You and me. You're insane."

"Look," he said, sticking a cigarette in his mouth, "it's proba-bly hard for you to trust me when I say you'll be perfectly safe with me. My interests are your interests. And I didn't steal a thing. I found the letters, and I'm giving them back. You're going to make money you couldn't have made otherwise. You have no reason to complain."

A small orange cat slunk along one of the walls on the opposite side of the street. It sat and stared across at them haughtily, as if asking what they were doing in its neighborhood.

"We're both needed for this," Oliver said. "There are things in the letter that only you will understand. I have the letter, and you have the knowledge. All I want is for us to go and get the pieces. That's it."

Oliver calmly lit his cigarette and took a long draw, waiting for her reply.

"I'll think about it," she said.

He nodded and pushed off the wall. "You know where to reach me."

The Pool

Though it was only a little after four, the sky had gone dark and all the lights had been switched on: the illuminated ads on the double-decker buses, the light of cell phones pressed to hundreds of faces, the warm glow from the windows. Everyone was moving quickly, the final panicked moments before all the shops closed and Christmas began. London was sparkling and pulsing. Ginny allowed herself to be carried along with the crowd. She had gone beyond shock into a new and completely foreign state of almost aggressive acceptance. The summer had pushed her into some weird places. She had handled it then—she would handle it now.

When she got off at Angel station, she saw a man selling trees in the shopping plaza. Decorate. That's what she would do. She would decorate, and she wouldn't think about anything *but* decorating. It was Christmas, and she wanted to make it nice for herself and Richard. It would keep her busy, and busy was good. She purchased one of the trees, a tiny one, maybe three feet high. It didn't weigh much; she could carry it with one hand. She walked around with it, looking blankly in store windows until she found some decorations to go with it. There was nowhere to leave the little tree outside—she couldn't exactly lock it up—so Ginny brought it in with her. She bought up pretty much everything she found on one of the display tables full of two-for-one Christmas balls and lights and shiny objects. She bought far more than she could reasonably carry, so she carried it unreasonably, the bags cutting harsh red lines into her skin, the tree banging into her ankles as she walked.

"Do you need help with that?" a man asked, as Ginny dragged the tree along the sidewalk.

"No, I'm fine . . . thanks. Merry Christmas."

He nodded, but looked very uncertain.

Though she had gotten a lot of things, some improvisation was still necessary. First, she had forgotten to get a tree stand. This meant finding a bucket in the closet, then getting the tree to stay upright by lashing it in place with some string, then covering the bucket in tinsel. Some of the ornaments came without hooks, so she was forced to make the hooks out of some paper clips she found. When she ran out of those, she just taped them to the tree, hiding the tape as best she could. She bought way too many lights, so she strung them everywhere—up the stairs, around the mirror above the sofa, around the television.

She decorated until there was nothing left to hang, nothing left to cover. Then she sat on the sofa and waited.

Paris. Oliver wanted her to go to Paris. She couldn't deny a minor thrill at the thought. Their conversation played in her head on an endless loop. There was nothing she could have done differently. If she'd said something to Cecil, Oliver would have bolted. So she would go to Paris. She had done it before. And at least this Oliver, Oliver, Oliver loop was a distraction from the Keith, Keith, Keith loop. That was something.

This internal debate continued until a black cab pulled up out front. There was a jingle of keys, and Richard was at the door with three large Harrods bags.

"Hello!" he said. "I have . . . bloody hell."

"I decorated," Ginny said, pointing out the obvious.

"Yes, I see that."

It was hard to read his reaction. He wasn't ambivalent—his eyes were wide and he rubbed his hairline.

"It's . . . wow. I don't really ever . . . I suppose I don't have time . . . it's marvelous."

Richard shifted the weight of the bags around a bit and continued looking around at what she'd done. He looked stunned but happy.

"I have half the food hall in here," he finally said. "The roast dinner! Need to put this in the kitchen."

Ginny followed him, watching as he casually slipped one of the bags behind a chair. Just as casually, she looked to see what it was. Wrapping paper peeked out the top. He had gotten her some gifts.

"It was absolutely mental," he said, dropping the remaining bags on the counter. "I must have sent out two hundred Christmas hampers this morning. Some people don't realize that if you want to send someone fifty pounds of chocolates inside of a decorative birdhouse for Christmas you should really ring me before eight in the morning on Christmas Eve."

"Any celebrities?"

"A few. Nobody was too bad this year. I didn't have to find any exotic animals or enriched plutonium or anything like that."

Richard wasn't exaggerating about the roast dinner. There were easily thirty different containers in the bags. When the last one was put away, Richard took a beer out of the refrigerator. "I'm too tired to drink this," he said, looking at it mournfully. He put it back in the fridge and shut the door. "I have to sleep."

He stopped halfway up the steps and had a look at the lights strung there. "Someone from your family has always decorated my house for Christmas," he said. "Peg did last year. Her decorations were a bit weirder, as you might imagine. She suspended the tree upside down, for a start."

"She what?" Ginny asked.

"By drilling a few holes in the ceiling and suspending it. Right there, in the corner." He pointed to just above where she was sitting. Sure enough, there was a series of small holes there. Aunt Peg, once again, had been down this road before.

"Was it a big tree?" she asked.

"It was enormous."

"And she just . . . hung it?"

"She did. I'm glad she didn't bring the ceiling down. Even if she had, she probably would have turned the rubble into more decorations. I still don't know how she did that. I suspect she had help. In any case . . . I'll see you in the morning. Merry Christmas."

That night, as Ginny lay in bed staring up at the collage on the wall, her brain drifted back to a brutal summer's day in New York City when Aunt Peg said, "Let's go swimming. My friend has a pool."

This was about three years before, when Ginny was a freshman in high school. It was right before Aunt Peg vanished from their lives. Ginny didn't know it then, but this would be the last time she stayed in Aunt Peg's apartment in the East Village. New York City summers are punishing affairs—intense heat magnified off steel and glass, more heat coming from the subways underground, heavy, blanketing humidity that makes you feel like you weigh ten extra pounds. New York is a watery town. It sits between rivers, has a huge harbor, and a swamp. For environmental and aesthetic reasons, Aunt Peg did not believe in air-conditioning. Plus, her apartment was directly above a Chinese restaurant. The apartment that was so cozy and warm in the winter from all the rising heat below was torturous in July. It was like taking a sauna in fat fumes.

So Ginny had been pretty miserable until this pool was mentioned. She was also confused, because having a pool in New York City meant you had to be insanely rich. Aunt Peg's friends were not insanely rich—more just insane. Ginny also didn't have a bathing suit with her. Aunt Peg dug out an old pair of shorts and a thin, ripped T-shirt, declared that to be exactly bathing suit–like, and took Ginny down, deeper into the Village, to a funky, run-down building on Avenue A. There was an alley that led around to the back, where some artist had created a metal "garden" out of car and bicycle parts. There was a Dumpster in the middle of this garden with a ladder up against it.

"Ready?" Aunt Peg asked, shedding her shirt, revealing the bikini underneath. She started to make her way up the ladder, into the Dumpster.

That was *not* a pool.

"It's clean," she assured Ginny. "It's safe."

She jumped inside with a loud splash.

Those things seemed highly unlikely. But, as she always did, Ginny followed her aunt. She slowly climbed the ladder and peered in. Pools usually look bright. They're painted a cheerful blue on the bottom to give the water a pleasant color. Climbing into a dark pool violated some evolutionary instinct. It just wasn't right, even if it did have an inflatable alligator bobbing around. Rust, disease, dirt . . .

"It's fine!" Aunt Peg said again. "I swim in this all the time! Trust me, they cleaned it really well."

Ginny got to the top edge, sat there for a moment, sticking her feet into the water. It was warm, and it reeked of chlorine. That was a positive sign.

Aunt Peg was looking at her, waiting for her to take the plunge—literally. Aunt Peg was the one person Ginny hated to disappoint, so she took a deep breath, inched herself forward, and dropped.

The water was about five feet deep, but the walls of the Dumpster were about eight feet high. It also wasn't very big. It was exactly what it looked like—a big metal box filled with water in the backyard of a building in the Village. But there was something great about it—it was a pool. It was an incredibly stupid pool in the middle of New York. And she had done it. Aunt Peg made the call, and Ginny had answered.

"You know what?" Aunt Peg said. "People would say that it's impossible to have a private pool in the city, unless you were some kind of mogul and had it on the roof of your penthouse or something. But it's not illegal to have a really clean Dumpster, and if you want to fill it with water, and if you want to get in it . . . well, that's your prerogative. People always say they can't do things, that they're impossible. They just haven't been creative enough. This pool is a triumph of imagination. That's how you win at life, Gin. You have to imagine your way through. Never say something can't be done. There's always a solution, even if it's weird."

Ginny nodded away at the time, and by the next day dismissed the sentiment as stupid artsy crap, even though she liked the pool. The day after that she found that she had an infected scratch on her arm and told her mom she got it on the garage door.

But the idea never left her mind. The adventures of the summer had been a triumph of imagination. You could make something amazing out of something awful. So, Keith had a girlfriend. So, she was essentially being blackmailed. She was here. She had made it to London for Christmas. She was with her uncle. She had jumped into the garbage pool before.

Before Ginny could think the matter over anymore, she rolled over and reached around in the dark, finding her computer on the floor. It blinded her for a second when she opened it. She blinked off the shock and turned on chat to see if Oliver was there. It didn't surprise her to see that he was.

When and where? she wrote.

He instantly began typing a reply.

Meet me at St. Pancras Station at 10 a.m. on the 28th, at the meeting place. I have two tickets for the train to Paris at 11:37.

What meeting place? she asked.

You won't be able to miss it. After Paris, there are two other places we have to go.

Where?

47

I can't tell you that yet. I have to protect my interests. I've planned it all out. It will take us four days, total.

Ginny stared at the chat window glowing in the dark. Four days? When Oliver said they were going to take the train to Paris, she assumed he meant they would go there and back. They didn't even have to stay over—that was the magic of going to Paris from London. It could be a day trip. But four days? Multiple cities?

We'll have all the pieces by the 1st, Oliver added, *and then you never have to see me again. Deal?*

She was on the edge again, looking into the murky depths of the garbage pool. This time, there was no voice reassuring her.

Fine, she wrote. *I'll be there.*

Nothing for a moment, then he began typing again.

Merry Christmas, he wrote.

She closed the computer in reply.

The Feast

Ginny woke up on top of her computer, which had snuggled under the covers with her at some point in the night. She extracted it from her bed, looking at it a bit suspiciously. Downstairs, Richard was flopped on the sofa in a pair of running pants and a sweat-shirt, watching a *Doctor Who* Christmas special and sipping a mug of tea.

"Sorry," she said. "I overslept."

"It doesn't matter. This is casual Christmas. We do as we like. I'm drinking tea and watching television. Go make a cup and join me!"

Ginny went into the kitchen. The kettle was still warm from its last use. She flicked the switch and it speedily reboiled the water as she got out one of the heavy striped mugs. This was one English ritual she loved. She never drank tea at home. Tea was for England. Tea was at Richard's house.

"I have something very important," Richard said, when she

joined him in the living room. He reached around to the side of the sofa, producing a long box, about the size of a board game. It was full of what looked like paper towel rolls wrapped in shiny paper.

"Fancy crackers," he said. "Harrods' best."

"Crackers?"

"Christmas crackers? Oh, you don't have those. Here. I'll show you." He opened the box and removed one of the tubes, holding it out to her. "Count of three, you pull on that end, and I pull on this one. Ready? One, two, three . . ."

Ginny gave her end a halfhearted tug and the tube snapped apart with a loud cracking noise. Three small objects fell to the floor: a tiny lump of pink paper, a folded piece of paper, and a miniature metal elephant on a key chain. Richard handed Ginny the elephant.

"The prizes are usually rubbish, but these are nice crackers, so there you go. Small metal elephant. Quality. Bet you've been wanting one of those."

"Ever since I was little," Ginny said, as Richard unfurled the pink lump to reveal a small paper crown.

"I suspected as much. You also get a crown and a joke. The jokes are always bad. Let's see here. . . . 'Who delivers Christmas presents to all the little fish?'"

"I don't know," Ginny said, putting on her crown.

"Santa Jaws. Ho ho! That's a Christmas cracker joke. Now, presents!"

Richard had gotten her a number of gifts—a pile of books (chosen by his friend in the Harrods bookstore), a bag of makeup (put together by one of his friends at the makeup counter), and a sweater (chosen by yet someone else). He was a professional present-picker, with a team of literally hundreds of specialists working under him. It was no surprise then that the gifts were all perfect.

"I hope those are okay," he said. "I gave them as much information as I could. I would have chosen them myself, but it seemed stupid when I could just use experts."

Ginny handed over the three packages she had brought for him. Before she left home, she'd collected a number of pictures of Aunt Peg, along with drawings she'd left in a notebook. Ginny decided to frame them as a gift for Richard. Now that she was here, face-to-face with him, she wondered about the wisdom of giving Richard reminders of Aunt Peg. Maybe what he needed was to forget. He was very quiet as he opened them, and she could see that he was getting teary eyed, which made her get teary eyed.

"They're wonderful," he said. "Thank you."

He set them carefully on the coffee table and coughed into his fist.

"I forgot one," he said, his voice hoarse. "Let me just go and get it."

He was upstairs for just a little bit longer than was probably necessary to get something from his room. When he returned, he had one more box, which he handed to her. "I got this one for you when you first told me you were coming over. I forgot to put it with the others."

It was a phone, nicer than the one she had at home.

"I figured it would be good for you to have one for over here," he went on. "Your own English number. Makes it easier to reach me, or . . . whoever you want to call. The rules wouldn't let you have one of these last time, but there's nothing stopping you now."

Ginny smiled as she took the device out of the box. Her own English phone—a line to Richard, whenever she needed it.

"Thanks," she said.

"Now," Richard said, slapping his hands down on his thighs in a decisive manner that suggested he wanted to push through the emotional moment. "Since it's just us, we can have dinner whenever we want. I was thinking, why don't we make the food now? It's lunchtime. No reason to wait. There's a little bit of everything in there. What do you say? Not only did I get the roast dinner, but since the halls aren't open tomorrow, they give us everything that won't keep. Perk of the job. I've got amazing stuff in there."

He wasn't kidding. There was cold lobster and fresh mayonnaise, smoked oysters, stilton with cranberries, custard, half a dozen types of chocolates, glazed fruitcake, tiny cupcakes. . . .

"Partridge?" Ginny said, examining the contents of a labeled container. "As in, 'in a pear tree'?"

"The same, except not so much in the tree, and more in the oven."

"You eat them?"

"Don't they have partridge in America?"

"I've never seen it," Ginny said. "Does it taste like chicken?"

"Everything does! Except this."

He held up the fruitcake.

"Is *that* a food?" she asked.

"Ah. Good point. We'll just put that over here so we don't eat it by accident." Richard stuck the fruitcake on top of the refrigerator, out of harm's way.

They decided to eat in the living room, in front of the

television, purely because it seemed wrong. But they did it with style, setting the coffee table with everything they could find in Richard's cabinets. They had to drag in a few kitchen chairs to serve as a sideboard for all of the food. Harrods had not done them wrong. It was a feast. A feast largely comprised of meats. Meats and things cooked in meat.

"This would have been it for me," Richard said, looking at the food that was all over his furniture. "Sitting here eating all this by myself. It would have been very, very sad and very, very disgusting. Because I would have done it."

In that moment, Ginny was happy she came, for no other reason than this—sitting around with Richard and all of these containers in front of the television. They loaded down their plates, weighing them down with the vast quantities of gravy that had been provided. They ate and watched a movie. It was just so natural, so nice being here with Richard . . . and yet, she was leaving soon for Paris. She had to tell Richard now. She couldn't tell him the *whole* story, but she had to tell him something, at least that she was going. If he objected—well, she could ignore him and go anyway, but that would be wrong. That would be using him, disrespecting someone who was generous and kind and far from stupid.

She waited until the movie was over, and Richard was reaching over for another helping of potatoes.

"There's something I need to . . ."

. . . *talk to you about.* Yeah. That sounded bad. Richard froze mid-reach for the potatoes.

"Someone found the last letter," she said.

"Someone *found* it? It was stolen, wasn't it?"

"This guy . . . he bought the bag. He found the letters and got in touch with me."

"Well, that was decent of him."

"There's one last thing I have to do," she said. "One last piece of art I have to get. It's broken up into three pieces. I need to go and get them. And the first one is in . . . Paris."

Poor Richard. He didn't deserve this. Every time Ginny walked in his door she was on her way somewhere else. Then again, he had let Aunt Peg live in his house and married her, so clearly he had a thing for flaky American types who liked to sneak off in the dead of night. That was, as Ginny remembered it, how America won the Revolution in the first place. The English walked around in bright red coats in straight lines and took breaks for tea, and the Americans snuck around dressed in rags and hid in trees and stole their horses. Or something. Whatever. She had to do this—it was her *birthright*. It was what George Washington would have wanted.

"When were you planning on doing this?" he asked.

"The twenty-eighth?"

"Where will you stay?"

"The same hostel I stayed in last time," she said. "It's *really* nice."

"Are you going by yourself?"

"No. I'm going with a . . . friend."

Okay, *that* was a lie.

"Your friend from last time? Kevin?"

"Keith."

She could hear the drop in her voice. She couldn't hide it. Richard looked at her curiously.

54

"He has a girlfriend," Ginny said. "I just met her."

"Ah." It was a long, sad *ah* of understanding.

Richard knew the pain of having feelings for someone who didn't necessarily reciprocate. He had loved Aunt Peg for a long time when they lived together as friends and roommates. He had taken care of her through her illness, and married her to make sure she had care. And slowly, over time, she realized that she loved him too, that she had just been afraid of this straightforward, stable guy who had never hidden his feelings. Ginny had learned all of this from the letters. Aunt Peg died before telling anyone in the family what had happened, before she could even tell Richard how much she really loved him. Ginny found herself staring at his wedding ring again.

"Do you think it's a good idea to go with him, then?" he asked quietly.

"It's not him. It's . . . someone else. It'll take about four days."

Richard scooped up the potatoes and put them on his plate. He pushed them around thoughtfully.

"I can't stop you if you want to go somewhere," he said. "But it seems like you're asking my permission. Which is fair enough, I suppose. Let's make a deal. I know you've traveled before. So, be careful. Nothing excessively crazy. Check in with me at least once a day, and let me know where you are. And if you have any problems at all, any problems, you phone. You've got no excuse, now."

He tapped the opened box that contained her present.

"It won't be like last time," she said.

Last time, Richard had airlifted her out of Greece. Maybe she shouldn't have brought that up.

"Right . . . ," he said, giving her a forced smile.

It was done now. She had made her decision. She had permission. And if anything went wrong, she could call Richard. And when it was all over, once she'd worked out this mess, she could tell him the whole story.

She was going to Paris.

Boxing Day

Boxing Day. Ginny had heard this term before, but it seemed so ridiculous. Boxing Day sounded like the day when everyone beat the crap out of one another. Richard explained that it was the day that you . . . put things into boxes. Or moved boxes. Or did something with boxes.

Richard had been very concerned about leaving her alone again, but he had no choice but to go in to work. Apparently, Harrods after Christmas was about as bad as Harrods before Christmas, and Boxing Day was his own personal Armageddon. He was up and gone long before Ginny was out of bed. She had the entire day to herself, and no particular agenda. The day after tomorrow, she had to go to Paris with Oliver. She had no way of preparing for this trip. She had no information. Today, there was nothing to do but wait. Wait and think. And work on the essay. Outside, England was being English—it was raining. Rain here wasn't that bad. It made being inside all the more cozy. Ginny drew a hot bath, got a pad of paper, and decided to soak, listen to the rain, and think brilliant thoughts that would get her admitted to college. She spent several minutes setting up a towel and arranging herself so she could write notes without soaking the paper, but the second she moved to write something down, she splashed the notepad and soaked it completely. She tossed it over to the toilet and sank lower.

Describe a life experience. Well, how about this? How about coming back to England to find the guy you love dating someone else and some other random guy holding your dearly departed aunt's letters and her art hostage. How about that, admissions committee?

They would never believe her. They would think she was a fantasist. They would put her picture on the corkboard with a note under it that just read: PSYCHO. DO NOT ADMIT.

The bathwater cooled almost as fast as her desire to work on the essay, so she got out and dressed. Her timing was excellent, because as soon as she pulled on her shirt, there was a brisk knocking on the door. She jogged downstairs, shoeless, her hair still damp and straggly.

Keith stood on the doorstep, bundled up in a big army-green coat, a heavy black scarf wrapped several times around his neck. He stepped inside, dropped his umbrella in the hall, then yanked off his coat and scarf and threw them on a hook.

"It's pissing down," he said.

He walked straight back into the kitchen. This was how he used to come over in the summer—just walking in like he was fully expected, like he didn't have a girlfriend he'd kept secret from her. Ginny was too surprised to react in the moment, so she shut the door and followed along.

"Present," he said, setting a CD-shaped object on the table. "Go on, open it!"

The present looked like it had been wrapped in repurposed paper, full of telltale white crinkle lines and old tape marks. For some reason, this made Ginny open it very carefully, like the paper needed to be kept for another mission in the future. Inside, there was a homemade CD, complete with a fancy designed cover from the *Starbucks: The Musical* poster.

"Properly recorded," he said proudly. "So you can listen to it every day. So, what have we here?"

He examined the many containers piled on the kitchen counter and turned to Ginny with an expression of intense interest.

"We have a lot of leftovers," she said. "If you're hungry, there's a lot more in the fridge. . . ."

He was already rooting through the fridge and pulling out the tins.

"What is this?" he said, pulling off a lid. "It's not turkey. . . ."

"Pheasant," Ginny said. "Richard got the fancy Harrods Christmas dinner . . . because he works there."

Ginny passed him a plate, and he started piling it up with food. Keith could always eat, anything, anywhere, in any amount.

"So," he said, "I got the impression the other day that something brought you over here, but you didn't say what."

Ginny filled the kettle and said nothing for a moment. Her brain was still trying to catch up with the fact that Keith was here in the kitchen with her, that she was unprepared and wearing pajama bottoms . . . and now he was asking about the letters. But if anyone could take this weird story, it was him. And he had been there since the beginning. He had a right to know.

She set the kettle on its base and switched it on. Keith took a seat at the table to eat.

"Someone found the letters," she said. "All of them. Including the last one."

"Someone from Greece?" he asked. "Isn't that where they were stolen?"

"Yeah, but the person who found them is from here. He's English. He bought the bag. He used the information in them to track me down. The last letter, the one I never got to read before—it has more instructions in it. There's another piece of art. There's something else I have to do. I have to go to Paris day after tomorrow."

"Always the same with you," he said, shaking his head and taking a bite.

"There's kind of a problem."

Keith was chewing, so he waved his fork, indicating that she should elaborate.

"He won't give me the last letter."

"What do you mean he won't give it to you?" he asked, swallowing hard.

"He's keeping it, because he wants half the profit from the last sale. He bought the tickets to Paris. He's the only one who knows where we're supposed to go or what we're supposed to do."

Said out loud, it sounded even crazier and much, much worse. Keith set down his fork and tapped his fist lightly against his mouth in thought.

"You just made that up, right?" he said.

"Nope."

"So, you're saying that a complete stranger bought your stolen property, and is now demanding half your money . . . and that you are going to Paris with him. Because that is the sane thing to do."

The kettle clicked off. She busied herself with making the tea.

"What choice do I have?" she asked, yanking out two mugs. "He's not dangerous. He's just . . . he just wants the money. I need to get the pieces. I've had to do worse."

"Who is this guy?"

"His name is Oliver Davies."

"That tells me nothing. What's he like? How old is he?"

"He's, like, our age or something. It'll be fine. I'll just go with him. I've traveled with people I didn't really know before. I did with you."

"It's not exactly the same." His voice was rising. "We went to Scotland together once. We both happened to be in Paris at the same time. And I didn't steal your stuff and ransom it back to you."

"I didn't mean—"

"Gin, listen. Sit down." He was more serious than Ginny had ever seen him before. She picked up the two mugs of tea and sat next to him. "I'm all for weird stuff as a general rule, but you can't do this. What you're describing is some kind of travel horror story waiting to be written. In the best-case scenario this guy is some kind of a con artist, and that's me being optimistic."

"I know it's a problem," she shot back, unable to hold her frustration in any longer. "What choice do I have? If I *don't* do this, I never get the letter. I never find the piece. I never finish. And it's not like anyone can help me. What am I going to do? Call the police and tell them that someone stole my *mail*? He'll just disappear, and I can't let that happen."

Keith leaned back in his chair and pushed the front legs off the ground, sighing heavily. He stayed balanced like that for a moment, then brought the chair down with a thud.

"You said you're supposed to go the day after tomorrow, right?"

"Right."

"Explain to me how this is supposed to happen."

Ginny took a long breath. She was shaking now.

"I'm supposed to meet him at St. Pancreas. . . ."

"St. Pan*cras*, you mean. That's where the Eurostar leaves from. You said he wants you to take the train to Paris?"

"He got us two tickets. I'm supposed to meet him at ten. He's even set up the sale. He took me to see Cecil. Whatever it is we're getting, it's going to be auctioned off on the second of January, and I have to be there. So I guess he can't kill me, right?"

She tried to laugh, but it didn't quite work. Keith did not join in. He resumed eating for a moment, spearing a huge piece of pheasant that Ginny couldn't believe he actually managed to fit into his mouth. He chewed it to nothingness, his eyes flicking back and forth a bit in thought.

"It seems to me that all you need is the letter," he finally said. "Correct?"

"Right. But he's not going to give it to me."

"But he'll have it with him at St. Pancras, right?"

"He'd have to."

"All right then. We have a solution."

"We do?"

"You forget," he said. "I am a man of many abilities."

He stretched out his hands on the table and wiggled his fingers.

"You play piano?" she said.

"Do you forget my shameful previous life? I'm a thief. I nick stuff."

"I thought you mostly vandalized stuff."

"I stole a *car*," he said proudly. "And many other things."

"But you quit. You don't do that anymore."

"I gave up thieving for gain, but there's nothing wrong with using my skills for good, now is there? Everybody loves Robin Hood. And I haven't lost my touch. Oliver Davies takes the letter out, I steal it from him. Easy."

He scooted his chair closer, until they were directly side by side, his arm up against hers. Every hair on her arm stood up in unison, goose bumps everywhere.

"This is easily fixable, Gin," he said. "This is nothing. We will get the letter back, and you can get your aunt's art. Come on, now. No one messes with my mad one."

Oh god. She was tingling all over. She was going to become hysterical. She was going to grab him by the face and make out with him. There was nowhere she could look at him that made it any better. The way his new haircut revealed his ears a bit more, the way his T-shirt stretched across his chest, the string bracelets he had around his wrists . . . everything highlighted something about him that seemed unbearably wonderful. Her hands shook a little. She quickly pulled them down into her lap.

"Thanks," she said. She turned her head partially in Keith's direction. She could not look at his face. She had to find a dead zone somewhere on him that produced no feeling. She tried for the armpit, which she could look at easily because he had his arm extended, but even that made her pulse go faster.

"I have to go," he said. "I was just stopping in. But it's sorted now, yeah? I'll come by at eight thirty the day after tomorrow and we'll go over to the station together to work through the details."

He got up and pulled on his coat and scarf. The fact that he was leaving without saying why, or where he was going, or inviting her along told her all she needed to know. Ellis. They were going out somewhere. Or maybe she was already at his place for a cozy night in.

She commanded her brain to stop this train of thought. Keith was here now. He was going to help her. They would get the letter back. It wasn't exactly like before—it would never be exactly like before—but it was something.

"We'll get it," he said, as he stepped outside. "Remember, I have never failed at anything."

"Never," she said.

He reached up and gave her new haircut a shake with his hand.

"Still have to get used to this," he said.

"Me too," she replied.

Very wisely, he said nothing else, and jogged down the steps and to his car.

It Takes a Thief

St. Pancras train station is precisely the kind of thing Ginny went to Europe expecting to see, along with vast cathedrals, small cars, advertisements featuring casual nudity, and doctors smoking in front of hospitals. A good portion of the building is a massive Victorian Gothic work of art, made of deep russet-colored bricks and white stone. At the end is a clock tower—a sharp spire surrounded by shorter, sharper spires. The other part of the station is a pristine, supermodern glass temple. Along the massive arcade, dozens upon dozens of tiny brick archways are filled with every kind of shop or service, including Europe's longest champagne bar, almost three hundred feet long. Hundreds and thousands of people wander around with bags, some with little to no idea of where they are going—people figuring out train passes and connections and fumbling around with new currency.

It's exactly the kind of place a thief might like to spend some time.

Ginny and Keith stood along the rail on the second floor. Ginny looked up at the massive glass arch that formed the ceiling. Her suitcase was at her feet, and she had four hundred euros in her pocket. Even though she made over a hundred and thirty thousand dollars in the sale, most of that money had been set aside for college. Her own bank account was much smaller, and this was a pretty big hit to her balance. She would have to be careful to have enough to make it through the next few days. "All right," Keith said. "One last time. You're going to meet him over there at the statue . . ."

The statue was *The Meeting Place*, and it was as easy to spot as Oliver had suggested. Thirty feet high and made of bronze, it showed a man and a woman in a breathless moment of meeting, their faces close together, about to kiss. It was so nice to have a big, metal reminder of romance towering above her and Keith.

"I'll be watching from one of the arches," Keith continued. "And I'll have this." He held up the large, unwieldy London tourist map they had just purchased. It had been selected for sheer size, and when fully opened, provided a rustling paper shield.

"All you need to do is get him to hold it out for a few seconds. I'll do the rest. Once I get it, I'll leg it. I'll meet you outside."

"I just remembered something," Ginny said, leaning over the rail, pressing down hard, crushing it into her abdomen. "That's the same trick some street kids pulled on me in Rome. They came at me with these newspapers. They were flapping them around, trying to distract me and get my bag."

"Well, it's an old move, but a solid one. Did they get anything?"

"No. Some guy came over and chased them away."

What Ginny decided not to mention was that this same guy,

who was her age and kind of hot, then persuaded her to go to his sister's apartment, where he tried to make out with her. He was so extremely sketchy that Ginny had to run away. Why did she run into so many thieves and skeezes?

When the enormous clock above the statue hit ten, Oliver's long, black-coated figure passed below them, heading for the stairs. Along with the leather satchel, a small backpack rested on his back. Oliver was dressed less formally this time. He had on black cargo pants, a snug, somewhat ragged gray sweater, and a heavy scarf wound around his neck that came up well over his chin. Combined with the long black coat, he looked like some kind of operative about to go on a mission.

"That's him," she said.

Keith took a moment to make a mental note of his target.

"Black coat? Beaky face?"

Ginny nodded.

"All right," he said. "Showtime. Don't worry. I haven't lost my rapscallion touch."

He winked and peeled away from Ginny's side, wandering out of view. She took a deep breath and pulled up the handle of her bag, rolling it over to the statue. "Ready to go?" Oliver asked. "We have some time yet, but we might as well go through security now, unless you need something from one of the shops. . . ."

"I want to see the letter," she said.

"Why? You know I'm not going to let you *read* it."

Good point. Ginny tightened her hold on the handle of her bag and looked up at Oliver's face. It was a thin face, with strong, impassive features. The statue behind them was more expressive.

"Because . . . ," she said, "I started off every leg of the other trip by looking at a letter. I just need to see it, okay? It's how this is done."

Oliver rocked back on his heels and considered this, then opened the flap of the leather bag and held up some folded pieces of blue paper between two of his fingers. Immediately, Keith appeared from the hallway behind the statue and walked toward them briskly. He had the map out, feigning struggle and confusion, opening it this way and that, glancing around as if trying to get his bearings. "I'm at *The Meeting Place*," he said, in what Ginny assumed was supposed to be an American accent. It was a little strange—kind of like someone had taken a cowboy, a surfer, and a 1930s gangster and put their accents in a blender. "The statue. *The Meeting Place*. The *statue*. The frickin' huge statue of the people kissing . . ."

"Satisfied?" Oliver said, holding up the pages. He took no notice of Keith, who was coming closer and closer. He was not, however, close enough. Oliver was starting to put the papers away.

"Wait," she said. "Where's the envelope? I need to see the envelope too."

"I don't have the envelope with me."

"Why not?"

"Because I didn't need it. I only needed the letter."

Keith was just a few feet behind him now.

"The *statue*, not the *station*," he said. The closer he got, the more Ginny could hear the accent—and the more she heard the accent, the worse it sounded. Hopefully Oliver just thought that was what Americans sounded like. "What street are you on? No, the statue is in the station. . . ." *Bang.* Keith crashed into him, hard. For just a moment, the map closed around Oliver's outstretched

68

hand. Keith mumbled apologies before collapsing his map as if very embarrassed, and hurrying off. When he was gone, Oliver's hand was empty. It worked. It *actually worked*.

This was supposed to be the moment where Ginny laughed in triumph and delivered the speech she'd been preparing in her mind most of the sleepless night before. She was all ready to go, just as soon as the look of dismay and shock crossed Oliver's face. But it didn't come.

There was no use even pretending now. Ginny turned in the direction Keith had run off. He had stopped at the base of the steps and was shaking out the map and looking very confused. He looked up to Ginny, shook his head, and started making his way up the steps.

"I take it that didn't go as planned," Oliver said, when Keith had reached them. "Who are you, anyway?"

"I'm her hairdresser," Keith said. "She doesn't go anywhere without me. What did you do?"

"I got here an hour early. I stood right over there. . . ." He pointed to a spot on the other side of the second floor, maybe twenty yards away. "I watched you two arrive and do all your plotting. It wasn't that hard to work out what you were up to."

"So where's the letter?" Ginny asked.

Oliver reached up the sleeve of his coat and drew out the blue pages.

"Looks like we both do sleights of hand," he said to Keith.

"You are the ultimate div and obviously have no mates."

Oliver dismissed this evaluation with a shrug, and turned his attention to Ginny. "I'm getting on the train. This is a one-time offer. Either come with me now, or we're done here."

Oliver started walking in the direction of the boarding area for the Eurostar.

"I'm sorry," Keith said. "I thought I had it. . . ."

"It's okay," Ginny replied. "But I guess I have to go."

They had tried, and they had failed. Keith put his hands deep in his pockets and stared at the ground. She held up her hand in a lame gesture of farewell.

"See you in a few days," she said.

She had only gotten a few steps when Keith jogged in front of them and blocked their progress.

"I have a car," he said, holding up his keys for Oliver to see.

"Good for you," Oliver replied.

"As it happens, I also have a few days free. So I'll drive. Paris isn't that far. Maybe six or seven hours?"

"There's no way I'm going with you," Oliver said, stepping around him.

"I didn't offer to drive you. I'm offering to drive her. You can do what you like."

Oliver kept walking; Ginny didn't move.

"I'm going with him," she said loudly. "In the car."

This obviously threw Oliver for a loop. He didn't have a very expressive face, but she could just feel the displeasure coming off of him in waves.

"We need to do this together," he said.

"We can," Ginny heard herself saying. "We can meet there. How about the pyramid in front of the Louvre?"

"Good choice." Keith nodded. "Pyramid. Louvre. Noon tomorrow? Have fun on the train."

He clapped Oliver on the shoulder, hard, and linked his arm

through Ginny's to lead her away. It was all Ginny could do not to skip . . . to sing . . . to weep for joy. Okay, it wasn't *exactly* like the summer—but this *was* just the two of them, going off together. Going to Paris together. Driving along in his car for hours and hours, into the City of Lights. They would have meals together, and talk for hours. They would have to get a place to stay. . . .

"You're paying for petrol, of course." Keith smiled at her as he walked to the door. "And everything else. It'll be like old times! I think I want some cheeses. Lots of cheeses."

"So many cheeses," Ginny said, nodding.

The fantasy lasted all the way to the bus stop outside of the station doors. This was where Oliver caught up with them.

"Again," Keith said, not looking over, "I didn't offer you a ride."

"Well, I'm coming. Or this isn't happening. What are we supposed to do when we get the pieces? I suppose you'll just let me hang on to them, is that right?"

Keith let out a long sigh and looked over at Ginny. A light passing rain pattered on top of the glass bus shelter.

"We're going to have to bring him, aren't we?" he said.

"Probably," Ginny replied sadly.

"In that case . . . I want a hundred euros up front for petrol and as general payment for the annoyance of having you in my car."

"I bought the train tickets," Oliver said. "It's not my fault if we're not using them. I'll give you fifty and we'll work from there."

"And twenty pounds for parking and congestion charges," Keith added.

Oliver reached into his pocket and pulled out some money. He had prepared as well; he had a wedge of euros. After giving Keith one fifty-euro note and a twenty-pound note, he stuck a cigarette in his mouth and lit it, signifying that the deal was done.

"And you smoke," Keith said. "Lovely. Don't even *think* about trying that in the car."

Oliver obligingly stepped a few feet over. Conciliatory for a blackmailer.

"You realize," Keith said, eyeing Oliver's bag, "that your only value is the letter you have in the front pocket of your bag. It would be a terrible shame if you were separated from that bag and pushed out of a slowly moving car somewhere next to a French cow pasture."

"What, this letter?" Oliver reached into the pocket and produced the folded pages. "I can fix that problem right now."

He crumpled the paper and tossed the ball into the road. Ginny let out a gasp of horror as cars and trucks and buses rode over it. A few seconds later, it vanished, probably carried away by a tire.

"What did you just *do*?" she yelled.

"That was some blue paper I just bought in Waterstones. Like he said, I'm aware that my only value is having the letter. Don't worry. It's safe."

"Safe where?" Ginny asked.

"Safe from pickpockets with rubbish American accents."

The bus lumbered up to the stop. Oliver flicked the cigarette away and waved his hands, indicating that he would follow Keith and Ginny.

"I'm not a violent person," Keith said under his breath, as they climbed the steps to the second level of the bus. "But I've really been meaning to work on that."

One More for the Road

"Is my American accent bad?" Keith asked quietly, once they were on the bus.

"It was fine," Ginny said, looking down at her lap. The accent still burned her ears, but there was no point in telling him that.

"I've been working on it for a while. Mimicking Marlon Brando in *A Streetcar Named Desire*. And I've been trying to copy *The Wire*, but that one is kind of hard. . . ."

He trailed off as he typed out a long text to Ellis. It was hard not to hate Ellis. This wasn't her fault. But she could hate Oliver. That was a perfectly acceptable activity. He was sitting two rows in front of them on the top of the bus. His hair was cut very cleanly and precisely, with a ruler-straight line along the back of his neck. He had a mature bearing—seated straight, shoulders back. Not rigid, just very *adult*. Keith was more slouchy and scratchy and free-flowing. Keith looked like a student. Oliver looked like someone with . . . some kind of responsibility. *Evil* responsibility.

When they got off the bus Oliver kept about ten feet behind them as they walked to Keith's house.

"I'll wait out here," he said.

"Yes," Keith replied. "You will."

The house was cold and mostly dark, but the lights were on up in Keith's room. Ellis was already up there, looking out the window.

"Is that *him*?" she asked. "Down in the garden?"

"That's Oliver," Keith said, opening his closet, shoving some things aside and pulling a bag out from under a pile of stuff. "He's the wanker who's got Gin's letter."

"He's more normal looking than I thought he would be."

Ginny peered between the blinds on the other window. Just below, Oliver was patrolling the garden, his one arm behind his back, the other working the cigarette. He gazed at the cracked pavement like it was a map he was using to plot a siege.

"He's a prize," Keith said. "I'm just going to get my things from the bathroom. I'll be ready to go in a minute."

Then it was just Ellis and Ginny, smiling strangely at each other. It took Ginny a second to realize it but David wasn't home . . . which meant that Ellis had let herself in. Which meant she had her own key. And that . . . was not something Ginny was going to dwell on. She let the blinds go and they fell back into position, sending a spray of dust up her nose.

"So," Ellis said cautiously. "I have nothing in my diary for the next few days. And I packed a quick bag. I don't want to intrude, but if you wouldn't mind . . . I'd love to come. Really. Only if you don't mind."

In the bathroom, Keith could be heard crashing through the

medicine cabinet. Either he was intentionally being loud, or he had temporarily lost muscle control. He must have known this question was coming.

"It's all right to say no," Ellis said. "I know this is personal, and important."

That sounded very sincere. Ellis was genuinely asking Ginny if it was okay. But what else was she going to say? No? *No, Keith's friendly girlfriend, you cannot take a trip in your own boyfriend's car?* Even when it was her, Keith, and Oliver, at least it was two against one. They would stick together. But now, the dream was well and truly over.

"Sure," Ginny said, trying to sound enthusiastic. "Of course."

Ellis clasped her hands together in excitement. "Oh, I'm so glad. I've never been to Paris before. Weird, right? Since it's just a short train ride away, and I studied French for years. I grabbed a few things from Sainsbury's. . . ." She picked up a shopping bag by her feet and held it up. "Biscuits, crisps, fruit, water. Some Top Trumps for the long, boring bits on the train. We'll need to take the Chunnel—I looked up the route online. Plus, I bought a map of France just in case we can't get a signal."

Keith decided this was a good moment to return. He had an overstuffed backpack, and was punching the contents down with his fist.

"I'm coming!" Ellis cried. "Ginny said it was okay." Keith kept squishing and pushing the contents into the bag, trying to get it closed.

"Brilliant," he said. He gave the zipper one final tug and strode out of the room. "We should get going."

"Is that your car?" Oliver asked when they came outside. He

pointed to the humble, turtlelike automobile parked at a slight angle in front of the trash.

"Awe will soon take the place of jealousy," Keith said, brushing past him. "I've seen it before."

Keith opened the trunk and examined the contents. He had cleaned it out a good deal, but it was still fairly full. He removed two large bags, looked inside, and dropped them into an open trash bin. Though Ginny loved the little white car and had many fond memories of it, she understood Oliver's trepidation. It didn't exactly look like the ideal vehicle to take around Europe. For London, sure, it was perfect. It was small and pre-dented, ideal for zipping between buses and cabs and down narrow streets that were never built for cars. You could park it anywhere—you could probably park it *in the house* if you had to. Plus, it wasn't something anyone would want to steal. The white was faded, like old T-shirts that had been washed too many times with black socks. There were dings and scratches and tiny, coin-size spots of rust near the bottom. It screamed, "I have manual locks."

"We're not *all* going," Oliver said, glancing at Ellis's overnight bag and shopping bag full of food.

"Oh, but we are." Keith shoved his bag in first, then gestured for Ellis and Ginny to pass theirs over. Oliver tried to put his in as well, but Keith slammed the lid down before he could.

The car was a two-door—a fact that had never been relevant before. Ginny had always been in the front seat. Today, she would almost certainly be in the back. She never thought about the back of the car as being an actual place you could sit. It was tiny and dark and made for garbage.

"I'm shorter," Ellis said. "I'll get in the back with Gin."

"No," Keith said. "Let *him* manage in the back."

"Gin's taller than me. She should ride in the front. This is her trip. I'm intruding."

"It's fine," Ginny said. That conversation needed to end. "I'll take the back."

She folded down the front seat with a bang and plunged in headfirst, getting briefly tangled in the seat belt. The backseat was not a happy place. It was covered in musty-smelling fabric—fabric that had seen dirty sets and smelly costumes and piles of old take-out bags of hamburgers and fried fish and chips. In fact, the first thing it brought to mind was the swimming pool Dumpster, except it wasn't as big and it wasn't as clean.

What was mildly uncomfortable for her must have been torment for Oliver, who was at least six or seven inches taller. His head scraped the roof and he had to keep his neck slightly bent. He stuffed the backpack by his feet and held the leather satchel on his lap. The combined effect forced him into a squashed, leaning position, with his shoulder pressed up against Ginny's ear. She tried to move closer to the door, but there was simply no more room. Keith got into the driver's seat and immediately adjusted it back into Oliver's already cramped knees.

"All set?" he asked everyone.

He put the key in the ignition and turned it. The engine made a terrible screeching sound, then coughed itself off. "This car is never going to make it to France," Oliver said.

"Don't worry about the car," Keith said, jiggling the key. "Worry about yourself."

"Who are you two? Do you have names at least?"

"I'm Mr. Pink," Keith said. "She's Mr. Shut Your Face. Now,

tell us where we're going."

"Paris," Oliver replied stiffly.

"Yes," Keith said slowly, with mock patience, "you told us that already. But can you be a bit more specific than that? I don't know if you're aware of this, but it's actually *quite a big place*." He reached down and folded his seat back, completely crushing Oliver.

"I'll tell you when you get off my lap."

"I just want you to know what to expect from this trip," Keith said, folding the seat back up into a driving position. "Pain. Not nearly as much as you deserve, but we will try our best."

"I already worked it out," Ellis said, holding up both a map and her phone. "We take the M20 to Folkestone, then from there we get the train to France. The trip to Paris should take about five and a half hours, total, so we'll be there by dinnertime."

"I'll tell you the rest when we're closer to Paris," Oliver said coldly.

"'I'll tell you the rest when we're closer to Paris,'" Keith repeated, in an exact copy of Oliver's voice. He could do other types of English accents very well, at least to Ginny's ear. "Posh boy speaks posh. Bet you went away to school. You a public school boy? Sent away from home at a young age? Is that why you're so well-adjusted?"

"Yes," Oliver said. "That's why. Can we go now?"

The Talking Letter

Most of the route to Folkestone was a highway—so the next two hours were mostly spent looking at the backs of flatbed lorries, vans, other cars, and the many sheep and horses that seemed to graze along England's major traffic arteries.

Keith's car, never a prize, was even worse in the winter, in the backseat. It was thin and poorly insulated. The heater was a concept joke that was probably funnier closer to the vents in the dashboard. Ginny huddled inside of her jacket and zipped it up over her chin, breathing hot air back on herself. In the front, Keith and Ellis were talking, but Ginny could just about hear them over the terrible noise of the engine. Oliver had his headphones in the whole time. She was in a little bubble, all on her own.

Once they got to Folkestone, they made their way into a long line of cars at a dock, where they sat for half an hour. Then a man in a glowing yellow-green jacket was waving them along a train platform to a series of wide doors and directly onto the train.

This was an odd experience, being in a car on a train. All the cars trundled along through the silver train compartments. There were ads on the walls, and everything was bathed in a soft yellow light. Then another man in a vest flagged for them to stop. Doors closed and a heavy metal grate dropped down, locking them in. There were no windows around, not that there would be anything to see. They were going through a tunnel, passing under the English Channel—a kind of very long, sideways elevator ride.

Oliver tried to stretch a bit, accidentally digging his elbow into Ginny's ribs. She pushed it back.

"So," she said. "Are you going to show me the letter now so we know where we're going?"

"There's nothing to see," Oliver said. "I don't have it with me."

On that, Keith and Ellis swiveled around.

"You *don't have the letter*?" Ginny said. "You forgot it?"

"I memorized it."

"You *are* joking," Keith said. "I realize that you are not like the other children, but you *are* joking about that."

In reply, Oliver tipped his head back, closed his eyes, and began to recite.

"'Oh, you're still reading. Good! All right, Gin. You're in Greece. Greece is a fine place to be. . . .'"

Okay, so he wasn't joking. This was weird, listening to Aunt Peg channeled in a deep male English voice. This was like a horrible séance. In a car, on a train, under the English Channel.

"'Have you ever seen water like this? Felt sun like this? Is it any wonder that the Greeks were among the first to really start asking questions about the nature of beauty and art and life itself? This is the birthplace of Western thought. This is where the Big

Questions were forged out of the stuff that had been eating at mankind's collective brain for millennia—the big What the hell is going on? What the hell is going on? has been the central question of my life.

"'Sometimes I'm asking it in a big sense. Sometimes I mean it in a very small, immediate sense, like when I am trying to do my taxes. Lately, what with the brain cancer and all, I ask it all the time. I ask it about the TV remote (which, to be fair to me, is insanely complicated). I ask it when I can't remember which way it is to the grocery store. My disease has taken me on a journey of wonder, Gin. Wonder, and a lot of trying to buy bread at the post office.

"'Even I know that some of the things I have asked you to do are strange, and I'm a weirdo with a tumor the size of an egg in her head. But I have a method to my madness.

"'I want us to make a painting together. This painting is inspired by something my friend and idol Mari Adams did called Paint This for Me. She did a series of sixteen identical paintings—really simple ones—and then she left them in various places around Edinburgh to be touched, admired, rained on, stepped on, drawn on, sliced up . . . whatever happened to the paintings, that was all part of it. Then she collected them up and did an exhibition. I always liked the idea that the paintings were out there living their lives, being changed by the world. My idea is a little different. I am making one picture out of different materials that I have placed around in various spots. In order to collect them, you're going to need to revisit some places you've been, and go to one place you haven't. I'm marking your route home.

"'The first place you're going back to is Paris. No one "gets"

Paris after one visit. No one. How you get there is up to you. I know how I would want to do it—I'd jump ferries all the way across the Mediterranean, stopping in Sicily and Sardinia. Or you could stay along the coast of Italy and France, bouncing your way along the Rivera. Or you could just take a plane. Whatever floats your boat. Or plane. Just get to Paris. And what's there—the first part of this piece is the background—the sky.

"'Sometimes, Gin, I wonder what inanimate object I would like to be, if I could be any inanimate object in the world. There are so many good choices. I'd love to be an airplane that crossed the Atlantic twice a day. I'd love to be the Tivoli fountain, where poets have perched for hundreds of years, and tourists have come to understand the joy of living art. But the one I always come back to is much more humble. I'd love to be a tabletop in Paris, where food is art and life combined in one, where people gather and talk for hours. I want lovers to meet over me. I'd want to be covered in drops of candle wax and breadcrumbs and rings from the bottoms of wineglasses. I would never be lonely, and I would always serve a good purpose.

"'I suppose you remember going to my friend Paul's restaurant, the one I decorated? I made four tabletops for it. They're all made out of doors, and I painted each by hand. The paint I used wasn't really designed for the wear and tear of a restaurant, so they should all be well-marked. It's up to you to take the one you know is right. You'll know it when you see it. Use your instincts.

"'Paul knows that you will be coming back to take one of the tabletops. I asked him not to mention this to you when you first came by—so I hope you are pleasantly surprised that you are going back.'"

Oliver stopped and fiddled with the clasp of his bag.

"That's it for now," he said.

It was only then that Ginny realized she was clenching her stomach muscles to the point of nausea, holding in whatever reaction hearing this letter produced. It wasn't sadness or excitement—it was homesickness and nostalgia. It was like hearing the voice of a ghost. No one said another word until the train came to a stop and they made their slow way out and onto a French road, which looked more or less exactly like the English road they'd just left behind.

"It's in the café," Ginny said quietly. "Les Petits Chiens. That's what it's called."

It took about three hours of driving through France, punctuated by a few dodgy turns and bursts of swearing from Keith. Ellis navigated while Keith negotiated a car with right-side steering on what was, for him, the wrong side of the road. Oliver went back to his music and staring out the window. Ginny was left to her own thoughts, which was honestly the last place she wanted to be left.

They reached Paris right around five, just as the streets were snarled with traffic and the dark had descended and the streets glowed orange from the streetlights. It was bizarre how quickly generic highway could turn into . . . well, Paris. For the first time since she had gotten in this car, Ginny felt a surge of excitement. There was the Eiffel Tower, just illuminated for the night. There were the long stretches of creamy white buildings with their big gray-black roofs and their skylights. There were the Art Nouveau Metro signs from the turn of the twentieth century, with their sinuous green iron workings that looked like curling plants. This weird, impossible place that looked like a collection of palaces, a grubby city, a museum, a tight cluster of cafés—everything, all at once.

In the summer, the trees had been thick and green. Now, the trees were bare, but heavy with lights, so many lights, the color of champagne bubbles. Paris took its decorating seriously. The smells of the city seeped in—the bread coming from the bakeries, the toasty smell of a crepe truck, the occasional gust of sewer or garbage. Then, right back to the bread and crepes. Ginny's stomach grumbled loudly.

"I could eat one of those little dogs," Ellis said, pointing at someone walking a ratlike creature. "I am honestly that hungry."

"Me too." Keith swerved to avoid a pedestrian—or maybe toward a pedestrian. It was hard to tell. "I'm glad we're going to a café."

They drove on to increasingly smaller and more familiar-looking streets, finally arriving on a narrow artery where motorcycles had completely taken over the sidewalks for their driving and parking purposes. The car barely fit down the road. Keith stopped when he could go no farther and they seemed to be in the right area. They climbed out of the car. Oliver immediately grabbed for his cigarettes and shoved one in his mouth.

"I know where we are," Ginny said. Somewhere in her brain, she had stored the layout of these little passageways. She started walking, surprising herself with her own assurance. Sure enough, she turned a corner and saw the tree that blocked the front, now bare of leaves. Les Petits Chiens was dark. There was a sign stuck to the door, which was barely visible. It's never good when there's a note on the door of a shop or restaurant. It never means, "We're

84

open and everything is working just *fine*."

Ginny held up her phone to illuminate it.

"It's in French," she said. Her three and a half years of high school French had led her to this moment. "It says . . . 'Dear Customers, Jean-Claude and I have gone to Orange for the holiday. The restaurant . . . will open . . . something, something . . . on January third. Merry Christmas and Happy New Year. . . .' Oh my god. It's closed until January."

That was it. Instant failure, right out of the gate. Oliver cupped his hands around his eyes and pressed his face against the window to look inside. He tried the door as well, even though it was pointless. Keith immediately began laughing the tired laugh of someone who has just driven all the way to Paris in a backwards car.

"So we came all this way for nothing," he said. "Brilliant. Maybe this is something we could have checked on if we *had the letter*."

"All right!" Ellis said brightly. "This is just a little setback. We made it all the way here, we can figure this out."

No one replied, so she tried again, this time bouncing a bit as she spoke. "We haven't eaten properly all day," she went on. "We just need some food to buck us up, and we've got the best food in the world all around us. Let's find ourselves a nice little café and have some dinner. Then we can think about what to do next. Right?"

Nothing.

"Right?"

"Might as well," Keith said. "I'm starving."

He threw one arm over Ellis's shoulders. With the other hand, he beckoned Ginny over. She stepped over quietly. He draped his other arm over her shoulders, making them a friendly threesome. Behind them, Ginny could hear Oliver walking quietly in their footsteps.

The Card Cheat

They were in a café, four streets over from Les Petits Chiens. It had been chosen simply because it was the most café-looking of all the cafés they passed—very small round tables with marble tabletops, dark wood, a nickel-plated bar, and a simple menu written on a blackboard offering three courses and a glass of wine for eighteen euros each. It was still a bit early for Parisians to be having dinner, so they had the place almost entirely to themselves.

Oliver had been forced to sit by himself at a small table in the corner. Ginny could see that he was attempting to look dignified, even after his very public shunning and banishment. The way he sat there in his long black coat, deliberately sitting very upright, eating his plate of roasted chicken . . . Ginny almost felt pity for him. She had to tell herself not to look over at him. They had already each polished off a crock of onion soup, and now were making their way through the large dishes of mussels and the cones of french fries that cluttered the table. She had never eaten mussels before. They looked very odd, with their black, almost opalescent shells, each spread widely to reveal the globby little bit of seafood inside. But it turned out that globby was good, especially when swimming in a pool of white wine and garlic sauce, which you can then drink up in the empty shells and soak up in fresh bread. This was probably the exact kind of meal Aunt Peg wanted to see on her tabletop.

"Right," Ellis said, eating the last of a paper cone full of fries, "what happens now?"

It was an excellent question, and not one Ginny could answer, but they were both looking at her like she was about to start spouting streams of pure wisdom.

"I don't know," she said. "I mean, I want to get the tabletop. But Paul isn't here. I guess I could try find an email address or leave a note or something. Maybe he can send it to me . . . or something."

Keith picked at the remainder of his food and Ellis fidgeted a bit. It wasn't the most inspirational answer. Ginny stared at her mussel shells and the tiny amount of broth at the bottom of her bowl. She was still in Paris, eating Parisian food on a beautiful Parisian winter night. That was something.

"Does anyone want to hear my suggestion?" Oliver asked from three tables away.

"Not really," Keith said loudly.

Oliver picked up his plate of roasted chicken and potatoes and joined them, making room for himself on Ginny's side of the table.

"The owner of the restaurant already knows that you are going to come for it. The letter clearly says so."

"We aren't stealing the tabletop," Ginny said.

"It's not stealing if it is already yours. What we're talking about is breaking and entering—and we can do the entering without any breaking."

"And what does that mean?" Keith asked.

"We pick the lock."

Keith snorted and shook his head. He grabbed another piece of bread and ripped it in half.

"All I need is a little piece of wire," Oliver said. "I'm willing to give it a go, unless someone else has a better plan."

"You're going to stand there," Keith said, his voice taking on a slightly defensive tone, "in full view of the street, and practice all those lock picking tricks you learned on the internet, is that right? Sounds very slick."

Ginny had restrained herself so far, but now she had to speak. "We are *stopping* this *now*," she said. "My tabletop. My rules. Shut up and go back to your corner."

She was surprised by the firmness in her voice. Judging from their expressions, so was everyone else. Keith smiled. Ellis had to stifle a laugh into her napkin. Oliver did nothing at all for a good thirty seconds, then picked up his plate and stood up.

"Listen," he said, looking down at her and meeting her eye, "if we leave Paris without that tabletop then there is no point in going on, and our entire trip will be for nothing. This is your one and only chance. I still have a ticket home. Think it over."

It was quiet for a moment. Ginny listened to the muffled sound of French radio from the depths of the kitchen, the rip of the occasional motorcycle down the street. She was the captain of this disastrous operation, with no clue what to do now, or where to go next. She only knew what she didn't want, but that kind of information doesn't actually get you anywhere.

"Much as I don't like agreeing with him," Ellis finally said, jerking her head in Oliver's direction and lowering her voice, "I think he's right. What if we could go in there without causing any damage at all? You could do that, Keith. You know you can. I've seen you get windows open, get in all kinds of places."

"Yeah, I *can* do it," Keith said. "That's not the issue. It's Ginny's painting. And if she doesn't want to break in, well . . ."

They stopped their conversation when they were presented with the apple tarts and coffee that were included with their meal. Each was a beautiful, golden piece of pastry, fresh from the oven.

". . . but I could go over and see what our options are. Maybe there's a way in that wouldn't hurt anything. I mean, since we're here. It does seem pointless to walk away without even a second glance, Gin."

Ginny split her pastry into two pieces with her fork, releasing a little cloud of steam. The waitress came back and deposited a small jug of cream on the table. It was such a reasonable suggestion that Ginny didn't have much room to argue. It *was* pointless to walk away without even looking at the building again. A few tables over, Oliver blatantly stared, listening to every word.

"Okay," Ginny said. "I mean, if you want to look. Just . . . look. I guess that's fine."

Keith slapped the table and got up.

"You didn't eat your tart," Ellis said.

"It's all right." He broke into a worrying smile. "I don't like fruit."

Once he was gone, Ellis and Ginny were left to themselves. It was just them in the big, dark wood booth, staring at each other across the marble table. Ellis ate her tart happily, mumbling her joy about actually being in Paris and having real French food for the first time. Ginny felt mildly queasy, but forced it down in small, scalding bites. Once the food and coffees were done, there was nothing between them. No distractions. Just quality time to drink each other in. There was Ellis—everything that Ginny wasn't. Not just English, but a Londoner. Positive and unafraid where Ginny was cautious and concerned. Prepared. Cheerful. No wonder Keith was dating her. It only made sense.

Ellis toyed with her ring for a moment, then pulled the Top Trumps cards from her bag.

"Want to play?" she asked. "I know it's silly, but I used to love these things. I must have had twenty packs of them. It wasn't a holiday unless we had Top Trumps. Let's see . . . I have dinosaurs, Harry Potter, cars . . ."

Oliver slid into the booth next to Ginny.

"Want to see a trick?" he asked.

Without waiting for an answer, he reached over and took one of the packs of cards and began to run through a series of very fancy shuffles. Then he fanned out the cards on the table, face-down. It was the "dogs" pack.

"Pick a card," he said. "Look at it, but don't tell me what it is."

"What the hell are you doing?" Ginny asked.

"Showing you a trick. One of you, pick a card, look at it, and stick it back in the pack."

At least now Ellis and Ginny were back on the exact same page. They looked at each other across the table. Of the many aspects of his personality Oliver had demonstrated so far, "Magic Trick Oliver" was actually the strangest. Ellis laughed out loud.

"Oh, go on then," she said, taking a card. "You're clearly a mental."

Once she had looked at it and put it back, Oliver pushed the deck back together, shuffled it a few more times, and began flipping over cards.

"Do you think this means we're friends?" Ginny asked.

"No." He continued shuffling. "Is this your card?" He held up a card with a picture of a pug.

"No," Ellis said.

He flipped over some more, then held up a black Labrador.

"This one?"

"Nope."

Oliver flipped over card after card, but Ellis shook her head each time. When he reached the end of the pack, he sifted through,

"That's odd," he said. "That normally works. What was it?"

"A golden retriever," Ellis said.

The door banged open and Keith hurried across the café to them. The cold had lit up his cheeks, and his eyes were bright. "Right," he said. "We're in luck. There's a passage behind all the buildings on that street. I made my way down and found a window in the back of the restaurant. It'll be no problem at all to pop that open and slip inside. Nothing broken. No damage done. Trust me—I used to do this all the time."

Ginny searched her mind for something, anything that could slow this down.

"What if there's an alarm?" she asked.

"I seriously doubt there is. It's a one-room restaurant with four tables. There's a simple lock on the front door, which is almost entirely made of glass anyway. Anyone could smash into that place anytime, if they wanted to. He probably takes the cash box with him at night. Aside from that, there's nothing to take but the crockery. No offense to your aunt's decorating skills, but from what I could see through the window it already looks like that place has been vandalized. That place is like my car—too crap to be worth burglaring."

"Sounds fine to me," Oliver said. "I'll go."

"It's not up to you," Keith replied. "It's up to her."

All eyes were on Ginny. Out of the four people at this table, she was the only one who appeared to have any doubts about this plan. The radio droned on in the kitchen, and the clank of dishes grew louder. Outside, there was a lot of honking. Everything was swelling up. There was a growing sense that something was happening, and if Ginny wasn't going to take part in it, she would be left behind forever.

"What is it we're looking for again?" she asked.

Oliver put his hands flat on the table and blinked once. Ginny could almost see him flipping through pages in his brain.

"I think. . . ." He stopped and drummed his fingers, then nodded confidently. "'I *suppose* you remember going to my friend Paul's restaurant, the one I decorated? I made four table-tops for it. They're all made out of doors, and I painted each by hand. The paint I used wasn't really designed for the wear and tear of a restaurant, so they should all be well-marked. It's up to you to take the one you know is right. You'll know it when you see it. Use your instincts.'"

"Four tables," Keith said. "Won't be hard."

"Okay," she said.

"Wayhay!" Keith slapped the table. "That's the mad one I know."

"What about us?" Ellis said, indicating herself and Oliver.

"No point in us all going in. Ginny has to come, to identify the table, but you should stay with the car, El. I don't think we have much time left in that space, and the last thing we need is a large clamp on the wheel. Posh Boy will be out front. Not *directly* out front . . ."

"Yes, I could have guessed that, thank you."

". . . but nearby. You can stand around and smoke and look French. Any problems, you tap on the window. Are we all set?"

Ginny was not remotely set, but things were in motion. The bill was brought over, and she put down sixty euros while the others donned their coats.

"I'm just going to walk Ellis back to the car," Keith said. "Stay here. I'll be back in a minute."

Oliver set his lighter on the table and gave it a spin.

"I don't have any illusions about the two of us," he said. "I did the card trick because you looked nervous. When you're nervous, you need a distraction. I provided one."

"You're not *that* good at sleight of hand, though. I guess it's a good thing you're not picking the lock."

He shrugged.

"I'm nervous too," he said, getting up. "I'm going to have a cigarette. I'll be outside."

There was a little clink of a bell as the door shut behind him. Ginny absently ate the crust off Keith's untouched apple tart. She wasn't sure which was more annoying—the fact that Oliver had successfully distracted her and temporarily made her less nervous, or that he was being honest about his own nervousness. She didn't want him to have good qualities. Horrible people should be horrible all the time. That should be the law.

She stared out at the street, remembering the last time she was in Paris with Keith. They broke into a graveyard. And they got caught. Last time, they were let go. This time, they might not be so lucky.

Really, the only question now was whether she should call Richard before the police got them, or after. She reached into her pocket for her phone. Something came out with it and fell to the floor. Ginny leaned over to pick it up.

On the ground by her seat was a card with a picture of a golden retriever.

The Great Table Caper

Keith pulled his hat low over his head, pressing all the fringy ends of his hair down flat around his face. It gave him long sideburns and almost entirely obscured his eyes.

"I look shifty, don't I?" he said. "Good. Best to look the part." He clapped and rubbed his hands together eagerly. "I can't tell if you're enthused or about to be violently sick."

"Is there a third option?"

"Cheer up," he said, putting an arm around her shoulders. "It's me you're with. Would I ever lead you to do something stupid? Best not to answer that. Just follow me down this dark path over here."

Put like that, the idea had more appeal. Follow Keith into the dark . . . yes, that she could do, even if the alley that he had described was actually just a space just over a foot wide. It was a minor separation between buildings, nothing that people were really supposed to pass through. Keith turned himself sideways and started moving along quickly. Ginny could only see his out-line, and mostly followed by sound, trying not to scrape her face or knees on either wall. This had to be some kind of garbage alley for the restaurant. Whatever was underfoot was squishy and slippery—maybe boxes, maybe food—she refused to consider any other options. And actually, Parisian restaurant garbage smelled kind of nice. It was fresher than other garbage, sweeter, like over-ripe fruit. Maybe that was something she could put in her college essay: *There I was, creeping down the sweet garbage alley to break into the restaurant. . . .*

"You all right?" Keith asked. "Be careful when you get to the end. There's an old bike you have to step over."

"Fine," she said, trying to keep her tone confident.

Even though she'd been warned, she tripped over the bike. She probably tripped because she'd been warned and was tell-ing herself not to trip over the bike. She did that sometimes. It was often easier not to know what obstacles were in the way. The space behind the buildings was wider, but scrappy, mostly full of rubbish bins, boxes, and cast-off bits of furniture. Keith had turned on his cell phone for a light and was holding it up to a nar-row window about five feet off the ground.

"See." Keith grabbed the sill and pulled himself up to peer through the darkened window. "Easy."

What he was describing as "easy" would have been better described as "too high, too narrow, and too locked," but Ginny kept this thought to herself.

"All right," he said, hopping down. "I'll get the window open. Just need a tool for the job. . . ."

He poked around in the trash for a moment until he found an

extremely unstable-looking chair. If it looked risky in the dark, Ginny couldn't even imagine how bad it would have seemed if she could have gotten a good look at it. But Keith climbed up on it nonetheless and started working away at the window.

"Is it locked?" she asked.

"It's not a problem," he whispered. "Lower your voice."

At first, he must have been trying to ease it open, but when it didn't give after a minute or two, she heard his efforts getting louder, and his tone became more frustrated and determined. Finally, there was a splintering noise and he swung the window open in triumph.

"There you go!" he said, stepping down from the chair. "No problem. Up you get."

"Me first?"

"I'm a gentleman."

Ginny climbed onto the chair. The legs were wobbly and the seat was made of some kind of basket weave that felt like it was going to give at any second, so the sooner she stepped off it and got through the window, the better. She shoved her head and shoulders through. The room was pitch-black, with a terrible, vaguely septic smell. She could just make out that it was small, and that there was a white object just below her—the toilet. This made it impossible to slide in headfirst. In fact, there seemed no way in at all. She was just dangling there, about five feet up, half in and half out of the building, with nothing to hold on to. Plus, she was fairly certain that her hips would not actually fit though the opening.

"Come on," he said. "Have to be quick here. I'll give you a boost."

And with that, his hand was under her foot, pushing her up and in up to her waist. From there, she teetered between the world of the toilet and the world of the alley, her upper half facing a terrible fate, and her lower half flailing in Keith's direction. Her hips, as she had already guessed, caught her, leaving her to seesaw.

"Turn on your side," he whispered up to her.

"I know," she said. She tried to rotate herself slowly, so that some kind of graceful cartwheel maneuver could be pulled out of this. Once she began to turn, she started to fall forward again, right into toilet land. Keith had her legs now and was holding them for support, so now she was dangling over the toilet. Lacking any other choice, she scrabbled to put her hands on the seat. Her loose hair hung upside down, right into the bowl. There was no point in resisting now. She let her weight fall forward and slid gracelessly toward an old French toilet. And then she was on the floor, with the final, horrid indignity of a strand of her dampened hair landing in her mouth. She spit it out.

Keith had a lot more experience with this kind of thing and managed to pull himself up on the window frame and swing in feet first, stepping onto the toilet seat and landing silently and more or less gracefully upright with little effort.

"See?" he said. "Easy."

The bathroom was a very small place, no bigger than a broom cupboard, which meant that they were pressed in close together . . . not face-to-face, but face-to-side-of-head. She was close enough that she was sure she *heard* him smile.

"Shall we?" he whispered. She could just feel the brush of his lips through the hair that covered her ear. For a moment, she bitterly regretted not having her braids. There definitely would have been lip-to-skin contact.

This was too much. She was getting light-headed. It was lucky that it was so dark, that she had a good excuse for clutching at the door frame. Ginny took a series of deep breaths to steady herself and followed him out, through the beaded curtain that revealed the miniscule kitchen, the bar, and the room with the four tables. The front of the restaurant was mainly made up of two large windows covered with heavy purple velvet drapes. These were wide-open. Keith pointed at them. He pulled them closed on one side, and Ginny crossed around to pull them on the other. They were very effective light-blockers. Now it was pitch-black.

"Let's get the lights on and do this as quick as we can," he said.

This required a lot of fumbling around, feeling the walls. Les Petits Chiens was not a large place. Though they worked separate walls, they bumped together several times—a slightly unusual number of times, really. Finally, one of them hit the right spot on the wall and the tiny chandelier turned on. Suddenly she could see her aunt's artwork, which covered every surface. There were her collages, the pictures and the pieces of broken dishes that were mounted, mosaic-style on the wall—the hundreds of pictures of dogs, all eyes and tails and random fuzzy bodies. "All right," Keith said, surveying the four garishly colored tables. "Which one do you think it is?"

One was orange, one was plum, one was yellow, and one was blue. All were variously spattered with designs and dots of paint. She stood at the end of the room and passed her eye from one to the next, over and over.

"She wants a sky, right?" Keith said, pointing at the blue table. "This looks like a sky."

Her eye lingered on the blue table for a moment. It was covered in splatters that could have been stars. They were yellow and vaguely starlike. But Aunt Peg wouldn't paint a blue sky with yellow stars. She might paint the opposite, though. She turned to the yellow table. It had almost no other paint on it, aside from a few tiny flecks of red, which almost looked accidental.

"It won't be that one," Keith said. "That's just a plain one."

Ginny kept looking at the yellow one. It was deeply marked by stains from the bottom of glasses, orbs of red wine, scars from moisture. This was the table with the lightest color, the least protection. This was the one that would mark the most. She put her hand on its surface and reached for the plum-colored table at the same time. The plum-colored table had a cold, slick surface. The paint felt protective. This yellow paint was different.

"It's this one," Ginny said.

"The yellow one? You sure?"

"Look," she said, pointing at the rings and marks. "This is exactly the one she would want. She talked about people drinking wine, meeting over a table. And these marks—they're like the sun, or the moon, or . . ."

Well, that was it really. But she still knew it was the best choice. Keith got down on the ground and looked at the table from underneath. He produced a multipurpose tool in a case, with various-size heads for different jobs.

"Where did you get that?" Ginny asked in amazement.

"From my car. I had it in there from when I moved the set."

Since his head was under the table, Ginny could stare at the rest of Keith as he worked. This was a calming and pleasant sight, interrupted only by the unmistakable sound of a siren in the distance—one of those keening European ones that sounded like they were going *nee-neer-nee-neer-nee-neer*, and she could see the echo of a flashing light from somewhere down the street. Ginny drew back the curtain a little and found herself facing Oliver, who frantically waved for her to drop it.

"Oh my god . . . ," Ginny said. "Oh my god . . . stop. Stop!" Keith froze in place, taking in this sensory information.

"Is that for us?" he inquired.

"We have to go!"

"Right. Perhaps I was wrong about the alarm system. Oh well. You never know until you try. I've almost got this thing off, anyway."

He said it calmly, as if this was just a very interesting piece of trivia, then got up on his feet. He gave the tabletop a shake.

"Come *on*, you bastard," he said, grunting a bit to get the last nut loose.

"We need to *go*," Ginny hissed.

"No point in that now. Turn off the light and close the back window."

"What?"

"They'll probably just check the doors and windows and leave," he said quietly. "We just have to keep our heads and voices down."

Several seconds of utter panic ensued as Ginny tried to find the light switch again, then fumbled through the dark, crashing into the toilet to get to the window. Then another fumble back into the main room. Keith was invisible in the darkness.

"Get down," he whispered, now with a trace of urgency in his voice.

Ginny dropped to her knees, then scuffled her way along the

floor until she found the bar. She got behind it, curling herself into a ball. Outside, Oliver was talking very loudly to someone.

"I'm supposed to be meeting someone here, you see," he was saying. "This is where she's staying. I tried the doors. . . ."

Rapid French from some other person, and more protestations from Oliver, who was playing the confused tourist about as well as Keith had that morning. A slightly drunk, arrogant English tourist.

"Look," he said, "I don't know what's happening, but I was just waiting here. Do you speak English? She said twenty-five Rue de . . . wait. What street is this? What street is this? Can you just show me . . ."

"He's stealing my routine," Keith whispered from across the room. "Bastard."

They stayed liked this for several minutes, until the voices retreated. She heard Keith moving, so she peeked over the bar. He was standing up, pulling at the table again.

"We need to get out!" she said.

"Almost have it . . . stand over by the door, would you?"

"There are *police* outside."

"They've walked away, which means we have exactly right now to do this. Trust me, I've done this before. You trust me, don't you? When I say *now*, you throw open that door. So get the locks undone."

There was no time to think about this. She controlled the shaking in her hands as she felt around for the locks. There were two dead bolts on the door, plus a strange lock that took a lot of jiggling to undo.

"Ready?" he said.

"Um . . ."

"Now!"

The double doors of Les Petits Chiens swung open. Keith hoisted up the tabletop and hurried outside with it, setting it carefully down on the sidewalk.

"Take it," he said. "Get it to the car."

"What about you?"

"Don't worry about me. Be with you in a sec."

He stepped back inside and shut the doors, leaving Ginny in front of the restaurant with a tabletop made of a half a door. She had no option but to move, as quickly as possible. The tabletop was large, but not overly heavy. It was impossible to run with it, so she shuffled as quickly as she could. There was a little off-shoot street about twenty feet away, just as narrow as this one. She turned down it, having no idea where it went. It was nearly impossible to make it down this alley with half a door, but she also couldn't stay on the same street as the restaurant—so she wound her way down, turning to the left and right to squeeze past trash bins and bikes. The door whacked into bike handles and brick walls and various unseen objects.

This alley didn't go in a straight line, but wove between buildings on a long curve. She emerged on a much brighter, busier street, one lined with lots of small shops: a late-night grocery store, a packing supply store, a crepe stand, a Senegalese restaurant. After a few wrong turns, she finally got back on a street that she remembered and saw the white car at the end. People were giving her a lot of looks, but she soldiered on, working her way through the crowd with the tabletop. Ellis jumped out of the car to help her.

"Where's Keith?" she asked.

"Coming!"

"Where's Oliver?"

"I don't know."

Ellis opened the backseat and climbed into the other side and helped pull the tabletop into place. Then, without her even hearing him approach, Keith joined them.

"As it turns out . . . ," he said.

Oliver was right behind him, running hard. His height gave him a strange, hopping gait, making the ends of his coat flap up and down. For a moment, Ginny was transfixed by the sight.

"Get in, get in, get in," he said briskly, pushing her into the back with the tabletop. He squeezed in right behind her and just about got the door closed. They were still in a tangle when Ellis hit the gas and they took off.

To Belgium!

The scene inside the car had become much more complex in the last few moments. For a start, the tabletop made a wall between the front and backseats, with just four or five inches at the top left open for communication. Ginny and Oliver now had their own little room—a room that definitely couldn't hold both of them. There was double as much Oliver as there was Ginny. His knees were tucked up into their torso space, his arm span was much wider than the backseat. He was wedged in place. Meanwhile, the car itself was careening down a Parisian street as Ellis got used to the opposite-side driving. Ginny was bounced around in the tiny bit of remaining space, hitting Oliver, then the door, over and over. Most of the contact was of the shoulder-to-face and elbow-to-abdomen kind . . . with the occasional full-body slam.

On the good-news front, it didn't appear that anyone was after them.

"If I could just move this," Oliver said, trying to lift the tabletop enough to get his legs down and his feet under it. Keith peered over the tabletop and into the strange little world of backseat land.

"That looks really uncomfortable," he observed, leaning his chin and hands on the tabletop, crushing it down a bit on Oliver's toes.

"Do you mind?"

"You stole my patter from this morning. You're a bastard."

"And I saved your arse."

"I could have gotten us out of there. All we had to do was wait it out."

"Where am I going?" Ellis called. "Is anyone going to give me directions?"

"Do you think you could manage one of your little readings so we have some idea of what the hell is happening?" Keith asked. "Where does the letter send us next, oh knobular one?"

"Just get out of the city."

"We need a *bit* more than that," Keith said.

"I can't exactly reach my phone right now to look up directions."

"So tell us what our next stop is," Keith said. "We don't need you playing *Flight of the Navigator* back there."

"I'll tell you where we need to go for the night," Oliver said. "You can hear the rest tomorrow. And stop *leaning on the table*."

Keith released the table and retreated. Oliver continued his efforts to lift the table and get into a normal seated position. Through a lot of jerking and bumping around, he managed this. Further jerking and bumping allowed him to get his phone free. He was looking up directions.

"Why won't you just *say*?" Ginny asked, as her head knocked against his shoulder.

"Because I don't want to end up shoved out on the side of the road. The longer I know things, the longer I can put that off."

She had to admit, there was some sense in that. Actually, everything suddenly made a kind of sense. A minor euphoria came over Ginny, along with a fit of hiccuping. They had *done* it. They had made it to Paris and gotten this table. And though the circumstances were not ideal, Paris was still Paris, and success was still success.

They were on the Champs-Élysées, one of the grand boulevards of Paris. Ginny recognized it from her French textbook; specifically, from a dialogue called, "On the Avenue des Champs-Élysées." It was one of many dialogues in the book between Véronique and Sylvie, two girls who primarily spent their time reading menus out loud and reciting long strings of phone numbers. In "On the Avenue des Champs-Élysées," however, they stepped out of their comfort zone and took a walk and said how *formidable* everything on the Champs-Élysées was. They had a point. And now Ginny really understood why they called Paris the "City of Light." The Champs-Élysées during the holidays was nothing but light. Lights dripped off the trees. At the speed they were going (which was keeping up with traffic, which meant probably *way too fast*), all the lights blurred together into one wondrous streak. Aunt Peg was right. Paris wasn't a place you could get after one visit. A place this wonderful would take a lifetime.

"Oh no," Ellis said.

"Ah," Keith added as a follow-up.

"'Ah?'" Ginny said, shaking out of her trance. "'Oh no?' What does 'ah' mean? 'Oh no' what?"

They had stopped briefly. Directly ahead of them, bathed in

light in a great ocean of light, was one of Paris's great landmarks, the Arc de Triomphe—the massive white arch, so large that a small plane could be flown under it. And around that arch-circled traffic—lots and lots of traffic . . . hundreds, thousands, perhaps *millions* of cars, just going around and around and around. There had to be eight or ten lanes' worth, but there were no lanes. Nothing bound the cars into any particular position.

"What am I doing?" Ellis yelled. "Where am I going?"

"Hang on a moment," Oliver said, still working his phone.

"I can't hang on a moment!"

"Know what I heard once?" Keith said grimly, as the light changed. "Insurance is invalid in the circle around the Arc de Triomphe."

The little white car screeched into the melee and began going around the monument, cars merging in from all directions, peeling off, coming in front, slipping up behind. Cars were coming at them *sideways.*

"All right," Oliver said. "All right. You want the third junction. The one for the Place de la Porte Maillot . . ."

"What third junction? There are no junctions!"

A motorcycle buzzed by, just inches from Ginny's door. Ellis must have hit the gas, because the whole car lurched and shuddered.

"You want to play?" Ellis yelled. "All right, then! I played *a lot of video games* as a kid, bitches!"

"There!" Oliver yelled. "That way! Toward Boulevard Périphérique. There! There!"

The car swerved abruptly to the right. Ginny heard Keith swear for a solid ten seconds.

"Sorry!" Ellis called, merging farther and farther right with insane determination. She jerked the car off the roundabout in one final, bold turn.

"Turn right!" Oliver yelled. "Take the A1 toward Lille!"

"Where?"

"LILLE."

"A1?"

"YES!"

With one last screeching turn, they began the run out of Paris.

The A1 was just a highway, and the night was a wintry blank. It was colder than ever now. Ginny and Oliver had worked together to create some kind of peace with the tabletop, but the end result was that it sat on both of their feet and completely blocked any heat coming from the front. So they had two things making them go numb. They both went into a hibernation mode, silent, burrowing inside their coats. The one advantage to their closeness was that they got a little warmth from each other. Suddenly, there was a little burst of excitement from the front seat, and Ginny saw that they were pulling into a gas station.

"Petrol stop!" Ellis called.

Oliver and Ginny couldn't just get out of the car—they needed to be extracted from under the tabletop. Keith and Ellis worked from either side, one pushing and one pulling, to get it out of the car. Ginny and Oliver stumbled out, Oliver making an uneven path away from the car to smoke. Ginny's feet were completely pins and needles. It would be several minutes before she could walk at all. She leaned against the car, while Ellis went inside to find a restroom, and Keith filled the tank. She watched the little counter on the pump spinning what seemed like an incredible number of euros. Gas was expensive here.

"I need to give you money," she said.

"I'll use his for now. How do you feel, by the way? Being a proper thief?"

"Queasy."

"That's a sign you're doing it right. You did good back there."

"I still can't believe we did it," she said.

"Oh, you know how these things go," Keith replied. "You go to Paris, steal part of a table, and then spend all night driving to Belgium. God, when will they stop making this movie?"

"Belgium?" Ginny asked.

"That's where we'll be if we keep going on this road. Bet you've always wanted to go to Belgium."

Ginny searched for any mental files she had on Belgium, but came up with nothing, except a tiny memo about chocolate. Also, she hadn't called Richard. She had to do that now, before it got any later and they actually *left France*.

"I have to make a call," she said, holding up her phone. Keith nodded and continued filling the tank. Ginny endured the pain of walking on her dead feet and tried to keep her gait even and smooth as she walked over to the side of the station. Richard picked up on the very first ring.

"Hi," she said, trying to sound casual. "It's me. We're here in France. . . ."

"How's Paris?" he asked.

"Really . . . busy."

There was a lot of noise in the background wherever Richard was.

"Are you still at work?" she asked.

"Sadly, yes. Did you get into the same hostel?"

"Oh . . . we were just out. We're going to get a room now." Not a lie. Certainly the intention.

"You don't have a place yet? Isn't it after nine?"

"Yeah . . . but it's fine. We're going now. Really."

"I'm sure it is, just . . . text me to let me know you're safely in the hostel, all right?"

"Okay," she said. "I will."

When she got off the phone, Ginny looked up at the stars. The view here was incredible for that—black and clear. The only things around besides this gas station were a dark clump of houses up the road and a wind turbine in the distance. From here she could see about twice as many stars as she could at home, maybe three times as many. The sky was littered with them.

Ellis was over with Keith at the car. They were talking in low voices, laughing quietly. Even though they were probably talking about what they had just pulled off, Ginny felt a rush of jealousy. She hurried back to join them.

"Hey, tosser!" Keith yelled to Oliver. "Get in the car or we leave you here!"

Oliver threw his cigarette into the road and came over to them.

"Look how his coat snaps in the wind as he walks," Keith said. "Very dashing. He's like Batman."

The thing was, it actually *was* kind of dashing. The coat was extremely long and would have dwarfed a lot of guys, but it looked right on Oliver, and it *did* snap around his calves as he walked over.

"Are you taking us to Belgium?" Keith asked tiredly. "I need to know. It's late. We need to stop soon—we've been going all day now."

"We can stop in Ghent for the night," Oliver replied. "It's not too far. Maybe an hour. Keep going on this road."

"Fine. Time to pack the two of you back in the car. In you get."

Ginny took one last look at the sky, shivered under the size of it, and got back in the car where the world was smaller, though no easier to comprehend.

A Feeling of Shed

As they drove north toward Ghent, the clear skies gradually became more milky and pink, and a light snow started to fall. It was right around ten when they came into the city proper, and it was quite a contrast from the bleakness of the highway or the magnificent sprawl of Paris. Ghent looked like a congregation of cathedrals. Every building in the center was ornate, with a thousand little details and hooks and spires and miraculous accents carved into stone or made out of brick. A warm yellow light bathed the streets, which were now covered in a light dusting of snow. The city was situated around a river, which glowed under the lights.

"Well, it looks like we found Hogwarts," Keith said. "Now where do we go?"

"We try to find a place that's open," Oliver said. "It's late, and it's a holiday, so there's no guarantee that we'll find anything. I did have a place for us in Paris. . . ."

"So *why didn't you say that*?"

"Because we were escaping the police. I thought even you could work that one out. I had a plan. My plan would have worked. You changed my plan. Not my fault."

"God, no," Keith said. "None of this is *your* fault."

"What I'm saying—"

"Boys!" Ellis yelled. "Tired now! Bed! Sleep!"

"I *did* look up some places just now," Oliver went on. "I've looked up a few hostels and small hotels. There's a student area that should be loaded with them. We should try there first. I suggest we park and try it on foot. It might be easier to go door to door than try to drive around endlessly."

Keith stopped the car along one of the back streets, in something that might or might not have been a parking space. Again, Ginny and Oliver were extracted from their storage place. They stepped into the lightly falling snow—heavy flakes that already dusted the bridges and the sidewalks. The cold had permeated Ginny now—it was deep in her bones. But at least she was upright. She could move.

Ghent was pretty, and Ghent was also closed. In the center of town, every ivy-decked door looked locked, and every window wound with Christmas lights was dark. They walked through an empty central market full of small green stalls, all shuttered. They walked past a small castle with a spiderweb statue next to it. They found the street of hotels, which were all shut or full. They passed a hostel, but it had closed in October. They tried the surrounding streets, but found much of the same. After a while, they had clearly wandered off the tourist path into a residential area. Inside of the cozy houses and apartments, Ginny could see televisions and computers and people reclining on sofas. All she wanted now was somewhere to sleep. Anywhere.

"I feel like we're reenacting the Nativity story," Keith said, pulling his hat down over his ears. "No room at the inn, nowhere to lay our tabletop."

"What about this?" Oliver pointed at a sign in a window, which was written in several languages. In English it read: "Rooms for students or travelers, inexpensive and clean, ring bell." The building looked like a normal house—one of the more modern ones on the street. The windows upstairs were all dark, but there were lights on the ground floor, and a light on by the door.

"Is this actually a bed-and-breakfast?" Ellis asked. "It's not really marked or anything."

"It has this sign," Oliver said.

"Nothing to lose." Keith stepped forward and rang the bell. A minute later, an older man in a cardigan opened the door. Once their general purpose there was explained to him, and he adjusted to English, there was a lot of nodding.

"Are you . . . *allergic* . . . to cats?"

A quick poll was taken. None of them were allergic to cats. The door was opened wider.

"Come in," he said, "come in, but be quick."

They were ushered into a warm and cluttered living room. This was not a hostel. It was a house. A house that smelled like cat.

"I run a cat shelter," the man explained. "And with the cold, I have many more than normal. Today, I have . . . twenty-six."

"Twenty-six cats?" Keith repeated.

"Mostly it is a cat shelter," the man went on. "But sometimes I

117

rent the rooms. Sometimes. How many do you need? I have two. They are forty euros each."

It seemed fairly obvious that they would need at least that many, since there were four of them.

"We'll take both of them," Ginny said.

"Oh, good." The man nodded and picked one of the cats off the counter, where it was enjoying a nibble of a plant on the windowsill. "Please wait a moment. I will get them ready. If I had known you were coming, I would have had breakfast for you. Still . . ."

He gestured for them to wait and went upstairs.

"We're going to die," Keith said, the moment he was gone. "This man is a serial killer. We're going to die, and he's going to bury us in his garden and build a shed on us."

The place was weird, and yes, it smelled like cat—like so much cat—but they all seemed to be nice cats. And they were better off in here than out in the snow. Ginny reached down and picked up a little cat who had come over to rub her ankles. The cat was barely out of kittenhood, long and lean and wide-eyed, happily batting at her hair as he cuddled on her shoulder. Oliver didn't look happy about this at all. Two cats sat at his feet and just stared up at him. He looked at them warily.

"Who runs a combination *cat shelter and hostel*?" Keith asked. "With the cat shelter being the primary function? Only people who want to kill you with an axe and then put you in the garden and build a shed on you, that's who."

"They are ready!" the man called, a moment later.

"That was fast," Ellis said quietly.

The bedrooms looked like normal bedrooms. They didn't have

that anonymity that you found in hostels or hotels. And they had cats in them. Little golden eyes peered at them through the dark.

"Now," the man said, opening the doors, "I have one with two beds, and one with one large bed."

"We'll take this one," Oliver said, going into the two-bed room.

"I see how this works," Keith said grimly. "I drew the short straw."

"It's fine," Ellis said, nodding to Ginny. "We'll share the one bed. That all right, Gin?"

Ginny caught some little snatch of nonverbal communication that rippled between Ellis and Keith. It took her a second to decode it, and it came out a little garbled, but the essence was, "That could have been our room. We could have shared the one bed. But we have these two with us." They were sparing her having to share with Oliver.

They stepped into their respective rooms and set their things down. The rooms were just a few feet apart. She could see Oliver setting his things up on one of the beds, while Keith flopped on another. Their host lingered in the hall, in the patch of light between their rooms. Cats swarmed the general area, poking their heads inside to see who had come to visit. One large orange cat immediately hopped onto Ginny's bag when she set it down. Another scurried under the bed.

Ginny got out her phone to send Richard a text, letting him know they were safely in for the night. She glanced between their host, the cats, and her phone.

Here and safe for the night. Everything is fine! she wrote.

That was a relief. The only thing still on her mind was the

119

tabletop. It was out there somewhere, on the snowy streets of Ghent.

"Would it be all right if I went and got the tabletop from the car?" she called over to Keith. "I'd feel better if it wasn't out there."

"Car?" This instantly interested their host. "You have a car? You must bring it here. You may put it behind the house. Go get your car, put it behind the house."

"It's fine," Keith said, getting up and coming to their door. "We just need the tabletop. . . ."

"You must get your car and move it here now. You do not want to leave it on the street when you can put it here. Go and get it and put it here."

"Right," Keith said. "Gin and I will go get the car and the tabletop. We'll be right back."

For the second time that night, Ginny and Keith set out on their own, this time in a different city. Their footsteps crunched gently in the snow as they walked to the car.

"Didn't blink an eye," he said, when they were a street away. "Did *not blink an eye*. You would think that most people would ask, 'What do you mean, tabletop? Why do you have a tabletop?' But no."

"Maybe he didn't understand the English?"

"What he wants," Keith said, "is for us to move the car behind his house so no one will see it sitting vacant after he murders us. In fact, he will probably build the shed on the spot where the car was. Plus, he'll need the car, for his murdering."

"Stop talking about murder," Ginny said. "And sheds."

"I can't help it. This place fills me with . . . shed."

It was incredibly stupid, but Ginny couldn't help but laugh. He looked over and smiled, pleased.

They'd wandered fairly far in search of lodgings, and it took them a good twenty minutes to find their way back to where they had parked. It was a gorgeous walk, though. There was such a fairyland quality to the city. Brick buildings grew directly out of cobbled streets. The snow had gotten stuck in every crevice of the buildings, had dusted the ground. In the distance, there appeared to be a castle with a great square turret, topped by four flags at the corners. In short, pretty romantic.

Worse yet, Keith had never looked so good—the snow settling on his coat, his face flushed from the cold. He pulled off his hat, and his hair stuck up a bit. At that moment, Ginny loved him so much, she felt like her ribs were going to crack from the pressure.

"Keith Dobson," he said, skidding along in the snow, "a promising actor and playwright, considered by many to be one of the best of his generation, cut off in his prime, murdered by Belgians. It's just not how I wanted to go. I foresaw something else— drowned in pudding, eaten by werewolf, smothered by adoring fans. Not this. Not this. Ah, the auto. Did you miss me, girl?"

He unlocked the passenger's door and held it open for Ginny, then got in next to her. He put the key in the ignition and put his hand on the gear, but nothing happened. It made a horrible screech, then died. He tried again and got the same result. He gave up trying and turned in his seat to face her.

"She doesn't like the cold," he said. "Or the snow. Or rain. Or damp. She doesn't like moisture. Or . . . temperature." He stroked the dashboard lovingly.

"So what do we do?"

"Give her a few minutes. Do you have Monopoly in your pocket, by any chance?"

"I forgot it," she said.

"Too bad. Guess we'll just wait it out."

The snow dusting the windows made the car into a little cocoon. He rubbed his hands together for warmth.

"This trip certainly hasn't been boring," he said. "But then, it never is with you. That's twice we've had to run from the law in Paris, you realize that? The last time we almost got busted the circumstances were different, still . . ."

This was the first time he'd made any direct reference to what had happened before, and it didn't feel accidental. In fact, he had positioned himself so that he was straight on, facing her.

"I didn't think I'd come back," she said. "It's weird."

"You're weird. It's only to be expected."

"*You* weren't expecting me."

"No," he replied, after a beat. "I can honestly say I wasn't."

He did what he always did when he was uncertain—he started wiping his mouth with the back of his hand, as if trying to wipe the words away or keep something in.

"I should try again," he said, "shouldn't I?"

This could mean a lot of things, but in this particular case, it probably meant the ignition. *Probably.*

"I guess," she said.

He scratched his head thoughtfully, shifted back and straightened himself in the seat, and turned the key. This time, the car started.

"Look at that," he said. "She always comes through."

He flicked on the wipers and cleared the snow from the

windshield, flooding the car with street- and moonlight. It skidded a bit as he first got it into the road, but within minutes, they were safely back at the House of Cats.

Inside, Ellis had already gotten into her pajamas and was tucked into bed, reading some kind of life-affirming book called *Villages*.

"There you are!" she said, as Keith and Ginny came into the room with the tabletop. "I was worried that you really had been killed."

"Car wouldn't start," Keith said, as they set the tabletop down. "I don't think she likes the snow."

Keith took a final look at the bed Ellis and Ginny would be sharing and sighed.

"Guess I'll go," he said. "My roommate is waiting."

"Have a good night!" Ellis said, giving him a wiggle-fingered wave and a laugh.

"I hate you both," he said, smiling back and shutting the door.

Even though she had done nothing wrong, Ginny felt guilty. She quietly sorted through her bag, pulling out sweatpants and T-shirt. You had to be fully dressed when sharing a bed with the girlfriend of the guy you loved.

"I got the cats out," Ellis said. "We had about ten of them in here. I wasn't sure how you felt about sleeping with them. I like them, but . . ."

"I like them too," Ginny said. "But it's okay. I guess that's better."

Ellis slipped out of bed and squatted down in front of the tabletop to have a better look.

"So, this is it," she said. "Does it look like art to you? I don't have an artistic bone in my body. You're the expert."

That was an incredibly generous assessment. She had picked a tabletop in a dark restaurant and stolen it. She was able to detect small swirls in the paint, the markings of a tiny brush. And though it appeared to be one solid yellow, it was darker in some places and lighter in others. The wineglass marks generally were in the center, with little drips and shadows at the edges.

"I think it's the right one," Ginny said.

Ellis traced her finger along one of the wineglass rings, the strange orbs that floated all over the surface. Shivering, she hopped back up into the bed and pulled the blanket over herself. Ginny deliberated for a moment whether to go down the hall to change, before deciding that was stupid. She was about to get to know Ellis one way or another. She unhooked her bra under her shirt and pulled it through her sleeve, then took off her clothes and pulled the sweats on as quickly as she could.

"Do you want me to turn out the light?" she asked.

"Sure. I'm knacked."

Ginny switched off the bureau lamp and climbed into the other side of the bed. Even though the light was off, their bed was right up against the long, multipaned window, which had no curtain or shade. The sky was light and pink and cast a long pattern of elongated rectangles over them. When she put her head back, she looked directly up at the falling snow. The view was nice, even if it did make her dizzy to watch the path the snow was taking, sometimes driving down, sometimes weaving unevenly, coming and coming from an impossible distance and sailing past them to the ground.

Just she and Ellis. Together at last. Both staring up at the snow.

"I love the snow," Ellis said. "I'm glad we're doing this. Christmas week can be so boring sometimes. Nothing open for days. And I was so jealous that Keith got to go on your last adventure. Thanks for letting me come. Now I feel like I'm in the club."

Ginny had no idea what to say to this, so she made a noncommittal sound. Kind of an *ohurggghhhh*. It was, perhaps, a little too noncommittal and perhaps a bit on the sometimes-I-am-Frankenstein side. She had to do better.

"It's nice of you guys to drive me," she said. "Otherwise I would have been stuck with Oliver."

"He's so strange," Ellis said, propping herself up. "You would think that considering what he's doing to you, he would be more appalling. More irritating. He *seems* like a normal person. He's good-looking. Quiet. I don't know . . . he just makes no sense."

A cat yowled forlornly outside the door. There was a tiny scratching on the wood and a paw poked under the door.

"Poor thing," Ellis said. "I feel bad about kicking it out. Do you mind if I let it in to sleep with us?"

"It's fine," Ginny said.

As soon as Ellis opened the door, a white cat skittered inside, followed by several other cat-shaped shadows. Ginny couldn't tell how many, but there had to be at least four cats in the room now. The white cat hopped right up on the bed and explored for a moment, finally settling in the middle of the bed. Another one, the massive orange cat, jumped up on the end of the bed and stretched out on Ginny's feet, locking her in place. Ellis took her place in the bed and again, and they resumed their snow staring, this time, with furry company.

"So," Ellis said. "Keith told me you're applying to uni?"

"Yeah," Ginny said. She didn't mean to sound as unenthusiastic as it came out.

"Where are you applying?" Ellis asked. "I don't know many American schools. I don't even know how it works. I know you have to pay a lot."

"I'm applying to a few places," Ginny said. "Mostly close to home."

"What are you going to study?" Ellis asked.

"I don't know. I figured I would just do the core classes for a year and then decide."

"I think it's great you can do that. It's a lot more specific here. My school is very rigid. There isn't a lot of choice."

"Are you an actress?" Ginny asked. "Goldsmiths is arts, right?"

"Me? God no!" Ellis shuffled around on the pillow a bit. "I don't go to Keith's school. I go to LSE."

"LSE?"

"London School of Economics. I study social policy. I am a big, boring policy nerd. I wanted a degree that would allow me to be helpful, but I don't know if that's going to work out. I'll probably end up working for the NHS making charts or counting the numbers of beds in hospitals. A friend of mine from school goes to Goldsmiths. I went to a party at her flat back in November. That's how I met Keith."

November. Ginny did the mental math. That was around the time Keith changed some of his online habits, when he hadn't been in touch every day. Even though she already knew the outcome—she was in a bed in Ghent next to the outcome—it still stung.

"I suppose we should get some sleep. If I steal the blankets, just give me a slap, yeah?"

126

On that note, Ellis flipped over on her side. The cats reorganized themselves around the girls, and the bed thrummed with their purring. Ginny soon heard soft, even breaths. Ellis had fallen asleep easily and peacefully. Ginny was still wide awake, her brain breaking down every second of what had happened in the car with Keith. If anything at all had happened. Okay, *nothing* had *actually* happened. But still, it felt . . . it felt like something. If he *had* moved in to kiss her, would she have accepted it?

Yes. Oh yes. So fast. She wouldn't have even hesitated.

She turned to look at Ellis, who was half-smiling in her sleep, her hair splayed out over her pillow like a halo. When Ginny looked down, the white cat was looking back at her. It was an incredibly sweet-faced cat. The orange cat at the end had more of a dismissive, world-dominating stare. This bed was full of devils and angels.

Ginny wasn't sure which one she was.

The Law of Pants

Ginny opened her eyes to find herself face-to-face with Ellis, sharing the same pillow. There were five cats on the bed now, curled and stretched and lounging about, very happy with these new human heaters they had been provided. Ginny extracted herself very carefully, pulling her legs up slowly, inch by inch, trying her best not to disturb any of the six other living creatures that shared the bed with her. Ellis didn't notice a thing. The orange cat, however, was extremely put out and landed on the floor with a thud. It padded indignantly out of the room.

The tabletop was a little less exciting in the morning light— a scuffed yellow half-a-door leaning against the wall. Now she could see how roughly it had been sawn in half, how thin and streaky the paint job was. Maybe this wasn't the right one. Maybe there was a masterpiece back there.

Well, this was the one they had. She made a mental note to contact Paul as soon as possible . . . although, maybe it was best not to. Maybe there was video footage of what happened. Maybe he would see it and recognize Ginny.

Time to stop thinking about it. She gathered up her clothes, picking up each item delicately, as if Ellis could be woken by the sound of a sweater. Today, she would wear lots of layers, even those long underwear things her mom bought her for the trip and insisted she take. There were two more cats waiting out in the hall when Ginny stepped out, cozied up against the radiator. There was a large gold clock in the wall. It was 6:10 in the morning. The early start was probably good.

Ginny tiptoed to the bathroom and opened the door, only to find Oliver in there, dressed only in his boxers and a T-shirt, brushing his teeth. That was officially the first time she had ever stumbled onto a guy in the wild wearing only boxer shorts, and now the image was going to be burned in her brain. The boxers in question were maroon with a thin gray stripe. His legs were long, not overly hairy, but the hair on them was dark. It was hard to know where to look. She couldn't take her eyes off the boxers. Mostly, she had a view of the back, but he turned halfway when he looked over. She commanded herself not to look at the front flap, which, of course, was exactly what she honed in on.

He spit and put his mouth under the tap to get some water. All while just wearing underwear. All while she just stared at the crucial spot of the Action Pants.

"I'll be just a moment," he said, pulling the door shut.

"Oh. Sorry," she said to the closed door. "It wasn't locked."

"It's fine," came the muffled reply.

Why was she apologizing? He was the one who didn't lock the door.

130

Just as she was recovering, the door opened again and he walked past, still just in the T-shirt and boxers, shoeless, calm as could be.

"All yours," he said.

How was this okay? It wasn't like she or Ellis were going to stroll around the Cat Palace in their underwear. Why did Oliver feel like this was an acceptable morning outfit? Why didn't he put pants on to walk down the hall? Why could guys, who arguably had a lot more going on in that department, walk around in underwear like it was nothing?

Also, he had steamed up the bathroom from his shower. Not only had she been treated to two viewings of the Oliver Underwear, but now she was soaking in his shower steam. Also, she wasn't showering alone. The orange cat, still disgruntled about being disturbed, decided to join her in the bathroom and watch. The hostel owner had left towels, but no soap, so mostly, it was a hot rinse. Then she dressed quickly and got out of there.

While the snowfall had been constant during the night, it hadn't accumulated much. In New Jersey, an all-night snowstorm could result in a foot or two of sticky snow that wouldn't move for days, but this was only an inch or two and could be lightly kicked out of the way. Oliver was brushing the car off with his gloved hands, cigarette sticking out of his mouth. He looked at her over the car roof and gave her a little nod of acknowledgment.

Now that Ginny had seen him in his underwear, things were simply not the same. Maybe he had done it on purpose, to make himself seem more human and vulnerable. "Why are you awake so early?" she asked.

Ginny had no idea why she asked this. She didn't care. She just had to say something. Something conversational. Something to get the underwear image out of her head.

"Do you think I slept well sharing a room with him?" he asked, stubbing the cigarette out into a pile of snow on the car roof. "I'd like to keep my eyebrows, thank you."

"You act like he's the one causing problems," she said.

"Yes, well, I've learned a lot, sitting in that car with the three of you." He finished up his brushing efforts, dusted the snow off his hands, and started heading back to the kitchen door.

"What does that mean?" she said.

He stared down at her. In the direct sunlight, his eyes were an absolute clear amber color. In normal light, they were very dark brown, almost black.

"Hey!" Keith called from the window. "Stop touching my car."

"I was clearing off the snow," Oliver said.

"I don't care."

Oliver shook his head and went back into the kitchen. Inside, the hotel owner was busy trying to assemble some breakfast. He had set four places around his little kitchen table with cheerful orange plates and little red eggs cups.

"I am sorry," he said. "I wasn't ready for guests. I have four eggs, some yogurt, some bread. . . ."

"It's fine," Ginny said.

"It is not fine. I should have been prepared. Now, what will you have?"

Keith and Ellis came trooping down the stairs.

"Fried egg on toast for me," Keith said. "Bacon, if you have it."

"I am sorry. No bacon."

"Fried egg on toast for me too," Ellis said.

"Same," Oliver said.

"Can I have mine scrambled?" Ginny asked the hotel owner.

"Scrambled?"

"Scrambled . . . kind of . . . shaken? Or . . ."

"Of course," he said. "I understand."

She watched as he shook the egg in the shell, then cracked it and fried it.

They had an audience as they ate. The hotel owner stood over them, and the cats formed a circle around. One of them jumped onto the table and stared Oliver in the face.

"So," Keith said, "where to today?"

"Amsterdam," Oliver said, staring back at the cat. "Back to a place you went before—your aunt's friend Charlie's?"

Ginny looked up from her examination of her strange fried egg. This was a major disaster, much worse than a locked restaurant. This was the end of the whole trip.

"Wait," Keith said. "Isn't Amsterdam where . . ."

Ginny answered by putting her head in her hands.

"This would have been one of those times it would have been good to give her *her own letter*," Keith added.

"What's happening?" Ellis asked. "I don't understand."

Oliver looked around, also confused.

"Amsterdam is very nice," the hotel owner said. "My cousin makes wigs there."

They let this comment pass.

"Amsterdam didn't work out," Ginny said. "The directions were to find Charlie's house, but he'd moved. He's gone. I have no idea where he is."

133

Oliver just shrugged and continued eating his eggs.

"So we find him," he said simply. "Sixty Westerstraat. That's the address in the letter. We go there and we ask around. Someone has to know him, or know where he went."

"Where he went might not be Amsterdam. He could be anywhere."

"He might be. But this time you have lots of advantages you didn't have last time. We have phones. I have a computer. We have maps. And there are four of us. It might be easy. We might find it straightaway."

Keith looked to Ginny and shook his head.

"Yeah," he said. "I'm sure that's exactly what's going to happen."

Ellis and Ginny carried the tabletop together, bearing it gently over the snow, sliding a little as they went. Ginny and Oliver were installed into the backseat first, and the tabletop was carefully loaded in on top of them. (Well, it was smacked into Oliver a few times, but then it was put in with care.)

"If you push the seat back, you'll move the whole tabletop," Oliver added loudly. "It won't just be me you're making suffer."

The careful positioning didn't change much. There was perhaps one extra inch at the top, so that Ginny could now see the tops of Ellis's and Keith's ears. It was, in essence, a wall. It actually helped that she couldn't see them very well. The tabletop offered some protection from that particular reality.

They set off. More European motorway, full of small cars and flat-fronted trucks and motorcycles. Ginny got to know the names of the major Belgian and Dutch gas stations—a fact she was sure would come in handy in the future. Like Oliver, she put in her headphones. The many layers she had put on this morning were paying off, both in terms of warmth and padding. She was in a cocoon.

She and Oliver were accidentally sitting a few inches closer today. Their arms would bump occasionally. The one advantage was that he radiated some body heat, so it was marginally warmer sitting closer to him than it was sitting closer to the window. There was a faint smell of smoke coming off his coat, which wasn't unpleasant. She decided to think of him as a kind of low-quality fireplace.

About two hours in, she heard Keith shout something about the need for petrol, and they pulled into a service area, which, to Ginny's surprise, featured a large McDonald's.

"I picked this one to make you feel at home," Keith said, as he pulled out the tabletop, releasing Oliver and Ginny from their seat.

It was decided that they would take half an hour for some food and to stretch. The snow was heavier here, but it had gotten warmer, and it was all starting to melt into slush.

Oliver opted not to join them, staying outside in the wet parking lot, smoking and talking on his phone. They watched him through the window as they sat with their food.

"The constant smoking," Keith said. "Puff the Magic Wanker is going to kill himself at this rate, which certainly gives me a new respect for the tobacco industry. Who do you think he's calling? His mum?"

"Maybe he has a girlfriend," Ellis said. "Or a boyfriend."

"No." Keith took a long sip of his soda. "No. There is no way."

"You never know," Ellis said. "We were talking last night about how he isn't bad-looking."

"Were you now?" Keith shoved a few fries in his mouth and regarded Oliver again.

Ginny and Ellis were throwing away the trash and just stepping outside when Keith started the car, gunned the engine (as much as this was possible), then pulled out abruptly. He headed right for Oliver. Oliver looked surprised, but he didn't budge, even as the white car came right for him.

"What's he . . . ?" Ellis said. "Oh god."

It looked for a moment like this battle of wills was going to accidentally end in death, but at the last second, Keith turned the wheel hard, fishtailing around, sending a wave of dirty, icy slush all over Oliver.

Keith got out and surveyed his work with satisfaction. Oliver was trying to maintain his dignity, brushing himself off calmly. The force of the splash must have washed the Zippo out of his hands. He reached into an icy puddle with his bare hand and retrieved it. He flicked it a few times, but it didn't produce any flame.

"Doesn't work?" Keith said. "Oh, that *is* a pity."

Oliver carefully removed his coat and shook it hard to get out the worst of the slush and dirty water, then rolled it tight.

"Can I put this in the boot?"

"Boot's full," Keith replied.

"It's going to get *her* wet as well."

Keith rolled his eyes and reached for the coat, shoving it hard into a corner of the trunk, mashing it down as hard as he could.

"There you go," he said.

Once in the car, Oliver wrapped his arms around himself and faced the window, resolute and silent. He didn't even put in his headphones. He was trying not to show it, but anger crackled off him. If Ginny had touched him at that moment, she was pretty sure she would have gotten a shock. Though there was a part of her—a very, very small part of her—that wanted to offer him a sweater or a pat on the shoulder.

How did he do this? How did he manage to make her feel bad for him? There was something terribly raw about Oliver. In the winter sun, his face was utterly pale except for the dark shadow all around his chin. He looked like one of those guys who had to shave a lot, maybe twice a day, or the beast would come out. Even though he was tall and looked more than capable of defending himself, he sat defiantly, doing nothing. He seemed altogether too used to abuse.

But, she reminded herself . . . he was getting abuse for good reason. He was silent because there was no way he could possibly defend himself. He was the person doing wrong here.

She decided not to look at him anymore, not even a glance. She wasn't going to look at anyone. She had the tabletop to protect her from the front, and her headphones to block out the rest. She could just sleep. The last one sounded like the best option, so she closed her eyes and scrunched herself against the car door. Tiny streams of cold air stabbed her through the gaps in the window, and the door itself was like ice, but she tried not to care. She shut her eyes hard and commanded herself to rest, to turn it all off.

The last thing she saw as she closed her eyes was the underwear.

The Stain on the Page

When she opened her eyes next, Ginny found that her face was pressed up against the window, hard. Just outside the window was the gentle, constant tinkling of bicycle bells.

"We're in Amsterdam," she said groggily, her lips rubbing against the cold glass.

"Have a nice kip?" Keith called from the front.

Something was weighing her down. Ginny turned to find the sleeping form of Oliver slumped against her, using her as a pillow. It wasn't entirely unpleasant to have him there. He was warm, and not overly heavy. She had probably slept so well because of the body heat he was giving off. Still, he had to go. Ginny straightened herself up, and Oliver fell senselessly in the other direction, toward his door. This woke him up, and he reflexively rubbed his face and looked around.

"Are we there?" he asked.

"We're *almost* there," Keith said. "Not that we have any idea

139

where we are supposed to go. Where are we going, precisely?"

"We should leave the car outside the city and ride the tram in," Oliver replied. "There should be a car park coming up in a few minutes."

"Not actually an answer," Keith said. "Give us the next bit. Recite, freak."

Oliver was still waking up. He yawned hard, pressed his hand to his temple, and began.

"'From Paris, it's time . . .' Hang on."

He blinked a few times and stared at the car ceiling, moving his lips silently.

"He's forgotten it, hasn't he?" Keith said.

"Shut it. 'From Paris, it's time to return to Amsterdam, the city of canals, bicycles, and delicious, delicious cheese. The Dutch are famous for their open windows. No curtains. No blinds. Their houses are on display. Walk along the canal streets, Gin. You'll be right at eye level with every variety of human life. You can see into a thousand different worlds.

"'But here's the thing: You aren't supposed to look. This is an understood Dutch custom. Everything will be laid bare for you, but you can't ever turn your head and gawk. This is both elegant and incredibly perverse. The idea, I think . . .'"

He paused again.

"This is really much better than just bringing the letter," Keith said.

"'. . . is that whatever you are doing in your house, however you choose to live, is fine. You have nothing to be ashamed of and nothing to hide. But at the same time, you have to respect your neighbors enough not to stare.

" 'I don't know. I'm making this up. I don't even know if the Dutch know why this is the way of things. There's probably some complicated historical precedent involving the curtain makers' union or something. Also, I looked. I peeked in every window where anything even remotely interesting was going on. You can't put something in front of me and expect me not to look.

" 'So, for the next layer of the painting, I decided to make a Dutch window, except you ARE supposed to look through it. Charlie has it. I am sure you have already seen it. You just need to go back and collect it. I realize that it's difficult to carry around a tabletop, Gin. And now I'm asking you to carry around a tabletop and a window. That's why I didn't have you get these things the first time around. Once you've done that, take the ferry back to England. Head back home, to Richard's.'

"There. That's the whole section. We go back to where you started last time."

"So we're done after this?" Ginny asked.

"Not exactly," Oliver said.

"More riddles," Keith said, pulling off the motorway toward the parking lot. "Wonderful."

A half hour later, they knocked on the door of 60 Westerstraat. The person who answered this time was not the same person Ginny had met over the summer. This person also didn't know a Charlie.

"So, we just start asking, I guess?" Ginny said, looking up and down the street. Westerstraat was one of the non-canal streets, full of fairly modern buildings.

"Do you know anything else about him?" Ellis asked. "A last

name. A job. Anything?"

"The letter just gave his first name and address."

"Right," Ellis said. "So, we just start asking people if they know Charlie. We can do that."

There weren't many people around, and knocking on the doors to either side of number 60 produced no result. They spread the search farther down on either side, Keith and Ellis going to the left, and Ginny and Oliver going to the right. No one knew Charlie.

They stopped briefly to get some sandwiches.

"I don't think this is working," Keith said, examining a mysterious salad on his.

"Maybe Charlie is an English version of his name or something," Ginny replied. "What's important is the window. My aunt's paintings . . . they're kind of weird. Maybe we're asking the wrong question. Maybe we need to ask about the painting itself."

So they tried it again, this time asking about the window. This brought a result from the woman who worked at the flower shop.

"Oh, you mean the jungle window?" she said.

Ginny looked to Oliver, to see if he had any idea if a "jungle window" was the kind of thing they were supposed to be looking for.

"That could be it," he said, nodding. "The man with the jungle window, do you know where he went?"

"I didn't know his name, but I think he works at De Bevlekte Pagina. It is a bookshop. He is a . . . he is a very strange . . ."

"That's him," Ginny said. The label "very strange" fit most of Aunt Peg's friends.

De Bevlekte Pagina was a tiny place, just a few streets over. It was some kind of medieval nook, uneven in every respect, from the strange lean of the walls, the odd shape of the room, and the slope of the floor, to the step in the corner that led to a tiny door halfway up the wall. Ginny had never seen such a small store, or imagined you could get so much into it. It had one employee—a girl in a red crushed velvet jacket and a bob dyed to match. Her shirt was low-cut enough to reveal a glimpse of a large cartoon heart tattooed over her actual heart.

"Hi," Ginny said, approaching her. "We're looking for someone named Charlie."

"Are you readers?" the girl asked, barely lifting her head.

"Readers?"

The girl offered no other information.

"Does he work here?" Ellis asked.

"Work here?" The girl was contemptuous now. "He is not an *employee*."

"Can you please get him if he's here?" Oliver said briskly. The girl didn't look happy about offering any other information, but she did seem to like the sight of Oliver. She smiled flirtatiously before leaving the counter and went to the back of the store and pushed aside a velvet curtain that blocked off a passage.

"Charlie, *er zijn wat mensen hier voor jou.*"

A voice came from the depths.

"*Wie zijn het?*"

"*Geen flauw idee.*" The girl turned to give them all another appraising look. "*Ze zijn Engels.*"

"*Engelse?*"

"*Ze zien er uit als studenten.*"

143

She dropped the curtain, came back to the counter, and continued reading her book.

"Is he . . . coming?" Ginny asked.

"When he is finished," she said, not looking up. "Did you bring books for him to sign or do you want to buy them?"

"Books? No."

The girl sighed and shook her head. They were a terrible disappointment to her. Even her interest in Oliver fizzled out, just like that.

Nothing happened for several minutes. They wandered around the shop as much as they could, but it was barely bigger than their rooms at the hostel. The books were a mix of Dutch, English, French, and German, mostly used. Oliver got bored and went outside to smoke. Keith and Ellis had a low conversation in the corner. Ginny sat in the single spot of sun in an open windowsill.

Finally, the curtain was pushed back. A guy appeared from the darkness. He was shorter than Ginny, maybe in his mid-twenties, and absolutely emaciated. What he lacked in height and body mass he made up for in hair—straggly beard, untamed locks sticking up in all directions. He wore a heavy red plaid lumberjack shirt, completely unbuttoned and exposing even more chest hair. Three or four silver necklaces glinted just under this layer. He wore black leather pants that were cracked and worn from use, and no shoes. His fingernails and toenails were colored ink black—it looked more like pen than nail polish. He was like something you found on a nature preserve, if they made nature preserves where you could look at artistic frenzy in the wild.

This was definitely the right guy.

"Hi," Ginny said. "I'm Ginny. Peg's niece?"

He leaned forward. Ginny couldn't tell if he couldn't understand her English, or if he was sniffing her. "I'm Peg's niece," she tried again. "Margaret Bannister? The painter?"

This hit a note of recognition. His eyebrows went up and he leaned back against a bookcase and folded his arms across his chest. He exposed the underside of his arm in the process, and Ginny could see words written there, a whole screed of some kind.

"Do you speak English?" she said slowly.

"Of *course* I speak English."

Ginny had discovered this during her first time in the Netherlands—all Dutch people seemed to speak flawless English. He nodded and turned to the girl at the counter.

"Margaret is *een Amerikaanse schilderes. Ze is erg goed. Maar ik kan niet geloven dat deze meid haar nichtje is.*"

Ginny had no idea what he was saying, but assumed it probably wasn't too complimentary.

"My aunt wrote me a letter. She said I was supposed to come see you. I was here over the summer, but I went to your old address. You have something my aunt gave to you. Something she asked me to come get. A window . . ."

Charlie picked up a pen and began cleaning under his nails with the writing tip.

"The window is on the boat," he said matter-of-factly.

"The boat?"

"I have a boat," he said. "It is on a canal."

That thought kept him occupied for a moment or two.

"A good place for it," Keith said quietly.

"The boat is gone," Charlie went on. He almost sounded happy about this, like the boat had finally sought freedom and was now living a happier life somewhere else. "I hire the boat out. Someone has hired the boat today. The boat will be back tomorrow. You can have the window then. Or . . . is it the next day?"

This last question was to the girl behind the counter, who looked up and shrugged.

"We're not here that long," Ginny said nervously. "I don't want to bother you, but we really need it today."

"Well, today it is gone. Come back later. Say hello to Margaret for me."

Charlie seemed to be done talking and, with a wave of his hand, headed back to the curtain.

"She's dead," Ginny said.

This wasn't something she'd had to say out loud in a while, and she didn't like breaking the news to anyone. Charlie's demeanor changed completely. Even the girl put her book down and looked up in confusion.

"Margaret? Is dead? But, how? She is so young. Did she have an accident?"

"She didn't tell you she was sick?" Ginny asked.

"Sick? Sick with what?"

"She had cancer," Ginny said.

It was like she had sucked all the air out of the room with a straw. Charlie sat down on the floor, in the tiny space between the bookcases.

"The window," he said.

That was all he could manage for a moment.

"I met her in New York," he said finally. "She came here to learn more about Dutch painting, about the use of light. About still life. She stayed with me, and I showed her my boat. She loved it. She was painting a picture of it. It's a very distinctive boat. It is pink. Very bright pink. She said she wanted to make something for the boat—a view you could look through, both ways. She mounted the glass in the window of my flat and painted it while standing on a box, on the pavement."

Ginny could picture it perfectly. Aunt Peg, so tiny, so graceful—her long brown hair tied back in a knot, probably standing on her toes. She moved like a ballerina, even though she never took a dance class in her life and couldn't keep time to music.

"I'm a poet," Charlie said. "Maybe you know my work?"

"No," Ginny said quietly. "Sorry."

"The name of this shop—it means, 'the stain on the page.' We both loved that idea. Painting, writing. Both just stains on the page."

Charlie took a long breath and stared at the shelf of books in front of them, drew a long, jagged line on his bare foot, then put his head down on his knees. The girl behind the counter reached down and touched his head. While Ginny understood that other people were entitled to mourn her aunt as much as she was, it still irritated her that Charlie was allowed this little display. He hadn't even known she was dead, hadn't been involved in any way. But then, Aunt Peg had hidden her illness from a lot of people, including her family. Only Richard was there for the worst of it.

Finally, Charlie roused himself.

"The boat, I hire it to tourists and for parties. Someone has hired it for this week, but they return it tomorrow. Come in the morning. I will take you to it."

Once they were outside, Oliver was the first to speak.

"I booked a place to stay here," he said. "Two rooms. Perhaps we should go there."

For the first time, Keith made no comment about one of Oliver's plans.

The Koekoeksklok

The hostel Oliver had found was by far the nicest Ginny had encountered on any of her travels. It occupied an entire canal house, narrow and tall, with one massive window at the front and back of each floor. The windows had red shutters, large as doors. At the very top, near the roof, there was a clock, and all down the front, tiny paintings of blue birds. It was called the Koekoeksklok. Ginny didn't need a Dutch-to-English dictionary to figure out that meant "cuckoo clock."

The theme continued on the inside, which featured a large common room paneled in dark wood, with cuckoo clocks all over the walls.

"I hope these don't work," Ellis said, looking around.

The Koekoeksklok was staffed by students—no murderers with dozens of cats. The hostel had one central wooden stairway that wound up and through the skinny building, with just a few deafeningly creaky steps from floor to floor. Oliver and Keith were shown to a room on the third floor, and Ellis and Ginny got the room above them, at the top, facing front. The ceiling of their room was peaked, and high as the roof, maybe sixteen feet. The decorations were basic, but very clean, and the beds were loaded down with a multicolor pile of blankets.

They had a massive window—the cuckoo hole—which faced the canal. Ginny looked out at the skyline. All the roofs were different heights, and almost every canal house had a little ornate peak at the top. Many of the houses had a hook sticking out of the front. Ginny had learned all about these hooks last time. Because the houses were so narrow, you couldn't get furniture up the stairs. Things had to be hoisted up by rope and brought in through the windows. Windows were really key here.

Below, there was a steady stream of boats drifting along the canal, and on the sidewalks and roads, hundreds of people on bikes. Amsterdam was one constant, steady flow of energy—not manic, just as fast as a bike wheel or the chug of a canal boat. Ginny really loved this city, maybe more than Paris or London. It wasn't overwhelming. It was practical and beautiful and lively.

"There's not much we can do tonight," Keith said, dropping down on Ellis's bed. "What now?"

Inertia was starting to take over. Ellis was sprawled on the floor. Keith was looking at her, not in any particular *way*—he wasn't drooling or anything—but his gaze fell on her and stayed there. It made Ginny uncomfortable.

"I guess we should eat," Ellis said to the ceiling. "We should go out."

Ginny got up to use the bathroom and get herself ready to go. She was only in there for a minute or two, but when she came back, Ellis was sitting up, her back against the side of the bed. Keith had repositioned himself so that he was at her shoulder, just at her ear. Again, they weren't *doing* anything, but Ginny was pretty sure this was only because she was here.

"I can't move," Keith replied. "I think I have to sleep."

"Me too," Ellis said.

It was entirely possible they were just tired. Ginny was kind of tired. But there was something incredibly awkward about being around the two of them right now. Escape. It was the only way.

"I have to go call Richard," she said. "I'll be outside. I might take a walk."

Keith yawned and lifted a hand in farewell.

Over the summer, Ginny had to spend a lot of time by herself—time alone with no internet, no television, no music, nothing to numb her from the experience of being on her own. This wasn't by choice. The first letter spelled out the rules. She couldn't bring a computer, a phone, even a journal . . . nothing that could distract her from the experience of *being in Europe* on her own. At first, it had been unpleasant and weird, but over time, she had adjusted. It was okay just to be by herself, with herself.

Now, of course, she had lots of company to think about.

Ellis was . . . extraordinarily pretty, and spontaneous, and sweet. She matched the sharpness in Keith's personality. She didn't need to be coaxed into climbing over the fence and through the window—she wouldn't need to be boosted up and shoved over. Ellis would make the climb herself. And she was English. She fit in. She had London style and that understated London swagger. Sure, Ginny had lost the braids, but the fake red in her hair was already fading, and that newfound courage of hers was just a thin outer coating. She was the American—a little louder, a little out of step. Given the choice, she would have dated Ellis too. It only made sense.

She sat down on a bench along the canal and pulled out her phone to call Richard. He answered on the first ring.

"Hi . . . sorry. Is this a bad time?" she asked.

"No, you caught me at a good moment. I'm hiding in my office. How are you? Where are you?"

"Amsterdam," she said.

"Amsterdam? When did you get there?"

"A few hours ago. We're in a really nice hostel. It's sort of like a cuckoo clock."

"I see. What are you doing there?"

"We need to get a window," Ginny said. "I guess part of the piece is a glass panel. It's on a boat, and someone rented it out. So when it comes back, we'll get it."

"And where do you go then?"

"I'm not sure," she said. "We sort of have to figure that out."

She heard his other line ringing, and the sound of him shuffling things around on his desk.

"Let me think what I'm supposed to ask . . . have you engaged in any exceedingly foolish behavior while under the influence of alcohol?"

She hadn't been drunk when she stole the tabletop, so she had a pass on that one. "Nope," she said.

"Are you wandering the streets alone in a haze of legal marijuana?"

"No."

"Do you have any intention of entering the prostitution

business, which is also legal in Amsterdam?"

"Probably not today."

"Good, good. Is there anything I didn't cover? I'm new to this."

"You were pretty thorough," she said.

"You know I trust you, Gin," Richard said, almost sounding embarrassed. "I know you can do as you like. You're eighteen. I certainly did plenty of things. . . ."

The door to the Koekoeksklok opened, and Oliver stepped out. He brushed off his still-damp coat and looked around. As soon as he spotted Ginny, he headed straight for her.

"No," Ginny said quickly. "I'm good. And thanks. For everything."

"Well, you know I'm here."

Oliver lingered a few feet off until she had wrapped up her call. He may not have been respectful of personal property, but he was all about giving people their personal space.

"Where are the others?" he asked.

"They're tired. I think they're napping."

They probably weren't napping. Well, *maybe* they were. Probably not. She was not going to think about what they were doing.

"I was going to go look for the boat," he said. "Care to join me?"

They stared at each other for a moment, sizing up the situation. They were here, there was a job to be done. More importantly, it would give her something to do while Keith and Ellis did whatever they were going to do . . . which was nap, of course.

"Fine," she said.

"I've got some directions," he said, pulling out both his phone and a tourist map. "The canals surround the—"

"I know the city pretty well," she said, cutting him off. "I mean, the tourist parts."

"I thought it all went wrong."

"It did," she said. "But I didn't leave. I ended up in this really horrible hostel. So I ran away from that and ended up meeting this family called the Knapps, from America. They took me in for the week. They were nice, but they were super tourists. It was like they were competing for the Most-Touristy-Tourists-of-the-Year award. They wanted to see it, have their picture taken in front of it, get the T-shirt, and move on. They used to have these *printed schedules* for each day. . . ."

Ginny started walking, and Oliver fell into step behind her.

"So why didn't you just leave if they were so annoying?" he asked.

"They weren't mean people," Ginny said. "They just wanted to check everything off their checklists. Lots of people probably travel like that."

"Lots of people *live* like that. . . ."

That was the kind of thing Aunt Peg would have said. Was he doing that on purpose? She glanced over at him suspiciously.

"It still doesn't explain why you didn't just leave."

"I was just sick of being by myself," she said. "I don't know. I just stayed with them. Anyway, the center bit of the city is pretty small, and the main canals are around it in layers, a bunch of half circles. It won't take that long to look around the main tourist areas. Maybe a few hours. I mean, we're looking for a big pink boat. How many of those can there be?"

"This is Amsterdam. There could be a small fleet of pink boats here, for all we know. But I take your point. Should we start this way? We're pretty much at the top of this street, anyway."

They began to stroll down the canal, under the bare trees. The lights and the moon reflected off the canal in a way that would have been romantic if she had been with just about anyone else.

"You couldn't bring anything the last time you came over," he said. "No guidebooks. No maps. No computer or phone or anything. Those rules, they were a bit mental. Did you follow them?"

"Yes," Ginny said, scanning the boats along the canal. It was getting darker by the second, and harder to determine exactly what color they were.

"Why? I mean, who would have known if you hadn't?"

"I would have known."

"Yeah, but . . . all that time on planes and trains with nothing to listen to. No internet. Nothing. It sounds like torture. I would have brought everything."

"You're not me," Ginny said.

"Did you ever think that she *expected* you to break some of them?"

Remarkably, that thought hadn't occurred to Ginny before. She stepped out of the way of a bicyclist and directly into the path of another bicyclist, who expertly steered around her.

"I don't know," he said. "Maybe you like all the rules, the backtracking, the games. I think it's annoying."

"This isn't *for* you."

"I think it's annoying in general. She should have just given you the paintings. This traipsing back and forth is such a pointless exercise."

"Look," Ginny said. "We're not discussing her, okay? *You* do not talk about her, or what she did."

"I'm just saying, it seems like she was a rule breaker, so maybe she expected you to break the rules."

"So," she said, "is this how you justify what you're doing?"

"What I'm doing is maybe a little unethical. . . ."

"Maybe a *little*? You're stealing."

"I'm not stealing," Oliver said firmly.

Ginny stopped. They were on the unguarded edge of one of the canals. The water was high, and two swans and a few ducks drifted past and regarded them curiously.

"How is this not stealing?" she said, mostly to the swans.

"Someone stole your bag," he said. "Not me. I purchased the bag, not knowing it was stolen. Inside, I found some property. I used my time and resources to track you down to return your property to you. In return, I asked for a percentage. You agreed."

"Or you were going to walk away with my stuff," Ginny said. "My stolen stuff. Don't you legally have to return that to me anyway?"

"I'm not an expert on Greek law, and neither, as far as I know, are you. All I have of yours, anyway, is a bag . . . which I did offer to return . . . and a few pieces of paper. The paper wasn't in any kind of sealed envelope delivered by Royal Mail, which *would* be illegal to tamper with, so there's no problem there. And I have agreed to return these pieces of paper to you on completion of our agreement. Do you want to take me to court for a few pieces of paper worth less than a pound?"

"How come," she said, mostly to herself, "I only know two English guys and both of you are . . . well, one was a thief and the other is you."

"I think it says more about you than it says about us."

"About me?"

"About the people you attract."

"It's not me," she said. "It's my aunt."

"It is you," he said. "She's not here, in case you haven't noticed. You are the common denominator in all of this. And don't lump me in with him. I've never lied to you. I've been very careful about that. I hate lying. I'm not a thief, and I'm not a liar."

This was the first time Ginny had heard anything that might have been considered an emotion in Oliver's voice.

"So what *are* you?"

"An opportunist."

"What does that even mean?" she asked.

"I saw an opportunity, and I took it. That's what it means. I've been completely up front about it, and I'll continue to be up front about it."

"You're delusional."

"I'm not. I know what I'm doing doesn't make me a great person, but I don't tell lies."

"Well I guess that makes it okay," she said. "I mean, as long as you're being *honest*."

Oliver got the stupid cigarettes out again. He had a new lighter. It was just cheap and plastic, not like the fancy Zippo he had before. He drew in and exhaled slowly, blowing the smoke to the side, away from her. Now that she thought about it, he was the only person she knew who smoked. It was just such a ridiculous habit. The cigarettes were his prop, his way of avoiding anything he didn't feel like dealing with, putting distance between himself and other people.

157

She was being too deep about that, probably.

"You hate my smoking," he said.

"Does it matter? Are you going to stop because I don't like it?"

They were coming up to a few steps leading down into the canal. Oliver stepped down to the very edge of the water and dipped in the tip of the cigarette, extinguishing it. He held it up to show her.

"I'm not unreasonable," he said.

"Of course not," she replied.

A Night of Vice

They walked for two hours. In the open windows, she saw Christmas trees and lights, a few ornate menorahs. Ginny was pleased to find that she had a fairly good memory of the layout of Amsterdam. The canals varied in width, from perhaps one car-lane wide to six or so lanes wide. They radiated throughout the city like a spiderweb, with boats parked along the sides, all kinds of boats. Long, traditional houseboats were next to sleek new cruisers, which might then be followed by tiny, flat rowboats that looked like they would sink the second a person sat down in one. Every once in a while, they would pass a boat that had met a bad end, half submerged under the water, tipped sideways, ducks looking at it mockingly.

They passed into the red light district—Amsterdam's legal prostitution zone. There were long windows dotted between houses and shops, each with a thin frame of red light. Those windows either had someone standing in them, usually female, or a closed curtain, indicating the little shop was currently busy. The windows were bizarrely cozy. Sometimes the women would sit and read or paint their nails or just wave. Ginny had a fondness for those windows and the women in them. They had completely freaked the Knapps out.

"Know what I was thinking?" Oliver said. "When I read that we had to find a window in Amsterdam? I thought we were going to have to find one of those."

She had to admit, Oliver had a good point. Aunt Peg would have had a lot of fun decorating one of those windows.

"This is pointless," she said.

"But fun," he said. Ginny had no idea if that was supposed to be a joke. He was utterly inscrutable. He just gazed around, his hands buried in his pockets.

Along with the red windows, there were several coffeehouses on this street. These were the pot-smoking cafés. They looked like they existed mainly for tourists, with neon signs and pumping music. They passed a quieter one that looked like a regular little café. They had two menus out front—one of various pot concoctions, and another of food. Mostly pizza.

"I want to go in," she said.

"You want to smoke?"

"No," she said. "I'm hungry. They have pizza."

"Lots of places have pizza. It's fine if you want to smoke. I'm not going to judge you."

"I don't," Ginny said firmly.

"Then we can go somewhere that has good food. There's lots of it about in Amsterdam. These places aren't known for—"

"I just want to go here, okay?"

Oliver raised his hands in surrender.

Truth be told, Ginny didn't *want* to go into the coffee shop—she felt a perverse *need* to go in. The Knapps (at least, Mom and Dad Knapp) wouldn't go anywhere near the coffeehouses, and there was something inside Ginny that compelled her to do everything the Knapps disliked. And if she was being *very* truthful with herself (it happened on occasion), Ginny would have admitted that the coffee shops scared her too. Even though they were legal and clearly full of tourists, they had the air of the forbidden . . . literally. And Richard had just asked her if she was walking around in a haze of legal marijuana. Here she was walking into a cloud of it. She pushed the door open with much more force than necessary and marched in.

A cursory glance around the room revealed that the coffee shop wasn't that much different from any ordinary café. It was a little darker, maybe. The air had the distinct, sweet tang of pot smoke. But there was nothing particularly scary going on inside, unless you counted the tacky decorations. The place looked like a stoner's dorm room—cheap cushions and basket chairs, black light posters of smiley faces, and dozens of votive candles in bright glass holders, right out of the IKEA catalog. The menus, both for food and drugs, were written in neon purple and green on an illuminated board. It was a bit sad, really. Aunt Peg could have done an amazing job with a place like this. Her paintings would have *really* messed people up.

Had she been on her own, Ginny would have turned around and walked out; but since she'd made such a bizarrely big deal of coming in, now she had to stay here and eat some pizza. She and Oliver took a seat at a wobbly little table, half of which was taken up by a massive ashtray.

"Here you go," Ginny said, pushing it toward him. "A present."

"I don't smoke indoors."

The coffee shop wasn't very crowded, but that didn't mean that service was prompt. Their waiter, when he finally showed up, was openly confused by the fact that they had come there for the food—but being mellow and stonerish, accepted this and ambled off. She and Oliver were the only people sitting completely upright. They looked stiff and unnatural. She tried to relax in her chair, but the slouching was even more unnatural. Oliver pushed a votive candle back and forth and eyed her across the table.

"So," she said, "what do you do?"

"Meaning what?"

"For . . . life?"

"I went to university for a year," he said. "For political science."

"And you don't go now?"

"I left."

"Why?"

"There was no point in staying."

This kind of thing always amazed Ginny—people who just walked away from institutions. People who left school when they didn't see the point. Aunt Peg had done that. Ginny knew she never would. That either made her someone who worked hard and finished things, or someone who didn't have the guts to break away from the pack. Maybe both.

Of course, if she never wrote her essay, this would not be an issue.

The two pizzas were slipped down in front of them, along with a beer for Oliver and a soda for Ginny. They weren't great pizzas—kind of floppy and damp—but she'd had worse. She was going to eat it, no matter what, since she'd brought them here.

"How did you memorize that whole letter?" she said, cutting hers into pieces. She didn't even need a knife—the fork went right through the spongy crust.

"You really like asking questions, don't you?"

"You said you're honest."

He eyed her for a moment as he cut a large piece of the pizza and picked it up for a bite. It flopped around too much to be handled, so he set it down and continued with utensils. "I'm just good at memorizing things. I don't even mean to memorize them, half the time. I just do."

"You mean you have a photographic memory?"

"No," he said. "Because that would be useful. It's far more random than that. I can recite the entire first chapter of every Harry Potter book. I can recite all forty-seven pages of my school handbook. I can re-create eight episodes of season two of *Doctor Who*, with the Tenth Doctor, word for word. I memorized the driving manual. I just seem to memorize things that have some kind of significance to me—"

He cut himself off abruptly.

"It just happened," he said. "No control over it. Came in handy, though."

"You can recite all the first chapters of Harry Potter?" she asked.

"Yes, well . . . I can recite chapters one through four of book one, chapters one and two of book two, chapters—"

"Okay, wait," Ginny said. "I want to hear this. Because I don't believe you."

"Which one do you want?"

"The first book."

"Can I finish my pizza?"

She nodded graciously. Oliver continued eating, wiped his mouth, took a drink of beer, and sat back in his chair. He assumed the position—eyes closed, head tipped back.

"Okay," he said. "Book one . . ."

And so he began. Ginny didn't actually know Harry Potter book one by heart, but what he was reading sounded right. Normally, Oliver had a deadpan manner of speaking. When he recited the letters, his voice went completely flat. When he read the book, his face relaxed and his voice deepened. He was a very good narrator, actually.

After a few moments, they had attracted the attention of some very stoned people sitting two tables over. They openly stared at Oliver, their jaws hanging slightly open, their eyes bloodshot and full of wonder. They began to approach, sliding their chairs closer and closer, inch by inch. The waiter began to hover as well. Oliver seemed to enjoy having an audience—he continued on for a full three chapters, growing more and more expressive.

"Was that Harry Potter?" one of them asked.

"What makes you say that?" Oliver replied.

"You kept saying 'Harry Potter,'" the guy replied seriously. "And it sounded like it. It sounded like you were reading it. How did you do that?"

Oliver drew his black coat tight around himself, leaned right into the guy's face, and quietly said, "I'm Dumbledore."

Ginny burst out laughing, despite herself.

* * *

"Are we still trying to find this boat?" Oliver asked, as they left the coffee shop. "Or have we given up?"

"I think we give up," Ginny replied.

"Good. So we can take the same way back."

It was a cold walk, but a pleasant one, through the canals, over the bridges. They didn't talk, but the silence between them was peaceful. Oliver smoked, and Ginny wrapped her scarf around her face. It was only when they had almost reached the Koekoeksklok that Ginny remembered why she'd left—or how long ago.

"Oh god," she said. "I didn't tell them I wasn't coming back."

"So?"

"What if they're worried?"

"I don't think they're worried," he said, dropping his cigarette to the sidewalk and stepping on it. Whatever lukewarm feelings of tolerance the Harry Potter reading had provoked were instantly chilled by this offhand remark.

"What's that supposed to mean?" she snapped.

"Never mind," he said quickly.

Oh, but she could never never mind now. Her mind was already flying. What he meant was that they wouldn't be worried because they were glad she was gone. They were *busy*.

"You keep saying things like that," she said, unable to hide the emotion in her voice. "What's your problem? You *mean* something."

"Listen," he said, holding out his hands defensively, "I don't think you want advice from me, that's all."

"I don't want *advice* from you. I want to know why you keep saying this stuff."

Oliver sighed deeply and stopped walking.

"This is all I have to say about the matter," he said. "I have been stuck in the car with the three of you. I have nothing to do but watch. I don't know what went on between you and . . . Keith . . ."

He clearly didn't like saying Keith's name.

". . . but I know something did. I'm also guessing it was left somewhat unresolved."

"How do you . . ."

"Because it's *obvious*," he said. "It is the most obvious thing that I have ever seen. He flirts with you. You flirt with him. . . ."

"He's not flirting," Ginny said. "I'm not either."

"No guy drives all the way to France for a girl he just wants to be friends with."

"Oh," she said, "you're one of those people who thinks guys are never friends with girls. . . ."

"I said you don't drive *to France* for someone you just want to be friends with."

"He has a girlfriend," Ginny said defensively.

"Yeah. I noticed that too. I don't think that changes much. As I said, I don't think you want my advice, but I'd be . . . careful."

The insanity of this had come full circle. She was out with Oliver, who was telling her to watch out for Keith. Oliver, the extortionist. She pushed past him, disgusted with herself.

And, as it happened, Keith and Ellis were in the lobby, trying to make sense out of an ancient Dutch board game.

"Where've you been, mad one?" Keith asked. "You said you were going out to make a call."

Ginny cast a rueful look at Oliver, who followed her inside.

"We looked for the boat," she replied.

"*We* looked for the boat?"

Keith looked Oliver up and down. Oliver shook his head and went for the stairs. For a moment, conversation was impossible because of the creaking noise. These were the loudest steps in the entire world.

"I was out," Ginny said simply. "Walking. He was out. We looked for the boat."

"Did you find it?" Ellis asked.

"No."

"No surprise there," Keith said, turning back to the game. "Want to play? We have no idea how this works, but we've decided if you get five hundred points, you win. It's up to you how you get the points. I've been getting points by hiding Ellis's pieces down my shirt."

He grabbed a pocket of fabric down by his stomach and jiggled it. It made a rattling noise.

"Cheater," Ellis mumbled.

"I think I'm going to bed too," Ginny said.

"You do everything he does," Keith called after her. "You *love* him."

She felt his gaze follow her long after she disappeared up into the darkness of the stairwell.

Random Acts of Cruelty

Ginny woke the next morning to a scream. Luckily, it wasn't her own. It was loud, male, and from right below them. Ellis jolted awake in the bed next to her.

"What was that?" Ellis asked. "Did I dream that? Was that you?"

Now there was yelling, and a thumping noise. They jumped out of bed at the same moment and ran down the steps, slipping on the slick wood as they hurried. The door to Keith and Oliver's room was shut, and a fevered conversation was going on behind it.

"What do we do?" Ellis asked. "They're at something in there. Think we should break them up?"

Another muffled cry, followed by loud laughter. Keith's.

"Yes," Ginny said, stepping forward and opening the door.

Keith was standing closest, dressed in a baggy pair of sweatpants and the T-shirt from yesterday. Oliver was just in boxers and a T-shirt again, but this time she couldn't really blame him.

He was also soaked, and swearing profusely.

"Shut the door!" he yelled. This time, he was not in the mood to show off the boxers. And once again, Ginny found herself staring just a little. Keith did not shut the door. He reached over and opened it wider, letting the cold air from the stairwell in.

"It snowed," he said, craning his arm over his head and lazily scratching his neck.

Now Ginny saw it. Snow scattered all over the floor, all over Oliver's bed. So much snow—snow that could only have come from one source. Keith must have been very, very quiet, because those stairs were like a musical instrument. And it must have taken him a few trips, because there was a *lot* of snow. Oliver grabbed his bag and let out a groan of dismay when even more snow poured out. His clothes were utterly soaked.

"Oh dear," Keith said. "Those are going to be unpleasant and cold."

Oliver shoulder-shoved Keith and slipped quickly past Ellis and Ginny on the way to the bathroom. Keith let it go with a smile.

"That was mean," Ginny said.

"Mean?" Keith sat on his bed and surveyed the damage contentedly. There was snow on his bed as well, probably thrown there by Oliver. "That's nothing. I could have done much worse, and you know it."

There was just a little defiance in his voice. Ellis put her hand over her mouth, possibly to stifle a giggle.

"He's going to freeze," Ginny said.

"Again, I'm not seeing the problem."

Ginny walked away, taking heavy steps back up to their room. She wasn't really sure why she was angry at Keith for doing this, but she was. She grabbed for her clothes, not even bothering with a shower. She could hear the water running through the pipes, though, as Oliver took his. Ellis came in a moment later and shut the door quietly.

"He's trying to help," she said. "Honestly."

"I know," Ginny said. "I just don't want that kind of help."

Ellis nodded and pulled on her clothes as well. They went downstairs, where a table full of yogurt, muesli, bread, cheeses, and meats was waiting for them. Keith joined shortly after, humming cheerily under his breath.

"I'm starving. Anyone else starving?" He loaded up his plate and sat down at the table. Both Ellis and Ginny stared at him.

"What?" he asked.

"Ginny's right," Ellis said. "Enough's enough."

"Have you both forgotten what he's doing?"

"No," Ellis said. "But . . ."

The creak of the stairs broke the conversation. Oliver came into the room in his wet, clingy clothes. His pants were clinging to his calves. Even his shoes were wet. He took seventy damp euros from his wallet and handed them to Ginny.

"For the room," he said. "I'll be outside."

"I'll bet that coat's not quite dry after getting splashed yesterday," Keith said. "Such bad luck."

Oliver left without a word. Ellis punched Keith lightly in the shoulder.

"What?" he asked again.

It was even colder than the day before, so the walk to the bookshop must have been brutal for Oliver. He had his arms wrapped tightly around himself. Charlie was waiting for them outside of the shop, dressed in skinny white jeans, a black leather jacket, and huge mirrored sunglasses. His hair was even higher and scragglier.

"You're wet," he said, tipping down the glasses to look at Oliver.

"Fell in a canal," Keith lied, jerking his thumb at the canal behind them. It was to Oliver's credit that he didn't reach over and knock Keith backward into the aforementioned canal.

"Oh. That happens. Come."

Walking with Charlie in the lead was a strange experience. He walked a vaguely snaky path and occasionally, Ginny swore he skipped a little. Not high enough to click his heels or anything. He'd just pop up higher than normal. Then snake, snake, snake.

"This man is stoned," Keith said in a low voice. "Or, even worse, he might *not* be. What the hell is wrong with everyone your aunt knows?"

This question became all the more relevant when they saw the boat.

To be fair, the pink boat was not horrific as Ginny had imagined it would be. In her mind, it was going to be Pepto-Bismol pink and painted all over, even on the windows. In reality, it was at least four shades of pink and rose. It was still very pink.

"Margaret picked the colors," he said, reaching up to run his finger along the slender bare branch of a tree.

This much was obvious to Ginny. It was either Aunt Peg or a group of five-year-olds.

"Where's the window?" Oliver asked.

Charlie took off his shoes and jumped over to the deck of the boat. He walked around to the front (the bow, whatever they called it). And there it was, the very front window, essentially the windshield of the boat. It was a painting of a jungle scene, a cartoonish one: massive green fronds, huge orange flowers, and an oversized parrot. The picture mostly went around the frame of the window, leaving the center open, like an opening in the foliage. Whoever was driving would have to navigate through Aunt Peg's strange landscape as they made their way around the canals. It was interesting, if not entirely safe.

"Let me just get it off," he said.

"Ooh er," Keith said quietly. Ginny and Ellis both stared at him, and he shrugged sheepishly. He wasn't quite off the hook yet.

Charlie grabbed the window by the edges and started pulling on it, which wasn't exactly the removal method Ginny was expecting.

"Do you need help?" Oliver said, preparing to climb on.

Charlie waved him away.

"It's no problem," Charlie said. "I stuck it on with glue. Just glue."

He was such a strange, spidery person, wrestling with a window on a pink boat. He groaned and grunted, locking his spindly legs and yanking over and over, his head snapping back. His glasses slipped off his face. He looked like some kind of deranged Muppet that had decided to attack a sailing vessel.

"This is incredible," Keith said. "Can we take him home with us?"

There was a cracking noise, which made Ginny's stomach sink.

"Here you are," Charlie said, coming over to the side of the boat and passing them the window. The glass wasn't broken,

173

fortunately. The cracking noise seemed to have been the splintering of the wooden frame around the pane.

"I am sorry for your loss," Charlie said, putting his ink-stained hands gently on her shoulders. "It was a loss for everyone, for all, for art."

"Yeah," Ginny said quietly. "It was."

They took the Hoek van Holland ferry back to England, which was just south of Amsterdam. Ginny had done a monster of a ferry ride on her last trip—twenty-four hours on a ferry to Greece. Of course, she had spent much of that time basking in the sun, not huddling inside, avoiding the December air and the frigid spray. But this trip wasn't nearly as long.

Ginny was a little nervous about leaving the window in the car. She had taken all her clothes out of her bag and wrapped it carefully, just in case the boat was dipping and swaying. Ideally, she would have stayed in the car with it, but it was freezing in the car hold, and they didn't allow passengers to remain down there anyway.

The three of them sat around one of the welded-down café tables. Oliver was relegated to a different table. He looked even colder once he was inside, but he bravely took out a huge novel and tried to read. Ellis got the Top Trumps cards out again. "Come on," she said. "You know you want to play the horses pack."

She was obsessed with those cards. Her inner Little Ellis couldn't be at peace until someone played with her.

"Go on then," Keith said.

"Ginny?"

Ginny shrugged.

"You'll have to teach me," she said.

Top Trumps appeared to be a game in which you got cards, and the cards had a picture (in this case, of a horse), and told you all kinds of stats for that horse, how fast it was, how big it was, etc. Whoever had the better horse won both the cards. You repeated this until someone had all the cards. So, basically it was exactly like high school, except it only took three minutes. Which was really a bit more humane, if you thought about it.

"You feel like you're really on holiday now, don't you?" Ellis said, once they'd played a game.

"Strangely, yes," Keith replied. "But we've confused the American. Look at her. You can just tell she's never been on one of the seaside holidays where you sit in the car in the rain and eat sandwiches."

"Those are the best," Ellis said, nodding.

"You make these things up," Ginny said. "You're trying to trick me."

Keith slapped the table loudly, causing Oliver to jump. "Oi!" he said. "Where are we going next?"

"Dublin." Oliver stiffly turned a page.

"Dublin?" Keith repeated. "As in Ireland, on the other side of England from where we are now, on the Continent?"

"You *are* bright. Yes, Dublin. And since we have to go through England to get there, I suggest we stop there for the night. You don't have to come the rest of the way if you don't want to, since we're quite capable of handling this on our own."

"Dublin?" Ellis said. "That's New Year's! Dublin on New Year's would be epic. This *must* be done."

"She's right," Keith said, with a nod to Ginny. "It must. By the

175

way, I think you have the wet trousers contest all sewn up. You have my vote, and I *mean* that."

Oliver got up and went outside.

"Was it something I said?" Keith asked.

"I'm going to the snack bar," Ginny said. "Want anything?"

They shook their heads. Ginny went by herself, stumbling from left to right as the boat rocked. She saw Oliver through the window. Clearly, he had struggled between his dampness and his need for a cigarette. The latter won. He was on the deck in the freezing spray, flicking his lighter over and over, trying to catch a spark. The sight made her sad, so on impulse she bought two coffees and took them out. She handed him one. He looked at it in confusion.

"I'm sorry about this morning," she said.

Oliver looked at her and back at the coffee. He squeezed it like it was something rare and precious and maybe a little dangerous.

"Thanks," he said. "My plan is to find somewhere on this boat to hide and sleep."

"Hide?"

"The one thing I learned from going away to school as a kid," he said. "They never stop. Never let them find you asleep. My own fault."

Oliver's hidden sleeping place turned out to be the car. They found him in there when they were alerted to go back to the auto deck on arrival. He had gotten into the trunk, taken all of Keith's dry clothes, and piled them over himself. He was a sleeping pile of laundry.

"He really does read lock-picking sites," Keith said, peering at him through the window and knocking loudly to wake him.

"This car is like a bank vault. No one can get in."

"I once opened the door with a pen," Ellis told him.

"Don't tell me things like that."

"I did. Just a little flick of the Biro and . . . pop! Door open."

Oliver rearranged himself in the backseat to make room for Ginny, shoving all of Keith's clothes down by his feet. The extra packing meant they were wedged in together more tightly than usual. Back on his home soil, Keith floored it in confidence, the little white car banging and clattering down the motorway. As soon as they came into London, Keith pulled over to the side of the road. There was no Tube stop, nothing. He turned around and looked at Oliver.

"This is your stop," he said.

"Where are we?"

"I just said. Your stop. That's where we are."

"Fine," Oliver replied. "I'll just take the window with me. You can keep the tabletop."

Ginny grabbed the edge of the window as hard as she could. There was no way she was letting Oliver take it.

"Out," Keith said again. "The window stays."

Oliver considered for a moment, then turned to Ginny.

"Well," he said, "there's not much you can do with these without the final piece. About tomorrow . . . should I assume we're driving again, or can we just take the train and the ferry and do it ourselves?"

"I suppose it's too much to ask where exactly in Ireland we're going?" Keith said.

"Are you really asking me this as you're dumping me on the side of the road?"

"At least I took you all the way to London. I could have dumped you in Wales."

"I'll be in touch," Oliver said, opening his door. Keith started pulling away before he had a chance to get his bag out, forcing Oliver to walk all the way down the block to get it. As soon as he reached the car, Keith drove forward again. Oliver waited this time before approaching the car. When he did, Keith backed up, causing Oliver to jump back to the sidewalk.

"Keith!" Ellis said. "Stop it!"

The backseat was suddenly very roomy. It was too big. Ginny shifted uncomfortably in the space and looked through the back window. Oliver was already making his way assuredly down the road, as if he knew exactly where he was going, his coattail snapping. For some reason, the sight made her very sad.

When they arrived at Richard's house, there was no parking, so Keith stopped the car and kept the engine running while they carefully extracted the pieces from the backseat. They helped her get everything up the steps.

"So we'll wait to hear from you about tomorrow," Keith said. "Times, directions, whatnot. I assume we're going to have to make an ungodly early start."

"You guys don't mind? Going to Ireland?"

"Course not," he said. "We would never leave you with him, would we, El?"

"Definitely not," Ellis said. "I'm excited! This has been amazing so far!"

Ellis gave her a big hug; Keith, a friendly clap on the arm. No sooner had they pulled off, the car farting and spitting its way down the street, than Oliver appeared. Ginny didn't even have time to close the door. He was just there, like he had grown right out of a bush or popped out of a rubbish bin.

"Where the hell did you come from?" she asked.

"I was just standing over there, waiting for you to get home."

"I would have seen you. What, were you crouching?"

"I wasn't crouching. I was just over there. . . ."

"How did you get here so fast?"

"I took the Tube. I beat you by ten minutes. He actually left me at a very convenient—"

"How do you know where I . . . oh, the letters."

"Now that we've settled all that," he said, sighing, "wouldn't you like to know why I'm here?"

"Why are you here?"

"There's something you need to do, and I didn't exactly get a chance to explain in the car. I can at least help you get these inside."

He pointed to the tabletop and window leaning against the door. Had he come here to take the pieces? That seemed unlikely. Like he'd said, they were of no use without the last one. Maybe for some other underhanded reason? Probably not. Keith really had thrown him out of the car. He couldn't have planned for that.

"Are you going to let me in?" he asked.

"Fine," she said, shoving the key in the lock.

The House of Secrets

Unlike Keith, who always came in like he owned the place, Oliver stepped in with caution, head slightly ducked, stepping lightly, looking around at everything like there might be something waiting to ambush him from behind the sofa. He didn't wander into the kitchen looking for food. He didn't even sit. Mostly, he stared at the decorations that covered the living room.

"So, what did you come to tell me?" she said. "You could have just emailed the instructions about tomorrow."

"Except there's something we have to do today. Here. In this house."

He punctuated that statement by reaching up to touch the garland Ginny had strung around the doorway, accidentally pulling half of it down. He tried to stick it back up again, fumbling with it for a moment.

"Leave it," she said. "Just tell me what we have to do here."

He leaned against the door and assumed his recitation stance, his head tipped back and his eyes closed.

"'Here's a shocker, Gin. I made some paintings that are actually worth some money, and since you're back, you might as well go and get them. You'll find them up in my workspace at Harrods, locked away in the cabinets in the back. The key is stuck in the Blu Tak under the picture of *A Bar at the Folies-Bergère*. . . .'" Oliver's eyes opened and he looked over at Ginny. "Those are the paintings you already sold."

"I'm aware of that," she said.

Oliver cleared his throat and continued reciting.

"'I thought leaving it there would be a nice touch. I would have felt stupid leaving the key to my inheritance on an I-love-London key chain on top of the fridge. You have to have some style when you're leaving things from the beyond. In the cabinet, you will also find the name and address of a man at an auction house who is fully prepared to handle and sell the paintings. His name is Cecil Gage-Rathbone and he is very good at what he does. Cecil can also handle the sale of our work in progress, which is not yet finished!

"'Up in my room, there's a disused fireplace. I'm sure you saw it before. It's all painted over. Get in there, reach up, and behold, you will have the next thing you need. Take this with you to our final destination, which is . . .

"'Ireland! Bet you've always wanted to go to Ireland, Gin. I am here to oblige. Ireland is truly one of my favorite places, and the last one I visited.

"'Here's the thing, though. I can't actually remember how to get to the place I want you to go. Richard knows, though, and since you're there with him now, you can ask him. Say you want directions to "the place near his gran's." He'll know what you mean.'"

Ginny instantly headed for the stairs. She was at the door of her room before she realized that Oliver had not followed her. He stood at the foot of the steps, gazing up.

"What?" she asked.

"I can come up?"

It hadn't occurred to her that he wouldn't follow her up to her room.

"Just come on," she said.

Oliver's reaction on seeing the Christmas decorations was nothing compared to his reaction when he reached the threshold of her room.

"Bloody hell," he said.

Ginny's room—Aunt Peg's room—was quite the assault on the senses when you first encountered it. Oliver stared at the floor-to-ceiling collage of wrappers and assorted pieces of paper. Ginny was already on the floor, shoving aside the suitcase she had set in front of the fireplace. Ginny got on her back and slid her head into the opening. The chimney had been sealed off at some point, but there was still a frigid draft coming down through the darkness. Just a few feet up, an object was wedged sideways in the flue. She reached up and grabbed it, and it came down, along with a handful of dust and filth that landed on her face. She sneezed it out and retracted herself.

It was a long, narrow box, like the kind of box a collapsible umbrella might come in. It was made in two long pieces, which just needed to be pulled apart to open. There were three things inside—a long object, a roll of tape, and a small plastic bag. The bag contained fine art pastels—large, fancy crayons with labels written in Italian. There were four of them: a gray one, a white one, a deep green one, and a light green one. The long object was a piece of blank paper.

"Oh no," Ginny said.

To be fair to the paper, it was very *nice* paper. It looked handmade. You could see the fibers. And it was almost completely translucent. Still, blank paper implied drawing something, and that was bad.

"What am I supposed to do with this?" Ginny asked. "Does she think I can draw? Because I can't draw. Come on, you *know* what I have to do."

"You'll be fine," he said.

"I'd be better if you *told* me."

"Honestly, you wouldn't. It doesn't make any sense without knowing the location, but the actual task doesn't sound difficult. We could leave tonight. We could go without them. I'd bet you we could get some cheap flights, be there in no time. That's how I was planning on doing it before *they* got involved."

For just a split second, Ginny was tempted. No more staring at Ellis and Keith. Just go off, get it done now. But no . . . no. Keith was offering to drive. That was how she was going. That was how it had to be.

"We go with them," Ginny said.

"Then we'd better look up the ferry times."

Ginny's computer was on the floor next to her bed. She pulled it over. Oliver stood over her as she typed and leaned against the bureau, making him look about fifteen feet tall.

"There's a ferry to Dublin at one," she said. "It leaves from Holyhead."

"Which is in Wales. That's about six hours away. We're going to have to leave at five in the morning."

He said it like it was a challenge.

"Then that's when we go," she replied.

"Well, then, I suppose I should . . ." He looked down at an eyeliner Ginny had left on the bureau, picking it up and examining it curiously, like he had never seen such a wondrous object before. ". . . I should go," he said. "I'll meet you in the morning, at his place, I suppose."

He left the room. Ginny heard him hurry down the stairs and let himself out.

"You're so weird," she said out loud.

Richard was somewhat surprised to find Ginny sitting on the sofa when he returned home that night.

"You're home," he said. "And you brought . . . some scrap-heap challenge materials. . . ."

He pointed at the tabletop and window that had joined the many decorations in his living room. They really didn't look very impressive out of context. The tabletop was yellow, with several reddish circular stains, mostly in the center, but some on the sides. There was what also appeared to be a long black scorch mark along the side. The paint had flaked up completely in several places, revealing a duck-egg blue door underneath. The door had been sawed in half and barely sanded, leaving one rough edge. The window was more artlike because it had a painting on it, but it was still very dirty, and the wood frame was shabby.

"That's the piece," Ginny explained. "It's not finished yet."

185

Richard turned his head to the left and to the right, trying to comprehend how a rough yellow tabletop and a colorful but dirty painted window went together, then shook his head, apparently deciding this was not the best use of his mental energies.

"So there's more?" he asked.

"One more piece," she said. "We have to get it."

"And where is this piece located?"

"Ireland. The letter said I was supposed to ask you for directions to the place near your gran's."

Richard nodded and looked away, jingling his keys in his palm for a moment.

"Right," he said. "Of course. Well, I propose, if you're up for it, a trip to the Rose of Delhi. It's just down the road, and they do a very good curry. Let me change and we'll go."

Richard quickly changed into jeans and a sweater, and they were soon walking down the rain-soaked streets. It always rained in England when you weren't looking, giving the roads and sidewalks a glossy shine. The night was otherwise clear, and not too cold.

For the second time in her life, Ginny found herself in an Indian restaurant. This one had a distinctly dramatic flair. There were heavy velvet drapes over the door to keep out the cold. Inside was a world of bright rose-colored walls, covered in tiny elephants stenciled in gold paint. Bouncy Bhangra music was playing, and there were fresh flowers everywhere—a small arrangement by the door, little vases on all the tables, another vase full on the host stand. They were effusively greeted, given warm, moistened washcloths to clean their hands with, and tucked into a cozy window table. The waiter immediately set about rearranging all of the glasses and silverware. This always baffled Ginny. Why did they set it one way and change it as soon as you sat down?

A moment later, she was facing down a menu she didn't really understand. Korma, masala, rogan josh, vindaloo, chicken tikka bhuna, aloo gobhi, biryani . . . she had no idea what these things were. When the popadoms came—the large, crispy disks that were sort of the equivalents of tortilla chips at a Mexican restaurant—she felt slightly more comfortable. She still had no idea what was in any of the five small silver bowls of dips that went with them. She allowed Richard to guide her through the ordering process. He got her something not too spicy, and made of lamb.

"My family is from Ireland," he said, poking a hole in the center of the popadoms so that they could be broken up and eaten. "I was born there. I moved here when I was little, so I never had the accent. I'm the only Murphy who sounds like this. It's the family shame. The place you're going is just outside of Kildare, near the Curragh."

"What's that?"

"About twenty kilometers of open grazing land. It's where the sheep are. They wander into town at night and eat up all the grass in your garden and leave you with the gift of sheep poop."

"So, I'm going to an open field?"

"No," he said. "Not exactly."

"So, what's there?" Ginny asked. "What am I going to see?"

"Didn't the letter tell you?"

"I didn't read that page yet," she said. It was the truth. She hadn't. "I kind of read them as I go."

Richard broke off a large piece of popadom and tapped it on the edge of his plate. He seemed to be debating something with himself.

"Is something wrong?" she asked.

"No," he said. "Just thinking of the best way to get there. You're going from Dublin, I presume?"

"We're taking the ferry in the morning."

"Of course. I probably shouldn't have taken you for curry tonight . . . though I'm sure your trip will be fine. Just a little . . . choppy, sometimes . . ."

He snapped his popadom in half again and left both pieces on the side of the plate without eating them.

"So," he said, changing his demeanor entirely. "Dublin. New Year's Eve. You'll be with your friend, right?"

"There are four of us," Ginny said.

"Four? Where did the other two come from?"

"Keith and his girlfriend. He drove. It's . . . fine."

The waiter came by with a cart with their food, so there was a natural pause while he set up a hot plate and put down the steaming metal dishes of curries and rice and bread. It was enough time for Ginny to come up with a change of subject.

"How normal is it for people to go away to boarding school here?" she asked, as they dished up their food.

Richard could easily handle a turn in conversation like that. He was used to getting constant, random questions fired at him all day long.

"It's not *abnormal*, but it's not the usual thing either."

"I just met someone who went to one," she said. "You always read books or see movies about people in England going to boarding school. I thought maybe it was what most people did."

"No," Richard said. "I didn't go to one. I know a few people who did. They're very expensive."

"So you have to be kind of rich to go?" she asked.

"Well, it usually implies some money. Some people go on scholarship, some schools cost less than others. It varies. Generally, though, there has to be some money coming from somewhere."

So, unless Oliver had gone to school on scholarship, he had to have some money in his family. He was probably smart enough for a scholarship—but people who won scholarships didn't seem like the kind of people who would just walk away from university. And while his clothes were probably secondhand, they were still very high quality. He knew good stuff when he saw it. Her guess was that there was some money, at least in his past. So why would he need her money from the sale?

"I'll write down the directions when we get back," Richard said, returning to their primary conversation. "It's not far from Dublin. Shouldn't take you long to get there, especially if you have a car." He gestured to the food. "Tuck in. I think you'll like that."

Whatever it was, it did look delicious. It was a deep reddish brown color, like chili, flecked with bright green pieces of cilantro. It smelled like nothing Ginny had ever eaten before.

"It's okay," Richard said, indicating her plate. "Try it."

He was definitely talking about the curry, but she got the distinct sense that he was trying to reassure her about something larger, something waiting for her in Ireland.

She plunged her fork in and took a big bite. The dish, whatever it was, was just as delicious as it smelled, full of tender meat and freshly cracked spices. Richard never steered her wrong. Whatever was waiting for her . . . it was all going to be fine. She was sure of it.

The Emerald Isle

"Why are Americans so fascinated by Ireland?" Keith asked when he opened the door the next morning. "Ellis and I were just talking about this. Now we need you to explain. Explain, American. You all seem to think it's magic. *Ireland . . .*"

He said the last word in an Irish lilt. Ellis, who was sitting on the steps cradling a cup of tea, shook her head.

"Morning, Gin," she said. "I wasn't talking about this. He was. To himself."

Ginny smiled thinly, taking in Ellis's jeans and sweater from the day they had started their journey to France. Either Ellis had gotten there very early or . . . or she had never left and had no other clothes to change into. That was the horrible but entirely likely option. Ginny tried to beat down the creeping misery that came with this thought, the one that wound around her body like a vine.

"Plus," Keith added, oblivious to her suffering, "you all think

191

you're Irish. What's the appeal? Do you like the accent more? Is it all the magical rocks? Oh, look, a leprechaun. . . ."

That signified the arrival of Oliver, who was just coming up behind Ginny.

"Good morning," he said.

"Is it?" Keith asked. "*Is* it?"

Oliver took his normal course of ignoring everything that came out of Keith's mouth and got into the backseat. He had prepared for this leg of the trip by packing very lightly—just a backpack. No computer. Nothing he couldn't keep on his lap. Ginny could barely face getting back in the car, which was looking ever so slightly the worse for wear. The heavy driving in the rain and snow had covered it in a layer of grime that actually altered the color and tinted the windows, making it feel even smaller.

"Ahead of us today," Keith said, jiggling the key and coaxing the cold engine to life, "we have yet another long drive to a ferry crossing. Nothing like the Irish Sea in the dead of winter."

"You could drop us off at the ferry terminal," Oliver offered.

"Oh no," Keith said. "Wouldn't miss it. New Year's Eve? Dublin? You and me together? The magic of *you* combined with the magic of Ireland?"

This time, they headed north and west, to Holyhead, in Wales. This was the longest drive yet, well over six hours—about the same amount of time it took Ginny to fly to England in the first place. There was very little discussion. No one was quite awake enough for that. Ginny stared glassy-eyed at the changing English landscape. The signs were suddenly in English and another quite strange language that Oliver told her was Welsh. She hadn't realized that Welsh was something people spoke, or even that it existed. It was a bit wilder here, rolling hills and tiny villages, and long stretches of nothing but fields.

It was slightly terrifying to drive into the belly of the ferry, a cavernous space half full with huge trucks and a smattering of cars and motorcycles. As soon as they had parked the car, they made their way up the stark metal staircase to the passenger decks. Keith and Ellis both stretched out on some seats in one of the lounges, head to head.

"You getting some sleep, mad one?" Keith asked, as he positioned his coat under his head as a pillow.

"No," Ginny said.

"Make sure no one feeds us to the kraken, then, right?" He gave her a little smile and a wink.

They were both asleep before the boat even left the dock. Ginny sat across from them, wobbling in her seat as the boat listed left and right. She couldn't sleep that peacefully—not on this boat, and not in this position. Oliver went outside on the deck. She could see him through the drizzle-splattered windows, battling all of nature in his attempt to light a cigarette. The wind battered his coat and sent its tails flapping, his closely clipped hair pushed up on end. There was something mesmerizing about watching him try to do the same thing over and over. The flick of the lighter. The cup of the hand. The turn to try to find the one position where the wind wouldn't put out the flame. After a few minutes and two ruined cigarettes, he gave up and came back inside.

"Must be a smokers' lounge," he said. "I hate them. They smell terrible. But it'll have to do."

"They smell like smoke," Ginny said. "What do you think *you* smell like?"

This was a little unfair. Oliver didn't actually smell like smoke that often—maybe just a tiny whiff on his coat right after he came in. He walked away silently. Ginny looked over at the happily sleeping couple again, shook it off, and decided to go out onto the deck.

Then they were off, the Welsh coast vanishing into the mist. Though it was a cold and choppy passage, Ginny enjoyed the trip. The ferry in the summer had been smooth and even, the sun beating down on blue water. She enjoyed the slosh and chug of the boat. It was *active*. This was traveling. It had a pulse to it. She spent most of the four-hour trip walking loops of the deck, listening to music at full blast on her headphones. (No *Starbucks: the Musical*. She had considered putting some of the songs onto her playlist, but then realized she had enough of Keith in her eyes and ears at all times. She was learning.) She took pride in the fact that she could walk so steadily as the boat rocked and slammed on the water. She was starting to feel in control of this thing—she could handle being around Ellis and Keith. She could handle Oliver. A little loud music, a rough boat ride across the Irish Sea . . . she could take it.

When the announcement was made for all drivers to return to their vehicles, Ginny bought two coffees and went to wake Ellis and Keith, who were still sound asleep on the lounge chairs.

"Oh, bless you," Ellis said, accepting her coffee.

Along with a coffee, Ginny gave Keith the driving directions she had gotten from Richard the night before.

"It doesn't look far at all," Keith said. "If we hurry, we can get the piece, have something to eat, and get back up to Dublin for midnight. But we've said that before, haven't we? I suppose you know but you aren't going to tell us, because it's much more fun to drive around Ireland without a clue of what's going on."

This was to Oliver, who had emerged from whatever hidey-hole he'd secreted himself in and joined them.

"I don't know how long it will take," he said. "I don't even know where it is. Ginny got the directions."

"This is somewhere near Richard's grandmother's house," Ginny explained. "The letter just said this place she and Richard visited together. He didn't say what it was either."

"All a bit mysterious, isn't it?" Keith asked. "Still. Looks like we can get it done and get our party hats on. Shall we?"

Ginny immediately saw what Aunt Peg would have liked about Ireland—the colors. There were long stretches of almost nothing but fields, but the fields were a dozen different shades of green. Then suddenly a tiny stone church, a few boring box stores, then a small town with four pubs painted in yellow and red and blue . . . a row of houses in every pastel color of the rainbow. So many colors in defiance of the steel gray of the sky.

The sun had just gone down when they reached the spot Richard had marked on the map. The car coughed to a stop. They got out.

"This is a field," Keith said. "Are you sure that's right?"

"It says stop at the end of the road and look for the white gate, go up the steps." Ginny lowered the paper and looked around. It was too dark to see clearly. Keith produced a flashlight from his car and shone it around, until he landed on a little stone wall, which led to a chipped white gate, partially covered by shrubs.

"There we are," he said.

They started trudging through the mucky grass. The ground was like a sponge, and every step produced a sucking noise. Only certain patches were actually muddy, but there was nothing solid about this field at all. The chipped white iron gate was unlocked, and it led to a series of stone steps that had been stuck into the side of a small hill, cutting a path up through the trees.

"I think—," Oliver said.

"Don't care," Keith cut in.

"Shut it for once and listen," Oliver said. He reached into his pocket and pulled out some white photocopied pages.

"Copies?" she asked.

"I didn't want the letter to get damaged," he explained. "And I think you might want to do this part yourself. It's more . . . personal."

Ginny looked at the path ahead. She could only see the first few steps; then it was completely obscured by darkness and trees. It wasn't the biggest hill ever, but it was still a good climb.

"Really," Oliver said. "I think we should wait here."

Keith tentatively held the flashlight out to her.

"Whatever you want to do," he said.

"I guess I'll go," she said, accepting it. "It's just up there."

She stuck the phone into her coat pocket and pushed the gate open and started up the steps. The stones were coated in slippery green moss. Getting up them was a challenge, as there was nothing to hold on to but the occasional tree branch or the step above. She lost her footing several times, sending the beam of light dancing all over the place.

"You all right?" Keith called. She couldn't even see him anymore. The view down was just darkness.

"Fine . . . ," she said, scrabbling to the top.

She was standing in a graveyard.

It wasn't like any graveyard she had ever seen in her life. It was more like a strange stone garden. Some markers were plain, rough stones. Other monuments were ornate Celtic crosses. Some had been here so long that the ground had come up to meet them, coming up halfway, sometimes more. Some were just little rounded tips sticking out of the ground. Many were crooked, tilting as the earth had changed around them. The inscriptions were covered in white lichen and black creeping mosses and molds obscuring the words—when the words were still there. Some inscriptions had been worn away by years of rain and wind. Interspersed throughout were new headstones, cut from some gleaming, silvery rock. At some of these were gifts and tokens. Along with the usual flowers and candles, small stuffed animals perched on the branches of the crosses, half-full bottles of whiskey remained from some recent, drunken communion with the dead. It was an amazingly not-creepy place. It was peaceful.

The moon was low and bright enough that she could see pretty well, but she needed the flashlight to read the pages she'd been given. Even though they were just copies, it made a huge difference to have them physically in her hand, to read them herself in the place where she was supposed to read them. She was grateful that Oliver had realized that this was one step she had to take by herself.

```
I learned my most important art lesson when
I was ten years old. We had to do a project in
which we set our heads down on a piece of paper,
```

sideways, in profile, and then someone traced them. Then this was copied, and the two halves were put together. When you put the two sides together, we learned the lesson: The result looks nothing like you. Surprise!

Why? Because we're not symmetrical. What's happening on the one side isn't happening on the other. There's this scientific theory that humans think symmetry is beautiful--equal, even things, all in the correct measure. But we are asymmetrical, Gin. Our faces, our bodies--they're not the same on both sides. Your eyes are not identical. Your nose is not exactly straight. And trust me, your boobs are almost definitely different sizes.

What's art, Gin? What's beauty? What makes my strange drawings or pile of stuff a work and not just junk?

This discussion has been going on for the ages, and there is no definite answer. So I'm as entitled as anyone to throw my hat in the ring and make up some definitions. I think something is art when it is created with intention--serious intention. Even crazy intention. And I think something is beautiful if it reveals something important about what it means to be alive.

This place is beautiful. They are strange things of beauty, monuments of death, lopsided,

weathered . . . many generations gathered
together in one place. They aren't pristine and
ordered in rows. They are carefully maintained,
while they are also allowed to change and decay
as nature commands. And so, they are living
places. Look around, Gin. From here, you can see
everything.

I came here with Richard soon after I realized
I was sick and was tested. His grandmother lives
near here, and we came to visit. I actually got
the call with my diagnosis when I was here.
(Richard is half Irish. You should know this,
since you are related to him. That makes you just
a little bit Irish yourself, at least by marriage.
But I think our family is a little Irish anyway.)

Dammit. Keith was right about that Irish thing.

We had been planning on walking up here--it's
a famous spot locally. Richard didn't want me
to come after I got the news, because going to a
graveyard when you just found out that you're
going to die is kind of morbid. I don't think I
accepted it, really. He was more devastated than
I was. I left him with his gran for an hour and
walked up by myself, because I just had to see
this place.

I was immediately drawn to one monument. I
won't even have to tell you which one. If you look
around, you will know.

Ginny looked around. There were so many monuments, in
so many conditions. But she remembered to look softly, to just
let her eyes drift. "Paint with your eyes," Aunt Peg used to say.
"Sweeping gestures, just like a brush." Side to side. Gentle.

There it was, perfectly obvious. It was one of the few monuments that wasn't a cross or a standard headstone, but an obelisk.
She walked over to it gently, stepping around the plots, both the
open ones and the ones marked off by little metal bars, low to the
ground, and the large slabs. When she got close to it, she saw a
carving of a woman, dancing, with a book in her hand. What she
read next confirmed her guess.

The woman buried there was a poet. She lived
with her sister, who was a sculptor. When her
sister died of a "fever" (or so said the parish
register, which the priest of the local church
showed me--it's a huge book, each birth and
death handwritten in ink--the same book is still
in use), the sculptor spent the next two years
working on that monument to her.

Sculpting used to be considered a very manly
art, Gin. Rock, chisel, breaking marble with your
bare hands . . . A female sculptor working in 1887

would have been a pretty rare thing. Her hands would have been rough; her arms would have been well-muscled. She would have spent a lot of time alone in hard labor, putting her tools against the rock. That was not the Victorian ideal. It took a lot of women like that, a lot of women who said, "I'm not going to do what you expect me to do, because you have no idea what I'm capable of. I'm going to get dirty and use tools and live the way I want" to move the world forward. And this woman? She made her sister into a goddess and gave her a seat on the hilltop where she could dance in the wind.

When I saw that, I knew I wanted to dance in the wind here too. I wanted to join her. This is why I asked Richard to scatter my ashes here. By the time you read this, I am sure this will have been done. I am here. Now, let's do this together. The container you got in London, you have it, right? Get it. Open it.

Ginny's hand started to shake. She knelt down, her knees sinking into the ground, then set her bag down and retrieved the box. She cracked open the sticker seal and slid out the contents. She put these carefully on her bag and continued reading, not caring that her knees were soaking and probably filthy.

You are going to make the final part of this.

This is a joint work. You need to let your fears
go here. Don't worry that it won't be good enough.
Don't worry that you aren't going to do it right.
Take the paper and tape it to the monument. Then
get out the pastels. Just rip the paper covers off,
because you'll need to turn them sideways. Do a
rubbing of the image, using whatever colors you
like. Just one. All of them. Whatever you want to
do.

The picture is now complete. I leave it to you
to assemble it.

The paper fought against the wind, but Ginny held it firm
and taped it down. She opened the bag with the pastels. She
reached first for the green, because that was the color around her.
She started very lightly. Then she grabbed the gray. She rubbed
harder, alternating the colors diagonally, even doing a few strips
in white, leaving only ghostly traces.

This was really and truly the end. Aunt Peg could never know
that she would show up here on New Year's Eve, with the moon
hanging low and spreading a bright white glow over the hilltop . . . but she would have approved. The ashes had been put
here months ago, been blown around and soaked in the rain and
pressed into the earth. They were a part of the landscape now,
part of the dirt on her clothes, part of everything. It really was like
Aunt Peg would forever dance on the top of this hill, a place she
only ever visited once in life.

She rolled up the paper and put it back in its box. She took her phone out of her pocket and was happy to find that she had at least a partial signal.

"I'm here," she said, when Richard answered. "On the hill."

"Are you all right?" he asked.

"I think so," she said, looking around. "Yeah. I am."

Neither of them spoke for a moment.

"It's a good place," he said. "She said she liked it because she could be between England and America, keep an eye on everyone."

Ginny laughed, and wiped a tear from her eye. She hadn't realized she was crying a little. Richard laughed as well.

"Are you up there by yourself?" he asked. "It must be dark."

"They're waiting for me at the bottom. We're driving back to Dublin now. We'll get the early ferry back in the morning."

"Well, be careful. And I'm here . . . if you want to call. I think I'm having a quiet night in. Maybe go round to the pub later, so . . ."

"Thanks."

"Happy New Year, Ginny."

"Happy New Year," she said.

Ginny took one last look around, to say good-bye to this place, good-bye to the year. She felt like she was leaving something behind here—she wasn't sure what, she just had the sensation that something she no longer needed had come loose and fallen away. Down below, she could hear Keith heckling Oliver. Their voices carried on the wind. She checked one last time to make sure the paper was secure in her bag, then climbed back down the hill in the dark. Keith was bouncing around Oliver, doing some kind of strange step dance. Oliver stood patiently, smoking and ignoring him.

"What was it?" Keith asked, as Ginny appeared.

"Just some stones," she said quickly. "I had to do a rubbing."

She wasn't quite sure why she lied—maybe it was just too much to drop on people on New Year's Eve. Keith continued his strange kick dancing, and Ellis chided him. Oliver, however, knew exactly what was up there, and he was looking right at her.

"Come on," she said, brushing past him. "We have to get to Dublin."

A Death in Ireland

They had dinner at a small, empty café—the lone business on a street of rainbow-colored houses. The café was white and starkly lit by fluorescent bulbs. There were three metal tables with green Formica tops. The menu was painted on a large green board and stuck to the wall. The main choices were "butties." Bacon butties. Chip butties. Batter burgers. Curry chips. Drink choices were tea or Coke.

"I have no idea what any of these things are," Ginny said quietly. "Except for the tea and the Coke."

"They are all very healthy," Keith said. "I suggest the chip butty. I feel it's something you need to experience."

A few minutes later, Ginny was facing down a french fry sandwich on white bread, the insides covered in ketchup. Considering where she had just been, she was feeling surprisingly upbeat. She wanted to eat. She wanted to drive fast across Ireland. She wanted to get to Dublin. She wanted to do everything, right now.

"Right," Keith said, working his way through a plate of fries and curry sauce. "If we drive like hell to Dublin, we can celebrate New Year's Eve in proper style."

"What's proper style?" Ginny asked.

"Well, we can find a pub and do things the classic way—drinking ourselves into a stupor, vomiting in the street, and passing out behind some rubbish bins in an alley—an approach I have advocated many times in the past."

"What's the other option?" Ellis asked.

"Option two: We just sort of walk around until we find somewhere good, and then we stand there and see what happens to us. We have the mad one here. Strange things seem to find her. She's like a party in your pocket."

"That's me," Ginny said. She took a timid bite of her sandwich. The fries were thick and crisp and hot with fat, which soaked through the white bread, making it go limp and squishy. It was both horrifying and delicious.

"I think," Keith said, "that we should go for the second one, while keeping our hearts and minds open to the first. I, of course, don't drink and can't drink, as I am driving the car. But you are welcome to do as you like."

"I have to make a call," Oliver said, picking up his bacon sandwich and going outside.

"You know," Keith said, "since we have everything now, we could just leave him and go to Dublin. Nothing's stopping us."

"Are you goin' to Dublin?" the owner asked.

"We are, yeah," Keith said. "What's good to do on New Year's?"

"You'll want to go to Christ Church. That's where people go."

Ginny was chomping away as they talked and soon polished

off the french fry sandwich. She instantly felt ill.

"Do you have any ginger ale?" she asked.

"No, I don't, but the shop across the road does."

"I'll be right back," Ginny said.

She noticed, as she stepped out, that Oliver wasn't in front of the café. There weren't too many options for places he could be, though. It was a small road, with just a handful of two-story houses. There were some cars, and a milk van, and two boys wandering down the street with a soccer ball. All else was quiet.

The store across the street was locked, though the lights were on. There was a sign in the window that said BACK IN 15 MINUTES. Ginny got the feeling it had been up a lot longer than that. There was a little walkway at the side of the shop, and Ginny heard Oliver talking in a low voice. She peered around the corner. He was leaning against the wall and speaking intently into his phone.

"It's fine, Mum," he said. "I'll be back tomorrow. I promise. I'll sort it then."

A pause. Oliver kicked at the ground as he listened.

"No, they can't do that. I'll fix it. Just leave it for now. . . . No, don't call the counsel. There's no one there anyway. Just leave it."

Keith and Ellis emerged from the café, Keith chomping away on an ice cream bar. Ginny quickly snapped her head back.

"Mad One!" he called. "Into the sexmobile! Where's Sneaky Beaky? I'm telling you, we should leave. . . ."

"Right here." Oliver came down the alley, shoving his phone in his pocket. He gave Ginny a quick nod as he walked past, but she had no idea why.

It began to rain, coming down hard, pounding down on the roof with such force that it sounded like nails were being dumped on the top of the car. Keith took the swervy roads at a good speed, slowing down when one of the Gardaí (as it seemed the police were called here) cars or motorcycles was nearby. Signs in English and italicized Irish pointed the way back to the M7 into Dublin.

It happened fast—a boom, a black cloud blowing out of the back of the car, and then a general feeling of looseness, like nothing was powering the car anymore and they were simply adrift. A free-flowing river of expletives came out of Keith's mouth as he gripped the wheel, steering the car off the road, where it eventually slowed more and more and then hit a large rock and bounced to a halt.

No one said anything for a moment. The lights remained on, but there was no sound from the engine.

"I'm going to count slowly to ten," Keith said. "I'm not entirely sure what that will accomplish, but it seems like the right thing to do."

Oliver was out of the car as soon as Keith had finished counting and opened the door. They both headed for the hood. When Ginny stepped out, she almost fell into a deep ditch that ran along the side, possibly to keep the sheep from wandering into the road. A few inches farther, and the car would have gone right into it. Ellis screeched as she made the same discovery.

"Gin, careful!"

"I see it."

They both made their way over to the other side of the car to climb out—Ginny sliding and Ellis crawling over the gear stick and slipping under the steering wheel. A few sheep wandered over to see what was going on, staring over the ditch at them. The car was belching a terrible, burning smell. Ginny stepped on something hard and sharp as she walked around behind the car. She reached down to touch it, and almost burned herself on a scorching-hot piece of something.

"It looks like you've thrown a rod," Oliver said. "I told you this car would never make it."

"Thrown a rod?"

"Do you see the large metal rod sticking out of your engine? Don't you know anything about cars?"

"No, *actually*, I don't."

"Maybe we can get it to a garage?" Ellis said.

"That's fatal," Oliver said, shaking his head. He moved away from the smoking car, put up his umbrella, and lit a cigarette.

Ginny looked up and down the stretch of road they had come to stop on. It wasn't very promising. They were between a field and an even bigger field. The streetlights were fairly far apart. The predominant noise was the gentle mockery of the sheep. *Baaaaaaaa.* She pulled out her phone, but the signal was so weak as to be nonexistent.

"Does anyone have a phone signal?" she asked.

Phones were checked. No one did. She pulled out the paper map and walked over to the closest streetlight. It was difficult to manage her umbrella and the map at the same time, but she didn't want to get back in the car while it was still steaming and hovering on the edge of the ditch.

"I think we're on the edge of the Curragh," she said.

"And what's that?" Keith asked.

"About twenty kilometers of open grazing land," she said.

"I don't think we're going to see the police anytime soon," Oliver said. "I suggest we walk back to the pub we saw about five minutes ago."

"And leave my car?"

"There's nothing we can do for it standing here."

"That does look pretty bad," Ellis said.

Keith was experiencing what appeared to be an entire rainbow of emotions—laughing, swearing, back to laughing again, before bending over at the waist in defeat.

"The battery still works," Oliver said. "We can keep the lights on so no one will hit it. We walk back that way. We can't stand here. That is not going to restart, and who knows when anyone will pass on this road. It's New Year's Eve."

"He's right," Ellis said, wiping the rain out of her eyes.

After a few minutes, Keith scratched his head hard and nodded a few times.

"Fine," he said. "Fine. Let's . . . fine."

The bags were removed from the car, including the bag that contained the final piece. It wasn't pouring anymore, but it was still raining fairly steadily. The air itself was thick with a cool mist that got to all the places the rain couldn't hit, soaking Ginny all the way to the skin. There was an earthy, smoky smell—somebody, somewhere around here was burning something to keep warm.

The rain and the cold weren't the real problems, though—the problem was that the road had no shoulder at all. The walking choices were the road itself or the sliver of marshy grass that lined it. This was pitted and dotted with rocks, and it was so dark that it was very easy to slide right down into the ditch. So the road was the only real choice. But the road was entirely comprised of curves, and when the occasional car did come along, it would race at them blindly. They'd get about three seconds' notice to dive for the side of the road, where they would slide and trip and almost fall into the ditch.

So it took about half an hour to walk. The pub was fairly dark inside, illuminated by one yellow-shaded light. Three old men sat at the bar, all with their eyes glued to a rugby match on a television mounted on the wall. They all turned slowly to see who had joined them. The woman behind the bar greeted them all warmly, and there was considerable sympathy when they described their plight.

"Sit down there," she said, pointing at a table with a fistful of dishcloth. "Sit down there and have a drink. We'll get Donal."

"Donal's the man," one of the others said.

"He'll sort you. Have a drink."

"You know what?" Keith said. "I think I will. I normally don't, but I feel tonight it may be necessary."

The woman came over and switched on a light, illuminating their corner. A round of pints of something was ordered, as well as a few bags of crisps. Keith sat, quietly smiling and shaking his head.

"I'm really sorry," Ginny said, as the pints were set down in front of them.

"It's not your fault. It could have happened anywhere."

He drank the entire pint in three long gulps, then returned to the bar for another.

"It really would have," Ellis said quietly. "It's good that it happened now. At least it died doing something useful."

A few minutes later, a plain white van pulled up to the pub. Keith pushed back the white lace curtain and stared at it.

"Donal's here!" the barmaid called.

"Are we really about to get into this unmarked white van?" Keith said in a low voice. "Don't they only sell these to child molesters?"

"Exactly how much *Crimestoppers* do you watch?" Oliver asked.

"You're a div," Keith replied, tipping a bag of crisps over his open mouth and letting all the fine particles fall in.

Donal was a much younger guy—probably in his thirties—who didn't look at all surprised that he had been summoned. He was dressed in some fancy rainproof gear, like all-weather athletes wear.

"Donal can help you," one of the men said. "He's an engineer. He makes fridges."

"What's happened?" he asked, accepting a whiskey that was handed to him.

"They've had a problem. Their car is stranded up the road."

"Ah, well, we'll fix it," Donal said. He took only a sip of the whiskey before setting it down. "Come on, then."

"You won't," Oliver said, mostly to himself. "It's a blown rod."

They all piled into the van, which was filled with all kinds of bungee cord and climbing gear. Keith pointed to this silently and drew his finger across his throat. The men from the bar followed in a smaller blue car and took their pints. It was like a little group vacation. They retraced their route, the van making easy time around the curves of the dark road. The car was now the object of interest for a large group of sheep who had perhaps mistaken it for a larger, metal sheep. The men with the pints stood back and Donal came forward and shone a light under the hood.

"You've blown a rod," he said in the same matter-of-fact tone Oliver had used earlier.

"Which is . . . bad?" Keith asked.

"You can't fix that."

A small chorus of "no, no, no, you can't, no."

"Best to leave it," Donal said. "There'll be no one around tonight to get it."

"Just . . . leave it?"

"Nothing else to do. You'd best come back to the pub for the night."

"But we need to get to Dublin," Ginny said.

"You might be able to get the last bus. It'll take you about two hours, though, at the rate they go."

Keith stepped forward and put his hand on the car.

"I think I need to say a few words," he said. "This car . . . well . . . to call her a car doesn't do justice to her spirit, her sense of adventure. I will always remember the horrible clanging noise she made when I tried to start her. . . ."

Under normal circumstances, Ginny would have been amused. But considering that she'd just seen where Aunt Peg's ashes were spread, that *she* got no eulogy . . . Of course, Keith didn't know about that. He couldn't be blamed. It still bothered her.

". . . and though I know she was bound to fail her next MOT inspection and sent off to the scrapyard to be crushed into a cube, I feel she was taken from us too soon. You lived fast, my friend . . . well, not that fast, but fastish. . . ."

Oliver rolled his eyes and wandered toward the van. Their new Irish friends drank their beers and allowed Keith to go on as he liked.

". . . and if there is a car heaven, I know you'll be there, leaking fluids all over the place. . . ."

"Can we go?" Ginny asked.

Keith looked a bit surprised that she was stopping his routine, but he nodded. They got back into the van and were taken to a spot farther up the road. There wasn't even a bus shelter or even a sidewalk—just a worn-away strip in the grass where people obviously walked along, and a single sign with some bus numbers and a loose, nonbinding promise that something that came here went to Dublin. They had been left with the instructions: "When the bus comes, get on."

So they waited. It was dark. Again, the only noise was the gentle call of the sheep. Ginny couldn't see them, but they had to be all around. "This must be like speed dating for you!" Keith yelled to Oliver, pointing at the cluster of sheep that followed their leader toward town. "Hard to choose, isn't it?"

Oliver tossed his lighter in his palm for a moment and shoved it in his pocket.

"Sorry," Ginny said, in a low voice.

"What for?"

"I wish he would stop."

"He won't," Oliver said.

The bus arrived more or less when promised, and was packed with people. It was abundantly clear that this vehicle to Dublin on New Year's Eve was the last-ditch party bus. Ginny didn't see anyone drinking, but it was undoubtedly going on. Even the steam on the windows had a faintly boozy air. Noisemakers punctuated the chatter.

Keith and Ellis got on first, and were shuffled to two seats in the back. Ginny and Oliver ended up in a pair of seats closer to the front.

"Sorry, Gin," Keith called. "Yell if you need us."

There was something spilled all over one of the seats. Ginny chose to believe it was beer. Oliver scooted Ginny aside, pulled a shirt from his bag, threw it over the spot, and took that seat.

"Least I could do," he said.

She'd been upbeat until Keith's eulogy. Now something else was settling in—something more appropriate to seeing where your aunt was laid to rest. She didn't feel like talking. Luckily for her, as soon as the bus was in motion, there was a burst of drunken singing. Ginny didn't know the song, but apparently everyone else on the bus did—and they sang it, and a hundred broken variations of it, all the way to Dublin. Ginny and Oliver shared a small pocket of quiet. Oliver didn't disturb her, but she could see his reflection in the dark window. Every few minutes, he would glance over to look at her. They weren't pressed together as closely as normal, but his shoulder bumped hers, then remained there. It was very subtle, and possibly even accidental, but it was enough.

The Bells

"We made friends," Keith said in a very loud voice, as they were all shoved off the bus in Dublin.

Indeed, a small crowd of people said good-bye to Keith and Ellis as they disembarked. Ellis was giving a good-bye hug to a girl wearing shiny gold tights, who then promptly walked into a bench.

"You seem . . . better," Ginny observed.

"Oh, you know." He threw a careless arm around her shoulder, a boozy smell on his breath. "It had to go sometime. A fitting end to a fine automobile."

"Dublin!" Ellis yelled, throwing up her arms. "Did you have a good trip? We had a good trip."

"See those people?" Keith said, leaning into Ginny and pointing at the girl in the gold tights and her friends. "They know where to go. We will follow them, and all will be well. Look how shiny they are."

"All will be well," Ellis echoed. Then she burst out laughing.

"And they gave us this!" He held up a bottle of what appeared to be champagne, probably very cheap champagne. He popped it open there and then, taking a long sip out of the spray of foam. It dripped down the front of his coat. Ellis handed them each large paper cups, which they had also acquired, and Keith poured them both liberal helpings. At the moment, he had no animosity toward Oliver.

"Drink!" he commanded. "Or you will anger the good people of this nation."

The champagne was warm, and there was far too much of it sloshing around in a cup meant for water or beer. But it felt right. Ginny took a gulp, and Oliver did the same. She continued sipping from her cup as they headed out of the station and into the city.

Dublin was heaving. Ginny had never *seen* so many people out on the street. Herds of people moved along. Everyone seemed to be going in the same direction, flowing like a river out of the depot. They walked down through several streets, until they hit a wide, main thoroughfare called O'Connell Street. They crossed a wide bridge over a river, which Ginny knew from her internetting was called the Liffey—the central artery of Dublin, much like the Thames in London or the Seine in Paris, or, come to think of it, the Hudson and the East River in New York. Water always played a role in these cities. Water moved people, moved things.

A man standing on the opposite side of the bridge was playing "Auld Lang Syne," which was probably a pretty dangerous move in the freezing rain. Fireworks went off overhead—little pops and spurts that looked very amateur and unregulated, so they were close and low, illuminating and reflecting in the water. Ireland *was* a little magical.

The parade of people wound its way to Temple Bar. This was a street entirely filled with bars and the occasional gift shop where you could buy absolutely anything with an Irish flag on it, or top hats made of green felt covered in shamrocks. Someone dressed in a massive leprechaun costume stood on one of the corners, and people kept staggering at him to have their pictures taken. There were a few food stalls open, selling pizza and sloppy kebabs. Mostly, though, it was a street of pubs. Every pub seemed to have a line in front of it. It was hard to get down the street.

"Our friends told us about a place where we can get in," Keith called. "It's this way . . . I think."

Ginny looked in her cup and was surprised to find that she had consumed all of its contents at some point.

"I finished mine," she said to Oliver. He held out his empty cup in reply. Ellis noticed this and turned around to give them a sloppy refill, half of the champagne ending up on the cobblestones.

Keith pointed to a multistory pub, which looked like a very old shop, or maybe a small factory. It was painted a shiny black with various Irish words written on the sides in gold paint. Ginny could hear music coming from inside—fiddles and tambourines and drums. It looked like there was no way possible they were going to get in. People were crushed up against the windows. It was a clown car of a bar.

"You're joking, right?" Oliver said.

"So stay out here," Keith said with a shrug. "Smoke your face off. We're going in."

Oliver did just that, while Ginny, Keith, and Ellis started the long process of getting into the pub. They made it inside by remaining in constant motion—not pushing, exactly. Just moving with the ever-shifting throng. No one was still in Dublin tonight.

"Right!" Ellis yelled. "I'm going to the bar! Who wants what?"

"Guinness, of course," Keith yelled back. "When in Rome."

Keith and Ginny pushed farther inside. Once you got in far enough, there were tiny pockets where you could stand. They found one of these on the landing of the stairs, just opposite the musicians' platform. They got banged around a lot, but it provided a good view of the main floor and of the musicians.

"If I start dancing, don't try to stop me," Keith said. "When the muse moves me, I have to shake it. You know that. I know that. I cannot resist a bodhrán. I am sure you, being American, cannot resist a bodhrán."

"What's a . . ."

"A bodhrán," he said, pointing up at the wide drum one of the musicians was holding and playing feverishly. "Come on. You knew that. You're Irish. All Americans are Irish."

"You aren't going to stop with that, are you?" she asked.

He smiled widely and shook his head.

The band kicked into an even faster song—a flurry of Irish fiddle. The drummer was working away on his handheld drum like a madman.

"I see you looking at that bodhrán player. You're obsessed with him. You're in *love* with him."

"I am," she said solemnly. "That's why I came back."

"Why did you cut your hair?" he asked. "The old style was cute, but this is better. I like how fringy it is. Fringy, fringy."

He reached over and batted the tips of her hair. The hair touching set off a slightly more intense reaction, an all-over body melt. Her eyes felt like they were swimming in their sockets.

"I like fringy things," he said. "Fringe theater. Fringe fries. Also, fridges, strangely enough."

She gripped the rail behind her for support. He leaned closer.

"Listen," he said, "I'm not saying this because I like your money, though on a totally unrelated note you should give me a hundred euros for petrol. I'm just saying . . . I'm glad you came back. You know that, right?"

"I . . . guess?"

"What do you mean you *guess*?"

He rolled toward her, cutting them some private space. He looked at the ground for a long moment and had just raised his head to say something when Oliver appeared next to them.

"It's eleven thirty-five," he said. "And your girlfriend just ran outside, chasing after a hat."

Ginny wished she could grab the bodhrán and beat Oliver over the head with it.

"Wassat?" Keith said.

"I said it's eleven thirty-five," Oliver repeated. "And Ellis saw a hat she liked. A pink cowgirl hat with silver sparkles. So she ran out of the bar and chased the person wearing it. She could be miles away by now."

The balcony where the band was shook as the members pounded their feet on it in time with the music. Keith watched them for a moment.

"Let's go," he said, still staring at the bow of the fiddle, as if hypnotized.

Ginny didn't want to leave this hot, insane place. She and Keith had been on the verge of an actual discussion—an important one. There was something huge happening between them, in the shelter of the noise and the crowd, and if they stopped the conversation would never be finished.

But they were leaving anyway. Ginny walked slowly, trying to get blocked by as many people as possible. Keith managed to get next to her. He said something. It was either "It'll be all right" or "I'll make it right." Then he gave her a look. A *look*. The kind of look you give someone you want to kiss. A serious I-mean-it-now look.

Or something. Something had just happened. Something *hugely* weird.

Ellis was just outside, happily showing off the pink hat. She hadn't gone far at all.

"I traded my ring for it," she said proudly. "Worth it."

"I think Christ Church is this way," Oliver said, pointing up the street.

Ginny followed along beside him. It took her a moment to notice that Keith and Ellis had fallen pretty far behind them. Keith was talking, his hands deep in his pockets. Something serious was going on.

"I'll make it right?" Was that *really* what he said? What the hell did that even mean?

Ellis was wiping her face. Was she crying? Was it rain? Was he back there *breaking up with her*? Was that possible? Magic of Ireland and all that twaddle . . . maybe it *was* happening.

She turned away quickly. If he was, he could not be interrupted.

It would be terrible to break up with someone on New Year's

Eve, especially someone as nice as Ellis. Truthfully, Ginny would feel bad for her. Ellis had treated her like a friend from the moment they met. She wished Ellis no ill will in the world. Maybe it was the champagne talking, but she just wanted everyone, everywhere to be happy.

Another series of firecrackers popped overhead. They passed the leprechaun, who was walking in the same direction as them. Every few feet, Ginny snuck a glance back. The conversation was still going on, and Keith was doing all the talking. Dear god. Something *was* going on back there.

"Have you ever been to Ireland before?" she asked Oliver, to make some conversation and try to keep calm.

"No."

"Why not?"

"It never came up," he said.

"I like it here."

He gave her a sideways glance.

"Come on," she said. "It's nice, right? You're allowed to say you like the place. I'm not going to hit you. You never smile."

"I smile all the time," he said, deadpan. "On the *inside*."

It was obvious when they reached their destination. Christ Church was, unsurprisingly, a church—or really, a cathedral of gray stone, brightly lit and fully encircled by people. The cathedral and grounds around it were filled to capacity, so the crowds now filled the road beyond the iron gate. Once they stopped, people started to fill the gap behind them, and she lost sight of Keith and Ellis. She stood on her toes to look for them. They were nowhere to be seen. Ginny strained, putting her hand on Oliver's shoulder for support, scanning all around.

Oliver looked at her hand.

Bong. The bells rang out, and the crowd cheered. Ginny was still scanning, scanning, scanning. . . . Maybe they had fallen way back, away from the crowd. This was no place to have a breakup talk.

Bong . . .

And then, she found them.

They were kissing. Fully and legally and totally making out, in the way that boyfriends and girlfriends do. For a moment, she had to watch, had to strain on her toes to make sure she got a good, long look—that the sight burned itself into her mind.

Bong . . .

It was almost funny. She really had to laugh. For a few minutes back there, she had actually convinced herself that Keith and Ellis were going to break up based on nothing at all. It was astonishing what a good job she had done. *Bong* . . .

Also of interest, the sound of kissing around her. You may see other people kiss, but you don't often have to hear it. Except they were in a sea of kissing. This was one of those kissing events where you went for the kissing. Oh ho ho! Even funnier. Even funnier.

Bong . . .

It sort of sounded like chewing, like everyone around was gnawing the faces off their partners. Oh, she was laughing now, tears of laughter running down her face. Or was it rain?

Bong . . .

Yes, the sound of kissing was the least romantic sound in the world. It was, now that she listened closely, much like the sound of a cat eating wet food. A gnawing combined with a slurping.

Such a weird and terrible activity. So why did it seem so . . .

Bong . . .

Okay, how many times were these bells going to . . .

Bong . . .

This was maybe what it was like to go insane. You go to Ireland with the guy you love and his girlfriend and then you freeze to death while being gently hosed down in lightly pissing rain and other people's slobber as they made out to death. While she stood with . . .

Bong . . .

Oliver. Who at least was warm and had an umbrella.

Bong . . .

She was still laughing. She put her head against his chest.

"The bells," she said.

"They ring nineteen times," he said loudly enough for her to hear. "I just heard someone say. . . ."

Nineteen times? She laughed even harder. That was an eternity.

Bong . . .

He leaned down. When someone collapses against your chest and just starts laughing like that, you probably want to check to make sure they aren't carrying scissors or eating the buttons off your shirt. She tipped her head up to look at him. He was . . .

Bong . . .

Okay, he was handsome. He was. Sharply featured and silent and lean. He didn't have Keith's half-crazed energy, of course. Something more . . .

Bong . . .

Brooding? Was that the word? Those were some still waters, and they ran deep. Of all the people in the world, it was Oliver who provided the most stability at the moment.

Bong . . .

"This is hell," he said.

Bong . . .

He had a point. He was like her. Kinda.

Bong . . .

She lifted herself on her toes once again, almost automatically. She imagined Aunt Peg on her toes, painting the window in Amsterdam. She imagined that Keith and Ellis weren't there. When she closed her eyes, the bells stopped ringing. She found Oliver's lips blindly, either by instinct . . . or maybe he met her halfway. It was impossible to know. When her lips met his, she felt him physically start. But he didn't pull away, either. She was kissing Oliver. Properly kissing. No hesitation. Her whole body suddenly felt warm. She reached her hands inside his black coat, feeling the smooth lining. She could feel that he had hard muscles in his back, and he was bending down as far as he could so that she could set her heels back on the ground and not totter. He was supporting her so they could kiss even harder, and she was digging her fingers into his back to bring him closer.

There were no more bells. People were moving around them. Ginny squatted down a bit to detach herself from the kiss. He followed for a moment, then seemed to realize she was stopping. He stood up at once. Already, there was debris around them—streamers and confetti, bottles, the broken paper rims of hats. New Year's Eve was the quickest holiday—so much buildup, and then it was over, dropped in a second, instantly unimportant.

Keith and Ellis came bounding up to them, dancing. They were in some nonstop disco that only they could see and hear.

Ellis grabbed Ginny by both hands and started doing a dance with her. If they had seen what just happened, they certainly weren't acting like it.

Keith picked a wet, trampled paper crown off the ground and put it on his head.

"I am king," he said contentedly, making a slow circle, arms outstretched.

Her lips were still full of that pleasingly numbing kissing sensation, and her legs wobbled slightly. The champagne. It had to be the champagne. Whatever the case, *that* had just happened.

One last firework popped and spluttered overhead.

The Crossing

Not many people, it seemed, wanted to cross the Irish Sea at two in the morning on New Year's. But all the people who did want to do this were drunk. It was like the ferry itself was drunk. The boat was slapping itself around on the dock, knocking the already unbalanced people into doorways and walls. It was raining again, and the wind was lashing them, but Ellis insisted on staying on the deck even though it was slick and unpleasant and windy enough to knock her over. The landscape was pitch-black. The sea was black too. The Irish flag flapped stiffly overhead.

"I'll tell you what," Ellis said, staggering along. "I am *staying awake*. Worst thing to do now is fall asleep so I am *staying awake*. Do *not* let me fall asleep, yeah? I'm going to walk. I'm going to walk around the ship. Anyone want to walk around the ship?"

She adjusted her pink hat. It had lost a bit of its silver fringe sometime over the last hour. She pulled the brim low and looked at the bare spot sadly.

Out of the three of them, Ellis had either had the most to drink, or simply had some unlucky body chemistry. Whatever effects the champagne had on Ginny were washed away in the rain and sea mist.

This journey had not only ended twice, it had ended each time on a ferry. The first ferry moved slowly through the sun; this one moved erratically through the night.

At least this time she knew—the journey was over.

"I predict this is going to be a very vomity trip," Keith said, following his girlfriend down the deck. Oliver was messing with his cigarettes again, so Ginny went back inside and sat down on one of the chairs in the lounge. She wasn't aware of falling asleep, only of someone shaking her shoulder. She opened her eyes to find Oliver sitting next to her. His coat smelled of sea air and smoke and damp, evidence of a journey she had slept right through.

"We're here," he said.

Ginny sat up instantly. "Where are the others?" she asked, rubbing her face.

"I haven't seen them since they wandered off down the deck."

"So . . ."

"I've been sitting here. Your stuff is fine. But we have to get off now."

Oliver had been watching over her while she slept. That thought would have been impossibly creepy before, but now . . . now it was kind of sweet.

Oh, her brain was so broken.

They found Keith standing in the desolate terminal, leaning against a pole for support.

"Hey, Gin," he said wearily. "Ellis just went in there. The night combined with the boat . . . it didn't agree with her." He pointed to the women's room. "Could you, um . . . could you go with her? She went in there a while ago. I think she needs some supervision."

Ginny nodded. He was right about this being a vomity trip. The ladies' room looked empty, but Ginny saw a pair of shoes sticking out of the cubicle on the end. Someone was kneeling on the floor in front of a toilet.

"Ellis?" she called.

"Oh, hello!" Ellis was trying to sound cheerful, but her voice was like death. "Oh, I'm fine. I've just been stupid. Don't worry about me."

"I'm just going to stand out here, okay?"

"Oh, you're sweet. . . ."

A gagging noise, then a pause.

"Oh god . . . ," Ellis went on. "Is this place moving? Gin, I feel like I'm still on the boat. Gin, is it moving in here?"

The stall door wasn't locked, and it bounced open. Ginny pushed it closed and held it while some grim noises came from within.

"I'm so sorry," Ellis said, coughing. "This is so awful."

"It's okay," Ginny said.

"It's New Year's . . . I'm so stupid. I'm so stupid, Gin. Why am I so stupid? No one else did anything stupid. Why is it just me?"

Ginny laughed. She couldn't help it. "I'm not laughing at you," she said quickly.

"It's okay." Ellis sounded like she was going to cry.

"No, really. I'm *really* not." Ginny sat down on the floor by

231

the stall door and listened. No noise now, just palpable suffering. Ginny got close and patted Ellis's ankle.

"Ellis?"

"Yeah?" Her voice was breaking. Oh, this was probably a mistake, but Ellis was so upset. She shouldn't have laughed.

"You really weren't the only one who did something stupid." Ginny said quietly. "I kissed Oliver."

Ellis shuffled a bit, then forced the door open and slumped in the corner of the stall, facing Ginny. She had definitely been crying.

"Really?" she asked.

"Really. But don't—"

"I won't tell Keith," Ellis said. "I know. He hates him. I understand."

Ellis's chin sank to her chest and she took a few deep breaths. "I'll tell you something," she said. "I was so jealous of you when I first met Keith. Always talking about you, this adventure you'd gone on together. But then I met you and you're so nice, and you let me come along. Oh, did I really trade my ring?" Her focus had gone down to her bare hand. "It was cheap, but still. I'm never drinking again. Bugger, why did I do that? Maybe I can get another, only a fiver . . . never let me drink again, okay? If you ever see me drink, just slap me. Oh . . ."

There was a rapping on the door. It opened a crack.

"Train's in ten minutes," Keith called. "El, you alive?"

"I think so. Just give me a moment. We'll be right out."

Ellis grabbed the door to try to pull herself up. Ginny helped her. She managed to get herself into a bent position, but couldn't straighten up right away.

232

"I don't think what you did was that stupid," Ellis said, steadying herself against the stall.

Then she threw up on the floor between them. Not a lot—but a definite harbinger of things to come. Ginny winced and looked away.

"Sorry!" Ellis said. "Sorry, oh god . . ."

Keith must have heard this happen, because he let himself in. He looked at the vomit on the floor with a strange kind of satisfaction. "And so it begins."

"I have a plan," Ellis said, as he half-carried her out. "We'll get on the train, and I'll ride in the toilet."

"It's like dating royalty," Keith said.

The train was very sleek and modern, with lots of light-up buttons and computerized signs. It was also freezing cold and smelled like sadness and old beer. Keith got Ellis on board and positioned her in front of the bathroom.

"Just put me in there," she said bravely. "I'll be fine. I'll be wonderful. Just shove me in the toilet."

"All right, all right, enough with the sexy talk."

She waved them off and slammed the door shut. A red light came on, signifying that it was occupied.

"I'm just going to stay here for a bit," he said. "You might as well go sit down. You might want to sit a car over."

A grim noise came from the toilet. Oliver and Ginny quickly moved to the next car, which was completely empty. They sat opposite each other in a group of six seats. There was no looking at each other. No speaking. Keith was gone for quite a while, so that was a lot of time to artfully avoid each other in a casual way. When he did return, he did so quite loudly, plopping down

233

on one of the seats next to Oliver and gazing between the two of them.

"How's Ellis?" Ginny asked.

"She'll be all right. How are *you*?"

It was just the way he said it, the way he leaned in a little. He knew. Oliver must have sensed this as well, because he got up.

"I need a coffee," he said. "Do you need one?"

This was to Ginny. She shook her head.

"He's very solicitous," Keith said after Oliver had left. "When did you two get so cozy? I guess it was all of that time in the backseat. I don't suppose I can blame you. He's a catch."

Yeah. He knew.

"It was just a kiss on New Year's," she said. "I mean . . . everyone was kissing. And I had all that champagne."

"Well. Congratulations. You've made a wonderful choice. I'm very happy for you."

It was snide and cold. So cold that she wished she could slap him.

"What do you care?" she asked.

"Sorry . . . what?" He leaned forward. "What do I care? Of course I don't care. I think that's the point we've demonstrated in all of this, my lack of caring. That's why I just destroyed my car. That's why I've been traveling with you for days so you weren't alone with the person who was ripping you off. It's all my extreme lack of care. But you seem happy now, so I'll just step aside then."

"It was one kiss," she said, a challenge rising in her voice. "I mean, why do you care who I kiss? You have someone. You didn't even tell me you had a girlfriend. . . ."

And, there it was. That wasn't the way she meant to say it.

234

This wasn't how she wanted this to go. It was out. It could never be put back.

"Do what you want," he said, throwing up his hands. He returned to the other car, back to his girlfriend. The glass door of the car shut behind him with a decisive hiss.

Reality Comes to Visit

That had gone very, very badly. That was like training for the Olympics, working up to one big moment that would matter for the rest of your life, and then just being careless and falling off the diving board or forgetting to correctly attach your skis. Poor form. No points. She began to sob, silently and pathetically, and completely unable to stop. She didn't hear Oliver return—she was only vaguely aware that someone had sat down next to her, and it definitely wasn't going to be Keith. He put a few napkins in her hand.

She shoved them up against her face. They stuck.

"I'm okay," she said. The words were barely understandable.

Oliver didn't point out how absurd this statement was, or try to talk her down. He just sat with her, first stiffly putting a hand on her shoulder, then extending his arm. At some point, she just gave up and leaned against him a little.

It took a few minutes for her to gather herself together again.

"It's fine," she said, her voice thick. "I just . . . we weren't a thing. Not a real thing. I just, really liked him. We said we were 'kind of something.' He wasn't supposed to like other people. Isn't that how it works? You just like the one person, forever, and then you stay together?" She tried to make it come off as a joke, but it didn't really work.

"I don't have a lot of personal experience in the matter," he said, "but I'm pretty sure that's not how it usually goes."

She looked out of the window at the gray morning. There was some beautiful landscape going by, but it was hard to appreciate. Her head was thrumming and her eyes were still leaking and dribbling. This wasn't how she was supposed to end this journey.

"I don't blame you for wanting to get back at him," Oliver said. "Did it work?"

"I don't know what that means," she said, hiccuping. Oh, good. The post-crying hiccups.

"Last night."

He stared at her as if she were very, very stupid. Oh. The kiss.

"What do you mean *did it work*?" she asked.

"You did that to get to him. Did it work?"

Is that why she had done it? That wasn't how she remembered it. She remembered the bells, the rain . . . she remembered the kiss. She didn't remember any motive. She just remembered that it had happened, and that it had been . . . nice. It had been good.

She was going to leave that alone. "Anyway, he didn't do anything wrong," she said. "He just should have told me. But now he probably hates me."

"So what if he does?" he replied.

That was too much for her to even contemplate.

* * *

They stayed in their separate compartments for the rest of the journey. Ginny saw Keith and Ellis again when they got off the train at Euston Station. Ellis looked a little better, but her face was still ashen. She raised a weak hand in greeting.

"I made it!" she said, her voice hoarse and scratchy. "I rode from Wales to London in a toilet. I should get a prize. I think . . . I think I have to go home now."

She leaned against Keith's shoulder. He put an arm around her waist.

"I'll let you know when the auction is tomorrow," Ginny said. "If you can come . . ."

Ellis was nodding, but Keith said nothing. He picked up his bag, hoisted it over his free shoulder. They went one way, and Ginny and Oliver went another.

In the end, it was Ginny and Oliver who returned to the house. Oliver stayed outside for a moment, waggling his cigarettes in explanation. Ginny went in and knelt down in front of the table-top and glass, and removed the paper from her bag.

The order seemed obvious. The paper went between the glass and the wood. That made sense. The paper was so fine that it practically vanished against the yellow background. The wine rings and stains on the table came through, shading the picture. She moved the glass back over and sandwiched the paper in place. The two dancing figures materialized from behind the ferns and plants and animals on the outside. She could see where the paint on the window had been affected by the rain and the elements, streaking and dotting it lightly. There was a light layer of grime all over the picture as well, but it only seemed to add to the over-all effect. The viewer was put into this strange jungle and was looking into some other reality entirely, with one of the figures beckoning the viewer inside. Beautiful wasn't the right word for it. It wasn't beautiful. It was rough and strange and bright. It was like a tangible dream.

Oliver knocked lightly and came inside.

"It's amazing," he said. "I would never in a million years have guessed that it would turn out that way."

"She was good like that," Ginny said. She stood up and sat on the sofa to look at it from a distance.

"It needs a name," she said.

"What did your aunt name her other paintings?"

"She didn't."

"So why name this one?"

"I don't know," she said. "The others were in a group. They called them the Harrods paintings. This one is on its own. It needs to be called something."

She sat back and stared for a long time, until her eyes went blurry. One good thing about Oliver—he could take long silences.

"When my aunt lived in New York," she finally said, "she took me to a pool one summer. Except, no one has a pool in New York. It was a cleaned-out Dumpster. It was a pool, but it wasn't a pool, you know?"

"Not . . . exactly."

"I mean . . ." It was annoying when other people couldn't get in your head and automatically catch up with your conversations. "I mean . . . people tell you what to expect. What things are *supposed* to be like. A pool is supposed to be this nice, clean thing in the backyard that's painted blue on the bottom, but anything with water in it can be a pool, even a Dumpster. She called it the triumph of imagination. It was how she did things. It's like, a fancy way of saying flaky. That's what I want to call it. *The Triumph of Imagination*."

"It's a good title."

Weirdly, her impulse was to put her arms around him. She wasn't drunk. She wasn't crying. Still, the impulse was there.

Before she could do that, she noticed something out of the corner of her eye. There was a white van pulling up across the street . . . just like the ones that seemed to disturb Keith so much. Two men in coveralls got out and started walking toward the house.

Oliver stared down at the coffee table. It was still littered with Christmas crackers and Ginny's silver elephant.

"I called them," he said.

The reminder was like a slap in the face. He wasn't here to be her support system—he was here to collect. He had stayed outside to call the delivery truck. Why was this a surprise? This was always how it was going to end.

There was a knock on the door.

"Miss Blackstone?" one of the men said when she answered. "We're here from Jerrlyn and Wise. May we come in?"

Ginny opened the door wider, and they stepped inside politely.

"Is this the piece?" he asked.

She nodded.

"We'll just get started then," he said.

They took over. Ginny and Oliver were relegated to the side of the room. The pieces, which had been manhandled and shoved into cars and bags and thrown around, were now treated like crown jewels. The men set down a packing quilt on the floor and lifted it gingerly. One held it upright while the other measured its

241

dimensions, examined its construction, and took some initial photographs. They had a long discussion on exactly how to pad it and box it and put it into the van. Ginny thought about asking them to let the piece stay long enough for Richard to see it, but it was all so official and efficient, there seemed to be no stopping them.

Oliver sat on the sofa, looking at Ginny's silver elephant. This was the reality of their relationship, Ginny reminded herself. It was all about finding this one piece of art and selling it off. The kiss, the trip on the train . . . it all faded away.

"We're finished now, miss," the first man said, presenting her with a clipboard. Ginny filled it out automatically, ticking boxes and signing on lines, not even reading. She stopped only in the box marked TITLE OF WORK and wrote in *The Triumph of Imagination*. When she was finished, they carried *The Triumph of Imagination* out the door, snugly wrapped in gray quilting and tape.

"There was a message from Cecil as well," Oliver said quietly. "The auction is at two tomorrow."

"Fine," she said.

"I suppose I should go."

"Probably."

"I'll see you tomorrow then."

She watched him from the window as he left. He never turned back, just made his way down the street, tossing his lighter in his palm. Like nothing had happened at all. She felt a strangely familiar pang in her heart, but she couldn't quite place it and didn't feel like trying.

The Dotted Line

The next morning was the first clear day since Ginny's arrival. The sky was bright and vividly blue with big, puffy clouds. Ginny stood in front of the white chalk steps that led to the front door of Jerrlyn and Wise. Occasionally, someone in a suit would pass by her and go up the steps. One or two of them glanced at her, perhaps knowing that she was the eighteen-year-old selling the artwork on show today, but the others passed without a look.

Ten minutes until the auction. Ten minutes, and no Keith. No Oliver either, for that matter, unless he was inside. She hadn't truly believed that Keith wouldn't come, but with every passing second, the reality set in.

She considered just going back to Richard's, then she hurried up and pressed the button before she could entertain this thought for very long. Cecil's assistant, James, opened the door, greeted her by name, and escorted her over to Cecil. The hallway was packed with people—easily double the amount that had been there for the last auction.

"It's so crowded," Ginny said, rocking on her heels nervously.

"Yes, a good turnout, especially considering the short notice," Cecil replied. "The last collection got a good deal of press in the industry, so we had a lot of interest."

Ginny scanned the hall, but Oliver was nowhere in sight. In the middle of this crowd, over by the table of coffee and strawberries, was a figure she instantly recognized. It was impossible to miss the massive crown of wiry, long, black and orange hair, the mix of gold Spandex leggings, the black mohair sweater that came down to her knees, and the face with the tattooed stars around the eyes. Ginny wasn't sure why she was here, but she definitely knew who it was. The woman gave a gasp and a wave, and set down a plate filled almost entirely filled with cream.

"Hello, darling!" she called in her booming Scottish brogue.

"I think you know Mari," Cecil said.

"Cecil told me about the auction," Mari said, answering the unasked question. "He's my art dealer down here in London. I put him together with Peg. I've know Cecil since he was just a pup. He didn't look like this when I first met him. You were pure poor art student then, weren't you, love?"

"I was indeed," Cecil said.

"You're going to take good care of this piece, aren't you?" Mari pinched Cecil's cheek. It looked like a hard pinch too. One that might leave a mark. Ginny couldn't help but be impressed at the way he took it without wincing.

"We certainly hope to," he replied. "Do you have everything you need? Glass of champagne?"

"Maybe just a small one, love. Virginia, you remember my Chloe, don't you?"

Mari indicated a girl leaning casually against the flocked wallpaper, next to a painting of a tiny boy in blue velvet with a bug-eyed dog. Chloe was Mari's assistant: part artist, part butler, part bouncer. She was dressed in biker boots, rolled jeans, and a shredded T-shirt that revealed a right arm tattooed from shoulder to fingertips in one large image of a mermaid splashing around in a purple and green ocean. The bleach blond mullet had been replaced by a shaved head with just a hint of peach fuzz.

An assistant stealthily put a glass of champagne in Mari's hand. It was in one of those wide and flat old-fashioned glasses that sort of looked like bowls.

"Let's go have a look at it," Mari said.

She guided Ginny over to the door of the auction room. The auction room was such a strange place, so heavily carpeted, so padded. There were a handful of upholstered chairs and four long tables. A dozen people sat in front of computers, talking quietly into phones. The piece sat on an easel at the end of the room, clamps along the edges holding it all together. In this light, Ginny could see just how dirty the window was. They'd made no attempt to clean it. The layer of grime and the runny paint . . . it was all part of the piece.

"It's always very strange to see them when they get here," Mari said, taking a long, loud sip of the champagne. "A bit like an operating theater. Have a bit of champagne."

Ginny felt a presence behind her—the hairs at the back of her neck tingled a bit. She didn't have to turn to know who it was.

"Oh, hello," Mari said. "Are you a friend?"

Once again, Oliver was formally dressed. He fit right in at Jerrlyn and Wise. Maybe the hair was a little too dark, the coat still a little strange fitting. "I'll be outside," he said to Ginny. "Just wanted you to know I was here."

"Aren't you going to stay for the auction?" Mari asked.

Oliver looked at Mari warily—processing the facial tattoos, the names on her hands and feet, the unnatural sunburst orange streaks emanating from her head. She saw him complete his analysis and decide that the best course of action was to walk away from both of them as quickly as possible.

"Oh, he's shy," Mari said. "He's different from the last one. Where do you find them all?"

It took Ginny a second to realize that Mari thought Oliver was *with* Ginny—in much the same way that she thought Keith was *with* Ginny. She was about to issue a denial, but then decided against it. For one thing, it was nice to have someone who thought she was such a collector of boyfriends. For another, Oliver's abrupt exit made her nervous.

People started to trickle past them into the room, taking their places at the tables, opening the computers and taking out their phones. Cecil put a hand delicately on Ginny's shoulder.

"Forgive us," he said. "Virginia and I just have a bit of business to complete. Please have a seat, Mari."

"I think I'll stand, darling. I like to think on my feet."

"Of course. This way, Virginia?"

He escorted Ginny over to his office and quietly shut the door. He didn't sit down, though. "Perhaps it's best if I speak directly," he said. "I don't know who Mr. Davies is, but I don't think he had anything to do with the creation of the work in the saleroom today. I don't know exactly what's going on, but I want you to know that that contract you signed does not bind you to selling this piece today. If you do not want to proceed, you can and should say so. We've pulled things from the block before. I don't want to go ahead with this sale if there's something irregular going on. . . ."

Before Ginny could react, there was a rapid knock on the door, and James poked his head in.

"I found him," he said, ushering Oliver into the room. James shut the door behind them. Now they were all crowded into the tiny space by Cecil's door. Cecil tapped his fist against his lips for a moment. Oliver pressed himself into the corner.

"Virginia and I were just having a conversation about the contract," he said. "I was explaining to her that it wasn't necessary for us to—"

"It's hers," Oliver said, cutting him off.

"Pardon?"

Oliver had gone completely pale, and was pulling his coat tight around himself, as if trying to disappear.

"I'm withdrawing from the sale. All the money's hers. Just sell it and leave me out of it."

"What?" Ginny said.

Cecil moved over to his desk and produced a piece of paper.

"I thought something like this might come up," he said. "I'll just need your signature on this rider, which supersedes the contract, directing all profits minus commission to Virginia Blackstone. You forfeit any claim."

"Good," Oliver said. He squeezed between the two wingback chairs to lean against the desk and sign his name.

247

"We're done here, right?" he asked.

"I won't need anything further from you," Cecil said. "If that's what you are asking."

"That's what I'm asking."

Cecil's office was so small that it was impossible for him to exit without squeezing past Ginny. As he did so, he shoved something into her hands. She looked down. It was the last blue envelope.

"Now," Cecil said. "We can proceed, if that's all right with you."

"Go ahead," Ginny said, running out of the office after Oliver. He was moving quickly. He had already left the building, and when Ginny got outside, he was halfway down the street.

"Wait!" Ginny said, jogging after him. "Where are you going?"

"Home."

"Okay," Ginny said, running around to get in front of him and stop his progress for a second. "You need to tell me what's going on."

He tried to step past her, but she blocked him again, putting her hands on his chest.

"Don't," he said simply.

"You need to explain. Why did you do this?"

"I don't need to explain anything."

He gently removed her hands from his chest and kept walking. She opened the envelope and read the letter in her hand. It started where the last part cut off in Ireland.

> yet.
>
> Gin, do you remember how I used to drag you to the Museum of Modern Art all the time and make

you stand in front of a crazy, huge painting of a woman on a sofa sitting in the middle of a jungle? Think back for a moment. I'll wait. . . .

From her spot in the street she could see inside through the window. She saw Cecil take his position at the podium. The sale was starting. Cecil was nodding and pointing politely at people she couldn't see, saying numbers she couldn't hear. Then he stopped. A few minutes later, people started trickling out. It was over. The piece was sold.

Mari stepped outside. She looked at the sky first, then took the steps carefully, holding on to the brass banister for support. She looked up and down the street, waving Ginny over.

"Ah, here you are," she called.

She carefully took a seat on the steps. She had to be over seventy, Ginny realized. Her joints were stiff. Ginny sat next to her.

"Did you two have an argument?" Mari asked, indicating Oliver's retreating figure.

"Not exactly."

"It seemed very dramatic, whatever it was. I love drama. But you missed the sale."

"What happened?" Ginny asked.

"The person who bought it was passionate about it. A hundred and sixty-seven thousand pounds."

A hundred and sixty-seven thousand pounds. Another large sum of money Ginny couldn't really compute.

"You don't seem excited," Mari said.

"I am . . . I'm just . . ."

"I know," Mari said. "Sales are strange. You make the art, and then suddenly, someone's paying for it. Suddenly it's a commodity. . . ."

"I didn't make the art," Ginny said.

Mari shook her head.

"Cecil told me you did the assembly and the rubbing."

"I just put it together," Ginny said.

"You don't just *put together* a work of art, love. It's not a sandwich. You were trained. Maybe you weren't aware of it, but you were trained. It's a very good work. I'm quite proud of that girl. Proud of you both. That's why I had to have it. There was a bidder from Tokyo who was giving me a hell of a time in there, for instance, but I was determined."

She smiled and let Ginny take in that piece of information before she continued.

"I'm good friends with a curator at the Museum of Modern Art in New York," she said. "I think that piece belongs there. So I'm going to speak to them about donating it. I think it should go home and be where lots of people can see it, don't you?"

"You bought it? And you're sending it to MoMA?"

The door opened again, and Chloe stomped past them, down the steps.

"I'll get the car, yeah?" she said.

"Thank you, love."

Chloe gave Ginny a firm nod, then headed off down the street in long strides.

"Chloe took a real liking to you," Mari said. "She doesn't take to just anyone. She's got good taste, does my Chloe. I'm going to get her paintings down here next."

From behind them, Ginny heard a car starting in the small private parking lot behind the building.

"Thank you," Ginny said.

Mari patted Ginny's shoulder with her gold-taloned hand.

"Money is for doing things, my love. Don't sit on it like a hen sits on an egg. It doesn't hatch. I should know. I've made enough of it."

A small, black sports car, some ancient model that was probably from the seventies, came peeling down the short gravel path and pulled blindly into the street, stereo pulsing.

"Make sure to come to see me in Edinburgh sometime," she said.

Mari walked slowly to the car and lowered herself into the seat. It was just barely off the ground. She and Chloe gave Ginny a little wave, and then they pulled off to terrify London traffic.

The Conversation

Well, we're done. But I have a little more to say. I don't want to be dragged off the stage just yet.

Gin, do you remember how I used to drag you to the Museum of Modern Art all the time and make you stand in front of a crazy, huge painting of a woman on a sofa sitting in the middle of a jungle? Think back for a moment. I'll wait. . . .

Ginny sat on the sofa and glared at the letter. For the first time, she wanted the letters to shut up and stop asking her questions. What she wanted, for once in her life, was a letter that provided a simple list of foolproof instructions. *Would you like to succeed in life and love and not be a crazy person? Do the following. . . .*

Yes. That would be nice.

It was her last night in London. Richard was in the kitchen, talking on the phone about some work crisis. They were supposed to go to dinner in a little while to celebrate the sale. She didn't really feel like celebrating. Yes, the piece had sold. Yes, she had more money. But aside from that . . . she had a ruined relationship and more questions than answers. She'd had the letter for hours now, and she couldn't even bring herself to read it. Even the one stupid thing she had to finish while she was here—the essay—wasn't done either. Failure on all levels.

Someone was ringing the front doorbell. Ginny almost fell over the coffee table in her haste to answer it. But it wasn't Keith. It was Ellis, hopping lightly in the cold.

"Sorry," she said. "I just wasn't in any state to say good-bye the other day. I didn't want that to be your last memory of me, chucking my guts up into a train toilet."

Ginny held the door open for her to come in, but she waved this off. "I have to go," she said. "I'm starting a volunteer job, doing an evening shift at a crisis call center. It's quite bad around this time of year, apparently. I just wanted to see you before you were off. So . . ."

She stood there bouncing for a moment. A gust of cold wind came in and flooded the living room.

"I don't want to interfere," she said, "but . . . I think you and Keith should talk. I think you'll both regret it if you don't work it out. And I think it would be a shame if you didn't take this opportunity to talk in person before you go. But . . . I suppose I've said enough. That was awkward. I'll shut up now."

She opened her arms and gave Ginny a hug.

"Anyway . . ." Ellis backed down one of the steps. "Hopefully you'll be back. I'm glad I got to meet you."

"I hope so," Ginny said. "And . . . I'm glad I met you too."

She shut the door quietly and looked around at the decorations in the living room, at the hole where the upside-down tree had been suspended.

"All set," Richard said. "Hungry? You're going to like this place."

"Could I have one hour?" she asked.

Keith's window was open, the lights around it being drawn inside by some unseen force. She thought about calling up, but then she decided to knock on the gold plastic door panel. David opened the door. That was lucky—Keith might not have done the same.

"Gin!" he said. "I heard you were here."

It was good to see a friendly face. David indicated that she could go upstairs as she liked. She took the stairs softly, but Keith seemed to know she was coming. He had dragged in half the strand of lights and was fiddling with the bulbs. What he was attempting to do, Ginny had no idea, but he looked pretty intent about it. He didn't even look up when she came in. "How was your auction?" he asked, not sounding very interested. "Are you rich now? More rich, I mean?"

"I can give you money for your car."

"I'm not really interested in your money." From Keith, that was a first—and definitely not a good sign.

"Why are you so angry?" Ginny asked.

"Angry? I'm not angry." His face was utterly composed and calm.

"So why didn't you come to the auction?"

255

"I was busy," he said, pulling in a few more feet of the lights. "I do have other things going on in my life, you know."

Though he wasn't exactly welcoming, Ginny sat down on the red sofa, pushing aside a few books and shirts.

"Are you taking them down?" she said, gesturing at the lights.

"No. I'm fixing them."

"I leave tomorrow," she said.

Keith nodded and continued fiddling away with the bulbs. This was how it was going to be. If she wanted this to happen, she would have to shove it into existence. "Why didn't you tell me?" she asked. "About Ellis. We talked every day. You never told me. And even after I came here, you never even told me. You never said a word."

"Told you?" he said casually. "You met her. . . ."

"You know what I mean," she said. "You said we were 'kind of something.' Why didn't you just *tell* me?"

Silence. Just the sound of the television from David's room. Keith yanked out one bulb and the whole string of lights went out. "Maybe I will take them down," he said, yanking the plug from the wall. "Don't want to start a fire."

He began pulling in the lights with greater force, each bulb emitting little pings of protest as they were pulled over the radiator under the window. For a few moments, it appeared that he was never going to answer, but finally he spoke.

"I told you about my old girlfriend, Claire?" he said, coiling up the lights into a messy tangle.

He had, on a train ride over the summer. It was the first time he really told her anything personal, how he had been in love when he was sixteen, and his girlfriend had gotten pregnant and

256

dumped him, unable to cope with the turn their relationship had taken. He'd gone off the rails. That was where Keith the thief started.

"She told me she wanted to be my friend," he said. "Then I went out and stole a car. She's the reason I have a criminal record."

"You have a criminal record?"

"I stole a *car*," he said, as if this was obvious.

"You didn't say you got caught."

"*Of course* I got caught. Several times. Allow me to show you my gallery of ASBOs."

"As whats?"

"Anti-social behavior orders. The chav badge of honor."

"I have no idea what you're talking about."

"My point," he said, "is that none of this explains what you did. Making out with the guy who was exploiting you, then throwing it in my face while I was trying to help you . . . yeah. Well played."

"You just said that when you and Claire broke up *you stole a car*."

"That's different," he snapped. "There is nothing personal about stealing a car. It's just a car."

"It might be to the person who owns the car." She was yelling now. "You took someone's property. I kissed someone, which I am allowed to do, even if you don't like him. Besides, he didn't take the money, so you can let it go now."

"He didn't take the money?" This gave Keith pause. "Why? Did whatshisname with the hair, from the auction house, did he—"

"He just didn't take it."

Keith just shook his head, as if unable to comprehend this new information. Finally he looked at Ginny, square on, his face open and honest.

"I thought I was doing the right thing. I didn't want to ring you up and tell you I'd met someone. It seemed wrong to do that to you over the phone."

"So you decided not to tell me *at all*?"

"You came here," he said. "You met her. What was I supposed to say? She was right in front of you."

"You were supposed to say, 'This is my girlfriend.' *I* had to figure it out."

"*That* would have been better? You would have wanted me to say, 'Oh, yes, this is my girlfriend? Behold her.' How would that have helped? I could tell from the expression on your face that you'd worked it out. I didn't want to make you more upset."

He had a point, sort of. Not the best point. Not a sharp point. But a kind of point.

"You had days after that," she countered. "There were plenty of times you could have said something. I just needed to hear it from you, that's all."

"Why?"

"I don't know," she said. "To make it official or something. I didn't want it to be true, but it would have been better coming from you, because I had . . . *hope*, or something."

Keith hung his head, his hair falling over his profile and hiding his expression.

"Gin . . ."

"You know what's funny?" she went on. "I *like* Ellis. A lot. I'm glad you picked her. Half the time the last few days I liked her more than you."

It took a lot of her to say that, but she felt better once she did. Stronger. She heard him laugh a little.

"That's fair," he said. "And you know how I feel. When I go old and stark raving mad, we can be in the mad home together. You'll keep sneaking up on me, and I'll keep taking your money, and your teeth. . . ."

Keith sat down next to her on the sofa and put his arm around her. This time, she knew why it was there.

"I have to get back," she said.

"I can't offer to drive you home, but I'll walk you there."

"I'm fine," she said. "I should take a cab, anyway. I promised Richard. We're going to dinner."

"I have a number for one."

The cab was fast. He had barely called when there was a honking out front.

"They're just around the corner," he explained.

No more good-byes. It was time to go.

She would come back to this house, maybe. Keith was a student. He might move out. But if she did come back, it would never be the same. She would never look up at those black blinds with the same anticipation, or stare into that piece of patterned gold plastic in the door and think when the door opened, she would be greeted with a kiss. All of those little fantasies, so carefully cultivated, were wiped away. Maybe this was what Aunt Peg meant all along—returning was a weird thing. You can never visit the same place twice. Each time, it's a different story. By the very act of coming back, you wipe out what came before.

Keith was watching from the doorway. She had to walk away, chin up. This was hard, but it was not impossible.

That was the amazing part. It was not impossible.

The Probably Problem

It was midnight. Ginny was in bed, staring at the wall. She wasn't tired. Now that her time in England was almost over, every second seemed precious. So much of this trip had been painful and strange, but she still wanted to hold on to it.

She got out of bed and looked out the window. There was a purplish ambient light over London, just enough that she could see the outlines and shadows of the things in the neighbor's gardens. She spent a few minutes trying to guess what the objects were—tiny, round chimneys, sheds, bikes, old boxes.

She was tired of guessing games. She crawled back into bed and pulled out the letter.

```
    yet.
    Gin, do you remember how I used to drag you to
the Museum of Modern Art all the time and make
you stand in front of a crazy, huge painting
```

of a woman on a sofa sitting in the middle of a
jungle? Think back for a moment. I'll wait. . . .

She didn't need a moment to think about this. She knew the
painting well. It took up an entire wall at MoMA. It was very
vivid, with deep greens and yellows. A naked woman lounged on
what appeared to be a maroon sofa, while around her, tigers peered
curiously through the grass, and a long orange snake wound along
the ground. In the background, another woman, half-hidden in
the foliage and oversize flowers, played some kind of instrument.

The painting is called The Dream. It's by Henri
Rousseau. Rousseau was always my hero, for many
reasons. The paintings, for a start. Their colors.
Their strange, childlike perfection.

Rousseau was entirely self-taught. He was
completely unaware that people saw his style as
in any way weird. He just assumed that people
would want to look at the paintings, that they
would be accepted. Critics called his style
"primitive." (Some called it worse things than
that.) He was considered groundbreaking by people
like Picasso, who bought one of his works off the
street where it was being sold for scrap canvas.

By profession, Rousseau was a toll collector
in Paris. He never saw a jungle in his life, but
he painted them over and over again. He painted

the ones he saw in his mind. He placed figures
in his paintings, figures that are as big as the
landscape.

As I write this, Gin, I know my mind is
dying. I am sitting on a sofa in London, several
thousand miles away from you. I am like that
woman on a sofa in the painting. I see things
around me that I know should not be there. Twice
today, I've reached out to pet a cat that I know we
don't own, that I know cannot possibly be sitting
next to me. But I happen to like my imaginary
cat, and when I reach out into what must be empty
space, I can feel her fur, and the soft rise and
fall of her chest. I call her Probably. As in,
"I probably need to take my meds, because I am
seeing the cat again."

The hallucinations aren't always that
pleasant, but I've been pretty lucky. And the one
thing I see most often, Gin? It's you. You walk
up and down the stairs. You crawl in the bedroom
window. You sit on the kitchen table. You talk to
me all day long when Richard is at work. You tell
me about school. We play 20 Questions (and you
win). You are all over this house. Honestly, you
should probably be paying rent.

Of course, I haven't seen you in two years, so
you appear in lots of different ways. Sometimes,
you are five years old. Sometimes, you are your

actual age. Sometimes, you are forty. Once, you had to be about eighty-five. But it's always you, Gin. There is a single, golden thread that runs through all the Ginnys. As I write these letters and paint my pictures, you are here with me, advising me. Encouraging me. These paintings are your paintings. And as for this last work . . . I can only see it in my imagination, because it's not done yet. I'm so good I can complete a work of art after I'm dead.

I'm fully aware that half the appeal bidders see in my paintings is that this madness that makes me see things will kill me, and I won't paint any more. There is nothing the art world likes more than a dying artist with a limited output.

Some people will say this is junk, that anybody could have messed up a tabletop, screwed up a painted window, and done a rubbing of a stone. Well, sure. But that's the usual argument. Anyone could have dripped paint all over a canvas. But Jackson Pollock did, because he knew it was right. Anyone could have painted a can of soup. But Andy Warhol did, because he understood more about modern society than those people. Idea meets execution. Feeling becomes action.

I don't know why people find this idea so hard to get. I mean, you can throw any two people

together, it doesn't mean they'll fall in love.
Everyone knows this. No one quite understands
how it works. It's just those people, where they
are in their lives, how circumstance throws them
together. Sure, it's happened before, but never
quite in that way. Maybe they seem to come together
all wrong. Maybe they've loved others. Maybe they
don't always do right by each other . . . but it's
still there, the love. The event. And no one would
dare criticize it just because it's common, it's a
little asymmetrical, and anyone can do it. It is
unique. It is theirs. It is beautiful. They have
made something that has been made a million
times before and has also never existed before
that moment.

   All right. Is that maudlin enough? When you
have cancer, people let you get away with murder,
I'm telling you. This is how Nicholas Sparks has
been getting away with things for years. Anyway,
Probably has come back up on the sofa and wants
her head scratched, so I gotta go pet my cat.

   I don't want this letter to end, so I won't
conclude it. I'll just pause as if I am still
writing and

There was no period. It just stopped in midair.
"You have to be kidding me," Ginny said.

She set the letter aside and stared at the ceiling. All these weird endings. Keith. Ellis. Oliver storming out of the auction house. One of these stories had to end properly. Who was Oliver, anyway? Why hadn't she taken the time to find out more?

She grabbed her computer from its spot next to the bed. She could write to him, but he wouldn't reply, that was certain. She would have to look him up. Google turned up a lot of Oliver Davies, but no pictures matched Oliver—at least, not clearly. There were a few large group shots he might have been in, but they weren't really useful.

There had to be a time where he gave some information. Had she seen his passport? No. Any ID at all? The only time he even had it out was at the train station, when they were going to Paris.

He bought the tickets to Paris. . . .

They made you give information when you did things like that. She rolled out of bed to the floor and pulled over her bag. She'd been shoving things in the front pocket. She unzipped it and felt around. Two crumpled napkins, a wrapper . . . and there it was, shoved down at the bottom, the unused ticket. Train number 234 to Paris. Seat number. Reservation number. Contact information for the railway company.

Oliver wasn't the only one who could pull off a trick.

Ginny was dressed and ready in the kitchen with the kettle on the boil when Richard came down.

"I didn't expect to see you up," he said.

"I just wanted to do a few things on my last day." She passed him a mug of tea, but he waved it off and continued tying his tie.

"Should we meet at the train station at ten? I may have to leave through a window to get there. January sales. If I'm covered in blood, say nothing."

"See you there," Ginny said.

She had already completed the first step in this plan. She had checked on the availability and obtained an email address on easymail.co.uk. Now she just needed to sound convincing. And a little stupid. Oh, there were advantages to having an American accent—a *real* one. Nothing could quite replace a *real* one.

The phone lines for the rail company opened at seven in the morning, which is exactly when she dialed.

"HIi," she said, dragging out the vowel. "I bought a ticket for one of your trains the other day, but I never got the receipt? I bought it online and it said they would email it. . . ."

"Reservation number?"

Ginny read it off the ticket.

"Oliver Davies?" the man asked.

"No. My name is *Olive* Davies. My email is olive273@easy-mail.co.uk. I'm an . . . exchange student?"

That was good. Make everything sound like a question. They'd just want to get her off the phone.

"Just a moment."

Sound of typing.

"Oh, I see what happened," the man said. "They put an *r* in there. They had oliver273. I'll just take that out and resend it."

Five minutes later, there was a message. Tickets issued to Davies, Oliver. Credit card number x-ed out. Address: 15A York Road, Guildford.

"Gotcha," Ginny said.

This time, there would be no loose ends.

267

This Is Not a Pool

Guildford, according to the good folks on the internet, was a town just a few miles outside of London. Market town, suburb, part of something called the "stockbroker belt," home of the occasional music festival. Made famous by the book *The Hitchhiker's Guide to the Galaxy* as being the home of Ford Prefect, who claimed he came from there as a way of seeming boring and normal and from Earth. There were plenty of trains to get there. Thank god for the English and their love of trains. So many train stations, so many trains at all times.

There was a line of cabs waiting at the station, which was larger than she expected. She tried to get in the closest one, but was told to walk all the way to the end of the line, to the first parked cab. Cabs lined up here, and cabbies did not jump their place in line. It wasn't a black cab either—just a regular car with a sign and a meter. The driver set his paper down as she got in.

"What brings you to Guildford?" he asked after she gave the

address. "You're American, yeah?"

"To see a friend," Ginny said.

"Whereabouts in America are you from?"

"New Jersey."

"I was in New Jersey once," he said. "I went to a mall there. A big one."

The ride was maybe a minute long. The hardest part was waiting at the lights and getting through the morning traffic. She was deposited at a row of identical yellow-brown brick houses with peaked roofs. On the corner, there was a pub, a fancy-looking mattress store, and a store that seemed to sell nothing but lightbulbs. There was a lot of construction going on in the street. Three of the houses were being worked on, so there was cement dust and bags and planks and wheelbarrows all over.

Fifteen A was a house with a half-broken stone wall and a collection of recycling bins in the stone garden out front. There were a lot of cat food cans in the bins. A lot. She knocked on the door, and a moment later, a woman in a pink fleece with her hair tied back in a ponytail answered. The TV was on in the background, showing some morning show, and an ironing board was open and in use. There was laundry hanging everywhere.

This was definitely Oliver's mom. They had the same dark eyes. Her hair was black with chunks of frazzled gray. She looked very tired, and nervous. She had deep purple bags under her eyes.

"Can I help you?" she asked. "Is this about the bins, because . . ."

"I'm looking for Oliver."

The woman looked surprised, like friends didn't just drop by for Oliver very often—certainly not this early and certainly not with this accent.

"He's at work."

"At work?"

"Yes. At the Elephant on the high street. Just opposite the Oxfam."

"The high street?"

"It's just that way," she said, stepping out and pointing. "Up to that crossroad and make a right. You'll see it right away."

High street, Ginny quickly realized, basically meant "Main Street"—and the high street of Guildford was a busy place in the morning. It was entirely paved in cobblestone and set on a hill. She was at the top, looking down at a long street of shops, ending in a narrow river. Every kind of store was represented. There was the McDonald's. There was the Starbucks. The many clothing stores. The drugstores, the bookstores, the stationery store, the supermarket . . . The middle of the street was filled with a variety of carts, selling jam, baskets, dried flowers, curry sauces, fresh roasted pig.

Elephant was right in the middle of it all. It looked like a family restaurant, or possibly a coffee bar. It had vaguely African decorations on the walls, and a stridently merry sign in a jungly font. There were big posters advertising world music CDs on the front. He wasn't hard to find. The place was almost empty at this time of the morning. There was one waitress in the back, setting tables, and one tall guy with black hair sitting at the bar, reading a clipboard and making some notes. It was a little strange to see Oliver in a black polo-neck shirt with a bright logo and a pair of khakis. His carefully cultivated image—the thrift-store designer coat, the dress shirts, the posh voice, the constant playing with the cigarettes. It was all busted.

He must not have been able to hear her come in over the near-deafening music—a chorus of cheerful children and heavy drums. She stood right behind him and tapped him on the shoulder. He jerked in surprise, sending his clipboard clattering to the floor.

"What are you doing here?" he asked in a low voice, as he retrieved it. "How do you know where I work?"

"You're not the only one who does their homework."

She had gotten that line ready on the train, and it was extremely gratifying to be able to deploy it so soon.

"What do you want?"

"I want to talk."

"There's nothing to talk about. You shouldn't have come here."

"You brought me here," she said. "You contacted me. You started it. Now I know where you live, and I'm not going to leave you alone until you explain what this was all about."

"Aren't you supposed to be on a plane back to America?" he asked.

"In a few hours. If you don't talk to me now, I'll give your address to Keith. I'll tell him where you work. He'll come and visit you."

That got his attention.

"Wait here," he said.

He went to the back of the room for a moment, had a quick word with the waitress, then reappeared with his coat on. He brushed past Ginny and went outside, the implication being that she should follow.

Outside, he started walking away at a furious pace. They

272

paused next to what looked like a medieval town hall, stark white with black beams and an ornate hanging clock.

"I told you," he finally said. "I found the envelopes in your bag. I did some research on your aunt's name and read about the sale online. I thought I could make some money off of it. That's the entire story. What are you expecting?"

"You could have had the money," she said. "You walked away. Why?"

"That's my business."

"And the letters were *my* business. You found out about me. Now I want to know about you."

He groaned and fumbled for his cigarettes. A crowd of high schoolers passed by, all in uniforms, laughing, talking, clutching coffees and PE bags. The guys were all in blazers and ties. The girls were all in matching blue skirts, with the same ties and blazers. The general effect was that everyone looked older and more dignified and fancier, but they all had that stunned oh-my-god-the-holidays-are-over-and-school-still-exists look on their faces. She would have that look on her face in two days.

"What good"—he shoved a cigarette between his lips—"what good do you think it will do, coming here? Why does it matter why I did it? It's over. I just didn't want to take it in the end. Do you want an apology? I'm sorry. There. Are you happy? Will you leave now?"

No. She would not leave now. She didn't know what good it would do, or even what she expected to hear. She just wanted more of *something*.

"So, you're a waiter?" she asked.

"I'm the manager."

"What kind of restaurant is that?"

"It's a fancy McDonald's with hummus. Is this Question Time?"

"You read the last letter," she said. "You know how it ends. It just cuts off. I'm sick of things cutting off without any answers."

"Well, then you're in good company. That's how everyone in the world feels."

He continued walking down the hill, through the crowds of shoppers. He was once again doing what Keith had derisively described as the "dashing" walk, his coat snapping around his ankles. Ginny had a hard time keeping up. The suitcase she had brought with her was too hard to drag over the cobblestones, so she had to keep to the sidewalk. He waited for her to catch up at the bottom of the street, once he'd reached the tiny bridge over the small river that ran through the center of the town.

"The station is that way," he said. "The crossing up by the Friary is tricky, so take care."

He pointed toward another offshoot of shops and restaurants and a very complex intersection. Ginny was not going to be dismissed like this, but she had no idea what came next. It was time to do something, say something. Anything.

"My aunt would have liked you," she said.

She wasn't quite sure where that statement came from, but she knew it was true the moment she said it. Aunt Peg would have liked Oliver's plan, even if it did involve taking half the money. She would have liked him even more for going to all that trouble and then not taking the money. She would have liked the card tricks and the memorizing. In fact, it was almost like Aunt Peg had planned for him to be there all along. But, of course, she hadn't. Oliver was right. Aunt Peg had nothing to do with the people Ginny met. She attracted people like Oliver all on her own.

Truth or not, the statement did not have the intended effect. Oliver made a rueful little laughing noise.

"Somehow I doubt that," he said, as he walked away.

There was no point in chasing him again. He didn't want to see her. It was time to face facts. She had to get on a train and go.

The crossing was tricky, like Oliver said. She had to wait with a group of people for the little green man to appear in the signal box, then stand on a traffic island and cross again. And then again.

She didn't notice Oliver come up behind her.

"It's a tricky path to the station," he said. "I'd better show you."

He extracted the bag from her grip and walked on—but slower this time, so she could walk beside him. It turned out that the path to the station was not nearly as straightforward as he had indicated. It wound through a multistory parking lot, past a movie theater, over another footbridge . . . Guildford was much more complex on foot. She would never have found her way back.

Oliver was shaking a little. His hands were unsteady. He tried to hide them behind his back, but before he could, Ginny reached out and took his hand and squeezed it. At first, it shook harder; then it slowed. He wouldn't look at her directly; he read the board instead.

"Your train is on platform five," he said.

He made a halfhearted effort to pull his hand free, but she wouldn't let go. He blinked and rolled his eyes up toward the ceiling. It wasn't a dismissive gesture. It was the kind of thing you did when you didn't want to react or get emotional.

"We used to have a little bit of money," he said. "It came from my gran. It wasn't a lot, but enough for my parents to send me away to school. Hence the accent. So I don't really know much about how my parents got on when I was a kid. It seemed all right. Not great, but all right. When I went away to university, my dad walked out."

"Sorry," Ginny said.

"He's a bastard," Oliver said plainly. "I don't care about him. It was my mum I was worried about. When she called me, she was completely falling apart. So I left for a few days to take care of things. Then a few days became two weeks, and then I had accidentally left university for the year. It was all supposed to be temporary, but . . . I didn't go back again this year."

"That's why you're not in school?"

"That's the reason," he said. "My dad handled the money. My mum has never been good at that sort of thing. She was a bit broken; she couldn't handle the bills and the paperwork coming in. So I came back and got the job at Elephant. She didn't want me to. She felt bad about my leaving uni, but . . . it had to be done. Anyway . . . around October, I couldn't really take it anymore, so I took a little of the money I saved and went off to Greece for a few weeks to think about what I wanted to do next. My bag broke, and I wound up getting yours. Then I found the letters. They were just so weird . . . I started looking up the stuff I read in them. They gave me some focus. That's when I found out about the sale. And I could see that you'd never opened the last one, and there was no record of a last piece like the one described, so there was something else out there. I figured if you had already made a bunch of money off the first sale . . . it wasn't like I was taking from someone who was broke. Then I could give my mum enough money to help her get by, and I could go back to school. But the only way I could do it was if I never blinked. So I tried. I tried to do it and be honest and up front about it."

A crisp voice announced the impending arrival of Ginny's train. Time was very short.

"If you'd *told* me that," she said, "I would have gone along with it. You wouldn't have had to do all this. I would have just given you some of the money."

"I know that. At least, I do now. And that's what makes it worse. It actually made it a lot easier that your friend came with us and was such a div to me. But you weren't."

Ginny unwillingly released his hand. It fell to his side. He was looking at her now.

"So now you know," he said. "Are you satisfied?"

"Not yet," she said.

She reached out and took his hand again and squeezed it. At first, it shook harder; then it slowed. She mattered to him. He was afraid.

She let go of her bag, stepped up on her toes, and kissed him. Hard. Egregiously and in public and right in front of the people trying to get out of the Costa Coffee. She wrapped her arms around him.

Kissing . . . real, proper kissing . . . makes you lose all sense of place and time. She was vaguely aware that they were blocking the people trying to move around them, that a group of little kids were making comments, that Oliver had scooped her up and was more or less supporting her so that she didn't have to strain to meet his height. This was one of the real ones that actually do make you feel like your body is going completely gelatinous, and you *like* it.

A peevish second announcement snapped her back to reality. It reiterated that the train was coming. It would be pulling in any moment. Snide, interrupting announcement. There wasn't time to say good-bye. Ginny reached around, trying to find the handle of her bag as Oliver released her and they slowly pulled their lips apart. She was dizzy, so it was hard to get her ticket into the little opening. In fact, she forgot that once she put the ticket through, Oliver couldn't come with her, so they were immediately separated by a metal bar. When she turned, he was doing something she had never seen him do before.

He was smiling.

Ginny took her place on the train, her head still spinning. It was crowded, full of people commuting into London for work, or maybe to enjoy the last day of the holiday. She sat across from a group of moms with their daughters, maybe ten or eleven years old, on a big day out. They were talking about going to a movie and discussing where they wanted to have dinner that evening. She wasn't entirely sure what had just happened or what it meant, she only knew she wasn't ready to go. She wasn't ready to leave everyone behind—Keith, Richard, Mari, Oliver. Even these little girls on the train. She didn't want to leave them either. They were all a part of one large picture, a picture Ginny loved.

But the train sped on efficiently through the bright and sunny morning, past woodlands and towns and fields with horses. It was taking her into the heart of London, and from there, another train would take her to the airport, and a plane would take her home.

Home. It was a nice thought. She had missed her parents, her friends . . . but the word didn't have quite the same meaning anymore. England was home too. So much of her was here.

The Question floated back into her mind. It had been lingering in the background, waiting for the right moment to make its presence felt. Like Oliver, she could also memorize things that were important (though this was only two sentences, which was a little bit easier). *Describe a life experience that changed you. What was it, and what did you learn? (1,000 words)*

Maybe now she had her answer, and it was one word: England. Sure, that didn't convey a lot of information, but these people had no right to pry into her personal life. They were college admissions officers, not therapists. It's not like they *cared* what her answer was. They just wanted to see if she was a functional student who could write three pages that made some kind of sense. She wasn't going to tell them the truth, that she wanted someone to block her path. She wanted this train to break down, for her flight to be canceled, for immigration to tell her that she wasn't allowed to go. She wanted London itself to rise up and refuse to let her pass out of its boundaries.

And then, just as the snack cart came by and accidentally whacked her on the elbow, she realized exactly what it was she had to do.

Over the course of fifteen minutes, somewhere between Clapham Junction and Waterloo Station, she figured out her future. Not the details . . . there was no point in thinking about details. Just the basics. She mentally paged through the calendar and did some math. The deadlines would probably be tight. There would be a lot of research and work to be done very quickly, but she had done harder things.

Richard was waiting for her at one of the coffee shops that lined the Victoria Station, doing a crossword puzzle. Ginny rushed toward him, and he looked up with a smile and a wave.

"You seem ready to go," he said.

"Well," Ginny replied, sliding into the seat opposite. "About that . . . what do you know about applying to universities here? And, like, having me around. For a few years. Not in your house, but, you know . . ."

It took Richard a moment to take in what Ginny was saying. He looked at his coffee thoughtfully and turned the cup a few times.

"I think," he said, "that if that was what you planned to do, then we could get that information. And that you'd always have a place to stay, even in my house, for as long as you wanted."

Now it all made sense. It wasn't like everything was fixed now, or every plan made, every answer in hand . . . but now there was a shape to things. And as they walked to the airport train and Ginny took a last look around the station, she knew it would be easier to say good-bye this time. It's always easier to say good-bye when you know it's just a prelude to hello.

Acknowledgments

First, I want to thank everyone who's written to me or otherwise contacted me since the publication of *13 Little Blue Envelopes*, asking me to write a second book. It's because of you that this story exists.

I have the good fortune to know many wonderful people. The following is just a partial list of people who are owed thanks:

Thanks as always to my agent, Kate Schafer Testerman. Without Kate, I would certainly have met some unlikely fate by now, like being accidentally shot off into space. To my editor, Zareen Jaffery, who guided this book with a clear and steady hand. Holly Black, Cassie Clare, Libba Bray, and Robin Wasserman, for all their help developing the story and generally listening to me chatter away. Sarah Rees Brennan, who hosted me for several days in Ireland and broke into that swimming pool with me. ("We didn't realize it was closed. It was just dark, and, you know, when we forced the door, it opened, and then we just took the cover

281

off. Of *course* these are bathing suits. . . .") Justine Larbalestier, Chelsea Hunt, and resident English guy Andy "Weasley Is Our King" Friel, all of whom read the book and gave me extremely helpful notes. To John and Hank Green, who introduced all of Nerdfighteria to Ginny and the crew.

More thanks to . . .

Scott Westerfeld, for the fob. Jason Keeley and Paula Gross, who feed me regularly. Rebecca "Lone Star" Leach, my de facto assistant, who does my strange bidding. Tobias "I love John Barrowman" Huisman, my pointman in the Netherlands. Donal Finnerty, Ireland's leading expert on fridges. The Accio Books crew: Maria Alexandra Flores, Luz Maria Flores, Alida Gene Sara Priest, Kerstyn Smith, Sophia Arnold, Hannah Gann, Jennifer McCall, Carissa Crossett, Marcus Walton, Megan Sprimont, Rachel Belanger, Jessie Johnson, Lois Carlyle, and Marlee Grace Abbott.

And to Hamish Young, who was born in the forest and knows all about badgers.